DATE DUE

DEMCO, INC. 38-2931

NOTHING RIGHT

Some Fun
Female Trouble
Living to Tell
Nobody's Girl
Talking in Bed
Family Terrorists
In the Land of Men
The Expendables

NOTHING RIGHT

Short Stories

ANTONYA NELSON

BLOOMSBURY

New York   Berlin   London

Published by Bloomsbury USA, New York
Distributed to the trade by Macmillan

All papers used by Bloomsbury USA are natural, recyclable
products made from wood grown in well-managed forests.
The manufacturing processes conform to the environmental
regulations of the country of origin.

LIBRARY OF CONGRESS CATALOGING-IN-PUBLICATION DATA

Nelson, Antonya.
Nothing right : short stories / Antonya Nelson.—1st U.S. ed.
p.   cm.
ISBN-13: 978-1-59691-574-9 (hardcover : alk. paper)
ISBN-10: 1-59691-574-9 (hardcover : alk. paper)
1. United States—Social life and customs—Fiction.   I. Title.

PS3564.E428N68 2008
813'.54—dc22
2008020318

First U.S. Edition 2009

3 5 7 9 10 8 6 4 2

Typeset by Westchester Book Group
Printed in the United States of America by Quebecor World Fairfield

CONTENTS

NOTHING RIGHT

NEVER SHAKE A BABY," the flyer insisted, "Never, never, never." The public service brochures displayed at the district attorney's office seemed to be speaking to Hannah, each pertinent and personal. The face on "Break the cycle of domestic violence" was one big yellow-blue bruise. "Substance abuse abuses us all," another insisted, a martini glass with a slash through it. The illustration was so highly detailed as to include a toothpick-speared olive.

Her fifteen-year-old son had demanded that Hannah wait rather than join him and his probation officer. Down the hall, a door banged open, a courtroom released. A young man in an orange jumpsuit emerged between two older, somber men, trailed by weeping women. His lawyers, his guards, his mother, sister, girlfriend. Like the brochures, this scene also seemed a warning; Hannah had passed from one kind of life into another. A small boy brought up the rear of the procession, one hand hitching his pants, one swiping at his running nose. Hannah felt close to bursting into tears. Ten years from now, that little boy would be wearing the jumpsuit, leading the pack.

1

Her own son seemed poised somewhere between these two, teetering.

"Ma," he brayed, suddenly beside her, nudging to indicate that his appointment had ended, they were free to go. Still free, Hannah thought, and her mood lifted.

"You take us to the most interesting places," she said as they exited the courthouse. This had been the third required monthly meeting since he'd made a bomb threat at school. Beside her, passing through the metal detectors, Leo pulled in a savoring breath. "*Good* times," he murmured. He'd been to jail, he'd worn handcuffs. He had a psychologist, a lawyer, and a probation officer; this current round of meetings was part of something called "diversion," and maybe it *was* sort of amusing. Leo's delinquency had to become *some*thing else, Hannah supposed, having already been terrifying, divisive, pricey, and heartbreaking.

He was her second son, and he'd never been the one she understood best. Recently, she'd found herself disgusted by him: she didn't want to share a bathroom or kitchen, bar soap or utensils with her own boy. His brother, who'd passed through adolescence sobbing instead of shouting, had not prepared her for Leo. The pure ugliness of a more traditional male's transformation to manhood—the inflamed skin and foul odor, the black scowl, the malice in every move—might eventually convince a parent to despair, to say to that child, "You are dead to me." Because it would be easier—more decorous, acceptable—to mourn the loss than to keep waging a hopeless battle.

Their next stop was Wichita Central High School.

"Leo's mother," the PE coach greeted her. He was precisely as billed: soldierlike, down to the bullet-shaped shaved head and stiff-armed formality. "G.I. Joe," her son called him. In his first-period class, Leo had recently pierced his own lip with a safety pin. In the divot beneath his nose, a pulsing bump he'd tried to pass off as a bug bite and then a pimple. Finally he'd just shown up at breakfast with the pin hanging there, clicking against his cereal spoon. A parent was required to come pay penance, help reclaim the old gymnasium. The smell alone could have brought back adolescence—sweat, fried food, patchouli—but this was also the high school Hannah had attended. Back then, this had been Central's only gym. In the years since, groups would intermittently creak open the metal doors and throw a party or host a science fair. The drama club had contributed a couple of sofas. Windows, metal-barred and streaked with pigeon droppings, let through a gloomy cold light; voices echoed. Hannah had played basketball here, once upon a time. More recently, her first son had acted in plays on the very stage that, today, G.I. Joe would lead the group in dismantling.

"Leo's mother, meet Dylan's father." Several fathers, Reagan's, Meagan's, Dusty's, and Jordan's; a roomful of uncomfortable men, glancing around with their hands jammed in their pockets, awaiting instruction. Hannah couldn't help prescribing makeovers for everyone. First, twenty pounds off each, that defeated weight of middle age, of parenthood. Next: therapy and SSRIs, all around. Hannah knew that whatever she saw as deficits in these people, they themselves recognized. They, too, wished not to seem sad and skittish. They wished they were trim and brave and confident. They wished they were young—not as young as their offspring, these children, clustered and glowering fifty paces away, also in the proverbial doghouse—but younger than their forty or fifty years. They knew their best years had passed, that they'd been sapped of something vital, and now could only make futile guesses at how to get it back.

The group had been told to dress "grubby," bring tools, and, now, to "buddy up." Hannah watched her son pair himself with a big slow-moving girl. This was the daughter of a dad making his way toward her, a man who'd covered his bland sameness with a vivid orange Hawaiian shirt. His long wavy white hair and bright craggy face suggested decades of overindulgence, specific decades, the seventies and eighties.

"I'm Chuck," he said to Hannah, thrusting out his hand, "and that's my girl Niffer."

"Leo's mom." They shook vigorously. He smiled quizzically, and Hannah smiled back. Perhaps they were both wondering the same thing: why their children had chosen one another. They glanced in unison that direction. Niffer was larger than Leo—taller, meatier—with soot-black hair pulled into a dozen little pigtails. She stood sullenly while Leo twitched alongside, talking at her eagerly, as if to sell her something.

"Finally, I meet the boyfriend's family."

"*Boy*friend?" Hannah repeated. To her knowledge, her son had never been accused of this before.

"Leo. The boyfriend. I had to nail shut Niffer's window to make him come in the front door. 'Stop your sneaky ways, son,' I told him. Frankly, I'm more worried about mosquitoes and West Nile than finding a boy in her bed."

Hannah sighed, her heart heavy with Leo's persistent deception, its busy proliferation. She took in Niffer once more, the faintly domineering power the girl seemed to have over her son, as if she might stretch out a paw and cuff him. "How old is she?" Hannah asked.

"Eighteen. Nineteen next month. This is her fifth year of high school." The parents appraised one another, still quizzical but without the smiles, trying to guess the trustworthiness of their children.

"You a doctor?"

"No, no." Hannah looked down at her green scrubs, which had been the required outfit of her former job. "I worked at a doctor's office."

"Well, you're not a doctor and I'm not Jimmy Buffett." He laughed abruptly, like a dog. "Not anymore, anyway. And I'm betting that fellow is not Abe Lincoln." An Amish father stood rocking on his heels, looking serenely about, his sons like sentries on either side of him. What bad deed had those boys done? Now Niffer's dad noticed Hannah's hand, from which she had removed her wedding ring. He didn't wear one, either, and for whatever reason, the absence made a difference. You didn't notice until you took it off.

For a couple of hours that afternoon the two of them hauled trash from the gym while others, those who'd brought sledges and crowbars, performed the more violent labor— enthusiastically, like cavemen. Despite the chilly October air, Chuck wore flip-flops. Hannah liked his casual use of profanity, as it made him seem not young, exactly, but immature, and therefore less likely to judge her. Having grown up in Kansas, she should have been accustomed to judgment, inured to the pity and superiority her neighbors felt toward someone like herself, with her foreign vehicle and secular Sundays, and yet it still hurt her feelings. Her neighbors would change her in ways she wouldn't want to change herself, she supposed, reconsidering her earlier notion of a mutually agreed upon ideal. They would send her to pantyhose and pumps, hair spray, Episcopal fellowship, potluck dinners, blood drives.

"Do you donate blood?" she asked Chuck, trying to balance her loathing of small talk against her tendency to appear bored or annoyed by others.

"Nah," he said. "I'm a nancypants around the needle. You?"

"Never."

When his cell phone rang, he cursed reflexively. "Fucking cow."

"Excuse me?"

"Ex-wife." This opened the subject of divorce, his of twelve years, Hannah's of four months. They discovered they'd been married the same summer twenty years ago, which led Hannah to speculate that if he'd stayed in the marriage, as she had, he probably wouldn't be as bitter about the split.

"Yeah-huh," he said skeptically.

"You could pretend that's what happened," Hannah suggested. But his wife had found a new love and life immediately, spawning a crop of younger, cuter children, Niffer's half brothers she never saw; Chuck helped at high school whenever he could because his wife had simply abandoned their now-aging teenage daughter.

"No way can I forget or forgive what that bitch has done to Niffer."

Hannah didn't mention that she'd been hoping her ex-husband would do precisely what Chuck's ex had, attach himself to another marriage so as to let Hannah off the hook. It was a particular kind of hook, and it was painfully embedded: the specific knowledge that she'd disappointed a good man, and disappointed him so deeply that he'd come unmoored, lost and adrift. There was no undoing that. She could only pray someone would arrive to save him. And she wasn't a person who prayed.

"I went to school here," she told Chuck now. "Go Cougars." She made the traditional Cougar fist, the one that was supposed to resemble claws.

"I went to East," he said. "Well, for a while I did. Then I just said 'Fuck it' and got my GED."

"I played basketball in this very gym," Hannah went on. "I was so stoned during one game I scored at the wrong end of the court. Right there," she added, pointing to the netless rim under the snarling cat. They each carried two bags of trash to toss on the growing heap outside. "How'd you misspend your youth?"

"Chasing tail. Racing cars. Taking drugs." He smiled his beach-bum smile, then shook his hair out of his eyes. "But I gave up partying," he said earnestly, letting the gym door close behind them. "Since the divorce."

"Oh," said Hannah, made uneasy, as always, by someone else's committed sobriety. Now, inhaling a deep breath of the fresh, cool air, she was afraid he would proselytize, attempt to sponsor her at AA or NA or whatever A wagon he'd climbed onto, and the spark of friendship she'd felt with him fizzled. But then he began slapping at his pockets until he hit upon his pack of cigarettes, offering Hannah one. She wasn't a smoker but joined him just from relief: he'd not relinquished this bad habit.

You had to have something with which to fill the hours.

"I like Leo," Chuck announced. "He set up my e-mail account, and he always says thanks. Although his fashion statement baffles me, him and Niffer both." He had the self-possession to look down at his own feet then and smile at his flip-flops. "Fungus," he explained.

"Ah," Hannah said, trying to exhale elegantly. "Leo thinks he's an anarchist." Her son had taken to dressing like a homeless man, baggy wool pants with exhausted suspenders, food-stained shirts and holey fedoras. Anarchy, despite its resemblance to clown-wear, felt like a state of siege; Hannah was coping as best she could. Because money was regularly missing from her purse, she had begun sleeping with it beside

her on the bed. She stored all the liquor in her car trunk after finding a water bottle of gin on Leo's nightstand; when
he caught scabies from his thrift-store clothes, she took
him to the doctor. And it was Hannah herself who'd given
him the idea of obtaining his fake ID, recounting to him her
own adolescent scam at the DMV, where she claimed to be
her older sister, acquiring a valid duplicate license with her
own young photograph on it, a full five years' difference in
their ages. "I just kept forgetting to respond to my sister's
name," she had told Leo, laughing. "Margaret," sent trembling into the liquor store with all the money. So how could
Hannah really complain when she found Leo's fake license
in his dirty pants, his photo over his brother's name and
birth date?

That was the thing: she both understood him, and was totally
flummoxed. For instance, why so angry? Why the hair-trigger
temper, so often? He was always breaking the telephone. Apparently, this aspect of his character was under control over at
Chuck's house. "Maybe teenagers should be shuffled around,"
she speculated. "Maybe they'd be more mannerly with people
they didn't know so well."

Niffer, it turned out, was depressed. "It's kind of like living
with two different girls," Chuck explained. "You never know
what side of the bed she's gonna get up on."

"I feel that way about Leo, too. And sometimes it seems
like *he* doesn't really know, either." There often appeared to be
a war going on inside Leo, the mild silly boy he'd been versus
the hairy, hoarse-voiced soul who'd suddenly moved in. The
divorce had contributed, no doubt, but her sons' behavior had
influenced the divorce, too—their childhoods abruptly gone,
leaving everyone feeling robbed. It just wasn't fun to be a
family anymore. Plus, Hannah had been fired from her job. A

bad year. "It's a combo plate of reasons," she acknowledged to Chuck.

"A cluster fuck," he agreed.

Hannah decided to tell him that her husband, like his wife, had seemed to give up on their child. This wasn't strictly true, but it made her feel noble, loyal to Leo in the face of so much disapproval and lack of confidence. His father was in the throes of grief, overwhelmed by losing both Hannah's passion and Leo's innocence in the same season. His response, finally, was to take their older son and retreat to his mother's home half a mile away, to his knotty pine bedroom with its desiccated ornaments from his youth. He hadn't given up on their son; he just longed for last year's model, cursed as he was by that most disastrous of devilry, nostalgia. But Hannah found it more interesting to construct a different story for Chuck, Chuck who was field-dressing both his and her cigarette butts, ready to rejoin the group.

"You have to stick with them," she said, of their teenagers. "It's like they're toddlers again." All the common household objects were dangerous once more, pills, razors, knives, liquor, glue. "Except toddlers are sweeter."

"And now we're older," he replied.

"Don't forget divorced," Hannah added.

Chuck shook his wavy hair—gold, it must have been, now silver—and opened the door. "I have to check out Niffer every night to see if she's cutting again. Up her arms, on her belly. It's just vigilance, my friend, round-the-clock vigilance. We do a UA every couple weeks. I am on the case. My ex doesn't know the half of it."

"UA?"

"Urine analysis. I take one, too, for solidarity. I'm letting her know I'm on her side, I understand how hard it is not to use. I'm telling her every day, in every way, that I am aware of the facts, and the facts are that life is a cage of pain, just a damn cage of pain."

"Must she be named Niffer?" Hannah asked that evening, trying to tease Leo.

He glared at the cheese and grater he held, as if he could imagine ways of injuring his mother with them. She had said a foolish thing; once said, it was not retractable. She was forty-three years old; why hadn't she learned that yet? When she and Chuck had left the gym that afternoon, they'd found their children' kissing by the portables. It was an alarming moment for Hannah. She'd never seen Leo touch a girl; until earlier that day, she hadn't known he was a boyfriend. His brother Justin had been so easily embarrassed by the questions she and his father had asked concerning desire or romance that they hadn't even broached the topic with Leo. They were a polite family who lived in the Midwest under those unspoken rules. The arguments she and Thomas had had—even the final, fatal ones—were marked by respectful restraint; for all she knew, Justin was gay. Where had Leo learned what to do? How had he known to grip Niffer's buttocks while chewing hungrily at her mouth?

Upon seeing the groping pair, Hannah's response was to turn away, avert her gaze from the slight pump of her son's hips, but Chuck had boomed right in, waving his arms, "Whoa, whoa, whoa, let's keep it PG, boys and girls!" Leo had leaped back as if electrocuted, then trudged sullenly after Hannah to their car, where they got stuck idling along behind the Amish horse and buggy.

Once home, Hannah didn't know how to be tactful about

the subject. Up close, the girl seemed brain-damaged, her face not angry so much as smeary, as if her features had been smudged by a giant careless thumb: hooded eyes, mashed nose, down-turned mouth. She reminded Hannah of a rabbit—not a real rabbit but a stuffed one, lop-eared and lifeless, costumed in torn black fishnets and red plaid skirt, a pair of mud-spattered combat boots.

This was Leo's first girlfriend. "I mean, couldn't you call her 'Jenny'?" Hannah asked weakly. "Jen? J.J.?" Leo folded a piece of bread around his pile of cheese and stuffed it in his mouth without answering her. They were taking a break from writing his English paper on *Macbeth*. Year in, year out, it was always *Macbeth*. Leo resumed his position prone on the floor, Hannah hers at the computer. She typed, he was supposed to dictate. Mostly she asked him if her wording seemed natural to him. The paper had to sound authentically teenage, that paradoxical charge of childish eloquence. When she'd asked Leo why he didn't like literature, he'd told her it was all fiction, as if that were self-explanatory.

"Yes, and?"

"It's not real. Just a bunch of imaginary crap."

She'd persisted. "*That's* your complaint?"

"Yes. That's my complaint. It's all fairy-tale bullshit, imaginary crap. Witches, kings, elfs."

"Elfs? And that"—she pointed to the lethal looking technology stacked under the television, the boxes and wires, the hand-held control instrument over which he had such fluid mastery, these objects of his obsession—"that's not imaginary?"

"No less so," he said. There was his challenge to her. It was Hannah's temptation to summon his former self, the little boy who loved being read to, who longed to climb into the books, go visit Winnie the Pooh or Mr. Mole. He couldn't deny he'd been that boy; for years he'd begged to hear the anecdotal evidence of his charming boyhood. But that was the maudlin terrain her ex-husband so willingly wandered, and Hannah was trying to avoid it.

"There's no narrative," she said, of his favorite video game, "no characters, no writing, just shooting. And that infernal moaning."

"There are so characters!" Leo said. "There's a story. It's a long story." He proceeded to tell it, with more enthusiasm than he'd shown in months for anything except perhaps mauling Niffer. "There's a Master Chief, that's you. Well, me, the player. And I'm a master fighter, and I'm fighting inside this ring around a planet. First I have to get thawed out, and then I go do battle against aliens . . ." The more he told her, the less solid her argument seemed. The game involved power struggles, bloodshed, and moral dilemmas; was it considerably less relevant than a weak king and his bitchy wife? Moreover, Leo might have learned *that* lesson in his own home. "And you know what else? The game doesn't always turn out the same every fricking time, unlike *literature*. We could play, if you want. There's a multiplayer option. Let me defrost you, Mom."

"A better mother might take you up on that."

He lay back on the floor, sighing. "Well, a better son might do his own *Macbeth* paper."

Justin, the first son, had also been a troubled youth. But his grief was different from Leo's. "Fine!" he'd cried, one desperate night in an argument with his father, weeping his excruciating boy tears. "I'll just *kill* myself!"

To which Hannah had made an instinctive and, according

to her husband, mistaken reply: "So will I! If you kill yourself, I'll kill myself!" The evening was out of control. This was where she and Thomas had first parted ways, as partners in being parents. Hannah's version of Thomas's strategy was that they should become militaristic drones, get tough with Justin; according to Thomas's interpretation of Hannah's ideas, they should capitulate, bend over backward, and do anything to prevent his suicide. They willfully misunderstood one another, courting their first son, neglecting their second. Leo, then age eleven, lay many evenings sniveling in his bed, burrowing into his blankets as if into a hole. Abruptly upon threatening suicide, Hannah had felt her adult qualities lift off and suspend themselves in a nimbus around her. It was liberating to act like a child, to *act*. The effect on Justin and her husband was to shock them, their disagreement instantly forgotten as they both turned toward her. A few years later, when Thomas moved to his mother's house, Justin joined him, his parting glance at his mother one of confusion, as if he did not recognize her. Thomas had won, she thought then, leaving her with the boy she understood less well. Thus, the family had been divided. Left behind, Hannah sometimes found Leo doing what she did, standing in the doorways of rooms, pondering the unused props, his father's desk, his brother's bunk. "Would you really have killed yourself," Leo asked her once, "if Justin had, would you have, too?"

"No," she had assured him, ashamed.

During this year in which she was letting her life fall apart, Hannah spent her afternoons like an invalid, reading books or want ads and drinking wine, dozing away upright in an easy chair, snug and hazy, waiting for the sound of Leo's bike clattering on the porch. You never knew what was going to pop into the house, hilarity or fury, the child or the burgeoning man. He might request that Hannah sing a song to him or rub his back, share a blanket on the couch as they watched videos together or did homework. Without prompting, he would drop his head on her shoulder and say that he loved her. "I love you, too," she would recite, the words offered in the rote, hopeful manner of the prayer; she wasn't sure she loved anyone, anymore.

Then again, he might enter enraged, prepped for an evening of negotiation, argument, inquisition—these tiresome things that constituted her relationship with her second son.

A month ago, he'd come home in the mood of a salesman, hastily selling his mother a version of recent events. "Remember when I told you my cell phone was stolen?" he started off. "Remember when I called from school and told you? Last week, Tuesday, I think? Remember, I said it was a good thing you got insurance last time around? Totally worth the extra four bucks a month? 'Member?"

It wasn't that Hannah didn't remember (she didn't), or that she couldn't trust him (she couldn't), but that she had no idea which of these was most lamentably the problem. Listening, from the depths of a near dream, half blasted, she could easily have failed to call in the cell phone loss. Just as likely, he had never notified her of it. Then a week later, he had roused her from her nap by slamming the refrigerator door. "Bomb threat," he said casually, when she asked why he was home early.

"Wow." She struggled into sentience. "They just let you go?"

He appraised her over the milk carton he held to his face. She didn't drink milk, so he got to do what he liked with the container.

She said, "When I was young, we had snow days."

"You're funny," he said.

That evening, they were called in to be questioned. It was his phone, his reputedly stolen phone, from which the bomb threat had been made. Clearly he had done it. Clearly she would lie for him, since he was already on probation. But clearly also she had been drunk, and inattentive, and somehow guilty besides. The problem with falling out of your life was that occasionally you got busted for doing absolutely nothing wrong. Doing nothing whatsoever—nothing wrong, yet nothing right, either.

Hannah was roused out of her dreamy fuzz on a frigid afternoon in December by a figure rapping at the front door, an insistent apparition that had pulled her from her chair and led her stumbling across the room before she gave the action any conscious thought. Leo's large girlfriend, there on her steps.

"You're a mother," Niffer said, after Hannah had gotten her in out of the cold and an odd fur hat, settled at the kitchen table, served with a soda while Hannah refilled her wineglass.

"Yes," Hannah agreed. Once, she'd told Thomas that she found it appalling—appalling!—that men could actually have children and not know it. Just little shots in the dark, and utter uncertainty.

Between her and Niffer a long quiet pause formed. Niffer did not appear to know that silence was intimidating. Also boring. For her, it was character. Hannah could not think of a way to fill the dead air between them.

"So *you* can understand," Niffer finally went on. "*Be*ing a mother . . ."

"Possibly," Hannah allowed.

The girl sighed, glancing slowly around the kitchen as if cataloging and dismissing its contents, the potholders and appliances and, admittedly, the somewhat useless decorative plates. "I'm pregnant," she said at last.

"Oh good God," Hannah said, blinking. The look Niffer directed at her now was blunt and opaque, large dark eyes without fear in them, without passion, either. Confrontation, perhaps, determination certainly—not quite like a stuffed rabbit, now. There would be no unsolicited advice, this look said. There would be no choice a grown-up could make except to go along. Maybe Leo liked being bossed around, the animated little bird pecking at the stolid pachyderm. Maybe that was what he needed, in the end, a girlfriend like an anchor, like a gun at his head.

"There's an ironic part, too," Niffer said, pulling in a deep noisy breath. "My mother's *trying* to get pregnant."

"I thought she had other children?"

"She wants more. All she has are boys. Three bratty boys. And me," she added, sighing. It was this sigh that permitted Hannah to begin liking Niffer. It wasn't much—hardly less trenchant or flat than anything she'd said so far—but it was enough to build on, a little exhalation of hurt. Niffer not only hadn't told her own mother yet, she hadn't let Leo or her father know, either. Her secret had been kind of fun, but now it was growing undeniable. She thought her father's response would be tears. Hannah, recalling Chuck at the gym, disagreed; shock, she said, then anger; men always defaulted to anger. And Leo? Shame, predicted Hannah, extreme embarrassment.

Happiness, declared Niffer, after another of her elephantine silences. "He likes babies."

"Hmm," Hannah murmured, never having seen this side of

her son, the baby-loving one. Yet he was full of surprises, that boy.

She watched herself carry on this halting conversation with Niffer while a confusion of other things leaped about in the back of her mind, all with exclamation marks: She was too young to be a grandmother! What if Leo wasn't the father! But babies were so nice to hold! How would she notify Thomas?! And, wait a minute, wait just one minute—what about the fact that Niffer was eighteen, an adult, and Leo, though full of adult mischief, was still legally a child!? This emphatic chaos—somewhat cartoonish and buoyed by a few glasses of wine—kept her busy while half attending to the girl, who professed self-righteously, dully, and far too familiarly her reasons for not having an abortion. But when she said, "Plus, getting pregnant means I won't do drugs anymore. Maybe I did it so I would stop doing drugs." Hannah abruptly dismissed her own thoughts.

"Say again?"

"See, it might have been subconscious. Kind of tricking myself. Like you know what I did when I wanted to grow out my nails?" She displayed her fancy talons, which were shining black and spangled with frosty glitter.

"What?"

"I spread Super Glue all over my hands. After it dried, I chewed on it, instead, like a substitute. And I smoked, so I wouldn't bite. But now I won't smoke, since there's a baby. But anyway, I know I have to have a goal, a real reason to not use."

"That actually sounds kind of smart," Hannah said.

"Huh?"

"I mean, if you can quit because you want to be good to the baby."

"Right. That's what I just said." And Hannah's little seed of affection for Niffer had sprouted a feeble root. "Anyhow, it's too late now for an abortion. I'm six months. Everyone just thinks I got fat," she said, lifting those heavy lips for a smile.

"You sure showed them," Hannah said.

"Six months?" Thomas said, incredulous. Sure enough, it was harder to tell him the news than it had been to receive it herself. She did appreciate the fact of the telephone, that she was not watching his face. "How could her father not know?" he insisted.

"Guess what, Thomas? It's just not fruitful to pursue that line of thought." There were a million things her ex-husband didn't know, many of them about his nearest and dearest family members. Did he know that Hannah had gotten fired for stealing a prescription pad from the medical office? He did not. Had she notified him of Leo's most recent arrest? Negative. Was he aware of the true amount of alcohol she put away in a day? No sir. "Other nonfruitful avenues are the ones about adoption, abortion, or statutory rape."

"Statutory rape?"

"She's eighteen."

"Eighteen?" Poor poleaxed Thomas; Hannah could almost enjoy shocking him, free as she was to simply hang up and not suffer his certain ensuing funk. There would be Justin for that, Justin as well as Thomas's martyred old mother, Bea.

"Eighteen almost nineteen."

"Sweet Jesus."

At the kitchen table, earlier that afternoon, Niffer had suddenly reached two-handed for her tummy, interrupted by movement inside. Her expression recalled for Hannah the sensation, the stirring revolution. Thrilling—you couldn't resist clutching at it, verifying it. "It's like having company with me all the time," she had said.

Exactly like, Hannah thought.

"I never feel lonely," said Niffer. And wasn't that the biggest teenage malady? Teenage, and middle age, for that matter— loneliness? Hannah found it hard to argue with Niffer's pregnancy; it was starting to seem like the preferable solution to many problems. She might have chosen pregnancy again for the same reason, to make herself grow up, to locate a line to toe. Pregnant more often, Hannah would certainly have drunk less over the years, spent fewer hours staring spellbound into the pages of a book and more on perfecting her motherhood. If there had been other children, no doubt Hannah and Thomas would still be married, too dizzy in the crowd to have yet uncovered the hollow space between them. And if they were still married, with more children, maybe Leo would have turned some of his spare annoyance on his younger siblings, maybe he would have been distracted by responsibility for them, less available to restlessness and boredom.

"Boredom is the reason for most bullshit," Chuck had declared, back at the old gym, back before he and Hannah knew they would have a grandchild in common.

"I know I've made a lot of mistakes out of boredom," Hannah had agreed. Boredom was like a revving engine stuck in neutral. Last year, when Leo had been arrested at the mall parking lot covered in paint—literally red-handed—he had claimed boredom as the reason for paintballing the signs. "Like *you* don't like to see a big splatter of blood?" he'd pleaded, confident of the universality of this desire.

"No," she'd said, stunned, scared. At least a baby didn't scare her. At least there was that. But Hannah's ex-husband wasn't a person who could be convinced of such freewheeling logic. He had hoped only for an ordinary life. It occurred to Hannah that drinking was responsible for some of the fluidity of her thinking, and that wasn't altogether bad.

"Another good thing?" Niffer had said, heading out Hannah's door into the winter afternoon. "My complexion has really cleared up."

"Hormones," Hannah said. "You shouldn't dye your hair, you know. The chemicals and all . . ."

"Really?" Niffer had said, looking worried under her coal black pigtails.

On the phone, Thomas had grown silent, pondering, reconstructing the world. His wife and sons were constantly knocking down what he knew and forcing him to put the pieces back together. It exhausted him, and the product probably seemed flimsy, flawed. Moving home to his mother's house had allowed him some relief, Hannah thought. Bea wasn't going to surprise him. "Leo's not responsible," he finally said. "This girl's an adult who took advantage of him. For all we know, she intended to get pregnant. She used him. It's rape, like you said."

"He was climbing through her window at night. And she's kind of slow."

"What?"

"Not retarded, but maybe damaged."

"My lord."

Hannah felt sad for her ex-husband. News like this took years off his life. He seemed to think not only that the past was something he could reclaim, but also that it had been ideal. He had been an optimist when she met him—and she'd not only divorced him but proven his outlook wrong. At least he wasn't crying, although he might never cease mourning.

However awful that conversation was, the one pending with Leo would be worse for being in person. "Don't get all pissed," he snarled at her when he finally arrived home, after midnight, eyes red slits.

"Were you riding your bike in the dark? High? With no headlight? It's *snowing* out there!"

"You are always focused on exactly the wrong things!"

"Niffer came to see me. I have been sitting here worried sick for the last ten hours, with no word from you whatsoever." She would also have to dream up some new punishment, and that was becoming a challenge. Already Leo had been grounded, suspended, and relieved of his allowance for the next indeterminate period of time. He'd been arrested, analyzed, medicated, interrogated, and put on probation. What was left? His father had been researching therapeutic boarding schools, whose brochures he dropped by for Hannah with yellow highlights on religious instruction or honor codes. There was one in Utah that especially appealed, the advertisement showing a group of earnest multicultural types sitting around a campfire, apparently in serious conversation about their remorse and rehabilitation.

"Don't make me go there!" Leo had wailed. And this was all Hannah had, the brochure she could flap before his face.

"I'm *glad* Niffer's pregnant!" he declared now. So the girlfriend had got it right; he was happy.

"Why are you glad?"

"Because it's what she wants. She needs a baby. Her own mother abandoned her, just left Niffer like a . . ." He searched for the simile. Hannah started to speak, to help supply a word, when he cut her off. "And don't start telling me how it's going to fuck up my life!"

"I wasn't going to." Hannah merely watched him. He was hungry and confused. Hannah recalled this feeling from adolescence: stoned in the night, lost, cold, exhilarated with apprehension. A shower of snow in the face like a premonition of the future, a promise held in the dark, something out there that was calling, toward which you were fervently headed. She said, "I'm of the opinion that it might save your life."

"How?"

"By forcing you to get your act together." Now was not the time to mention her concerns with Niffer's chromosomes. "By making you care about something more than you care about yourself."

"You can feel it rolling around in there," he said, turning to her with a passionate glance she hadn't been treated to in ages. "It's actually very cool, Mom."

"And you didn't know until today?"

"Nope. She wanted to surprise everybody." He couldn't help grinning at Hannah, giddy with what he'd managed to aid and abet in. And if you could possibly look past the absurdity of having this conversation with a *fifteen*-year-old, he sounded quite average in his response to learning he was to become a father. The news had restored him to humanity, Hannah thought. He wondered aloud if he and Niffer should get married before the baby was born, if that would be the proper move, and, oh, by the way, if Hannah would give her permission, since he wasn't old enough. And how did she like the name "Roscoe"? They had decided that if the baby was a girl, Niffer got to choose, and if it was a boy, Leo would prevail.

"Roscoe?" Hannah said, in this instance having a definite opinion—not a favorable one—where in others she'd been, so far, rather ambivalent. Ambivalent, or astonished, it was hard to say which. "I'm not wild for Roscoe."

"Amos? That was another I kind of liked. Niffer picked 'Ambrosia.'"

Her granddaughter, Ambrosia.

He was born seven weeks early, and even after ten days in the neonatal unit, still had "Baby Prentiss" markered on his ID tag. His temporary name on a strip of masking tape, slapped on a plastic case that resembled Tupperware.

"She doesn't want to name him until he's for sure going to live," Leo told Hannah, clutching her hand. His hand was large, a man's, but with a child's frightened need. Fatherhood of any baby might have made him scared, but this baby, whose odds of living were less than fifty-fifty, had left Leo traumatized; "scared straight," he might have been labeled. In any event, he held his mother's hand as if he would otherwise collapse.

Baby Prentiss was kept in a place like a church, replete with people prepared to genuflect and confess, bow their heads and pray, listen to what they were told with tears in their eyes, their responses mere whispers. Niffer had not returned to school after the birth—she would perhaps log yet another year in her lengthy matriculation at Central High—spending her days, instead, beside her infant on the other side of the glass, wearing a mask, reaching through the portals in Baby Prentiss's plastic container. She'd been forced to trim her nails, scour her hands till they were raw. Since she couldn't breast-feed, she'd bound up her large leaking chest with an Ace and taken up smoking again.

Some evenings Hannah and Leo found her at the hospital's

front entrance with the other smokers, huddled around a planter of dead foliage, clouds of smoke and steam over their heads. She fell upon Leo with too much emotion, heavy with need and sedatives; as Leo patted her back mechanically, Hannah saw that the power in their relationship was shifting. What would her son do with it, when he realized that it was his?

Up they rode in the elevator, first having to pass through the hall of healthy babies, the ones going home tomorrow in order to make room for the next wave, and then through the next, the legion of the normal, that ongoing birthday party of booties and Mylar balloons and laughter, and finally through weighty doors into an oddly awed silence.

This was the kingdom of sick infants. Moving into it from the celebration, you could be convinced you'd gone deaf. Behind soundproof glass, a horrific pantomime as the babies squalled. Yet when they reached Baby Prentiss, and Hannah watched his tiny face contort, his limbs turn suddenly an awful mottled purple, his concave chest flex in and out, bones like rubber bands, she felt his unbearable distress vibrantly in her head. Beside her Leo put his free palm to the glass. That pane was greasy with handprints.

On either side of Baby Prentiss, the babies who had been there yesterday were gone. One had been taken home, one had died, just like the law of averages.

Chuck joined them when his shift at the towing company ended, unshaven and wracked, hat in hand. The nights were so cold he left the truck running in the parking lot, within view of the seventh-floor window, his vehicle down there rumbling, putting up a stream of exhaust like a powerful living beast, like a dragon. He worried over the tiny creature in the quiet ward, but he worried more over Niffer. He believed she would kill herself, he confided to Hannah, if Baby Prentiss died. He hadn't foreseen this downside to her pregnancy. None of them had.

Only once did Niffer's mother come visit when Hannah and Leo were there. Hannah had met her at the principal's office back in November. The full complement of parents had been summoned to Central when Niffer announced she was having a baby, a compulsory meeting with not only the principal but the school nurse and a social worker. The social worker, who had been Leo's erstwhile emissary at school, shook her head disbelievingly. "I throw up my hands," she'd said, literally tossing up her hands, as if to release something heavy, like a rock, that she'd been carrying around.

"Now you'll have the pleasure of meeting my mortal enemy," Chuck had said cheerfully to Hannah. "Do you know that slag heap thinks she can just waltz on in and *adopt*?" Neither Hannah nor Niffer had correctly guessed *his* reaction to the pregnancy: it was all about revenge. He told Hannah there was no way in holy hell that woman was laying her mitts on Niffer's baby. He'd devote himself to another twenty years of single parenting to prevent such a thing. "Shit," he said at the principal's office, "I'll hire a fucking hit man."

It was terrible, Hannah thought, when only a hit man would suffice.

Her own ex didn't visit the baby very often, either. The last time Hannah had seen him had been just after the birth, when he came running into the maternity ward in the middle of the night, his face still wrinkled from sleep. Hannah felt some familiar, painful implosion whenever she met Thomas, some sad sighing hole in her chest. His clothes hung on him, as if he were shrinking, and the lines around his eyes were deeper, a series of runnels down his cheeks, as if his tears were corrosive. "Oh, sweetheart," she had said then.

"Hannah," he'd answered, trying hard to remain formal. They'd spent that late night with Niffer's parents, Chuck and Denise, four people either estranged or strangers. Hannah could only assume that the others shared her mixed feelings about the birth; maybe it would be best if the baby did not survive. It had been created by children, after all, and like other approximate projects—the sugar-cube igloo, the lumpy clay bowl—it was possible that they had not gotten it right; they'd used sticks and buttons, string and papier mâché.

But when she saw the baby—less than three pounds, without tear ducts or eyelashes, lacking the ability to inflate his own lungs—she could not wish him gone. Inside his plastic bin he wailed without sound, miniature body plastered with wires, limbs stuck with tubes, smashed blue face under a clear mask. Leo stood by, Hannah's son the delinquent, done up in surgical garb from head to toe; he was reduced to a set of floating frightened eyes. He turned on Hannah as beseeching a look as she had ever received.

They lived these weeks in limbo. "Literally," Hannah told Thomas on the telephone. "Isn't that where the babies go, when their future is undecided?"

"I don't know," he said. "I'll ask my mother."

And it was his mother, Hannah's former mother-in-law, who proved the most devoted in sharing the vigil at the premature babies' window. Finally, her steadfast patience would be put to good use. A janitor had found her a chair. There she sat, many an evening, tidy and meek, fingers polishing a rosary. The hospital itself was Catholic; at the elevator doors you waited under a portrait of its patron, Saint Francis. Now and then a clutch of nuns would round a corner, immediately silencing their conversation until you were out of earshot.

"I lost three babies," Bea told Hannah. "Two before Thomas, one after. Three girls."

"I never knew that," Hannah said, ashamed of her long dismissive estimation of her mother-in-law's humorless outlook.

"Don't tell Thomas," Bea said, rising from the chair to let Hannah assume the watch. "He doesn't need another worry." Her eyes were damp. She opened her purse to pour the rosary beads into it, then touched Hannah's arm as if to bless her. "Some days I would get so furious I had to go sit in the car and yell at God, just scream until I couldn't scream anymore."

Niffer rode the elevator up less and less often, eventually arriving at the hospital simply to stand with the smokers, finally not going at all, staying at home in bed, sick, too. "You have to visit her," Hannah told Leo when he returned from school.

"Why?" he answered. "All she does is take pills and pass out. All I do over there is watch TV. Watch TV, or listen to Chuck call his ex-wife a cunt. No thanks."

At the hospital, in the daylight, when the sun was shining, the ward seemed more hopefully lit. Day by day, while the baby slept and bawled and breathed and survived, Hannah watched through the glass. She could see him, through it, and she could see herself, in it, reflected back. The plastic chair awaited her, often still warm from having held Bea.

It was in that cathedral space, one random afternoon, that Hannah realized she loved the baby. The notion struck her cognitively, like the solution to a puzzle, no different from the day last spring when she'd understood—as if that bare forty-watt bulb had blinked on overhead, as if somebody had conked her—that she no longer loved her husband.

Love, she pondered: perhaps a bit more left-brained than you might expect, more science than romance. Invisible, yet quantifiable matter, it might evaporate and float away, fall elsewhere, freeze, boil; it could circulate in the blood, bitter as an infection, benevolent as a nutrient. Clear, tangible. It died. It was born.

He came home in March, more or less on his originally predicted birthday. "He would have been a Pisces," Leo reported, reading the horoscopes the day the hospital finally released the boy. "But now he's a Capricorn, I guess. He's only gonna have a two-star day. 'Read between the lines,'" he read. "'Tonight: close to home.'"

The baby weighed six pounds, like a brisket. He came to Hannah's house because his mother did not want him. Her milk had dried up; he would be bottle-fed anyway. "He bonded with nurses," she said to Hannah dully, under the influence of drugs meant to keep her from other drugs. "He'll probably like those outfits you always wear."

Would the story of Niffer and Leo's teenage romance, their baby's conception, their naughtiness, have been enough to carry them through a lifetime? No, Hannah thought. Adamantly not. But whose incendiary beginning—no matter its heat, or the thrilling flare it created—didn't end up, eventually, simply extinguished? She and Thomas had been happy for a long time before they suddenly weren't.

"There is no way to look cool with a car seat in your car," Leo said, snapping in place the elaborate plastic contraption. He smiled, delighted with their errand. Still happy, Hannah marveled, at having a baby.

The baby rode home with them that first day in what Hannah came to recognize as his constitutional calm. He'd perhaps cried so much, for so long, that he'd mostly cried himself out. He was a quiet baby now, not wise-seeming exactly, but shrewd, as if he would pick his battles, as if he would wait and see. Hannah had a lot of time to study him, first swaddled and vaguely immobilized in his chair, then, as the season grew mild, in clothing designed for babies younger than him, his steady stare and palpable rib cage. After several months he was still called Baby; his expression seemed to say he understood that his parents were not fully done themselves, and that he would be charged, now and later, with surviving despite bad odds. Better him, he seemed to indicate, than the fat oblivious models one met in the grocery or park, with their festooned strollers, those dimpled, gleaming butterballs with their robust sets of parents. Those babies need not have exerted a single effort on their own behalf. Not so, Baby Prentiss. He was sallow still, as if he smoked cigarettes, with more hair than seemed natural on an infant, and somehow covering his head like an executive's, with a defined part on one side. His nose was slender, his neck and elbows and hands refined, dexterous and bony as an older child's, and he rarely smiled, as if the world had taught him to challenge its charms.

The crib had been in Leo's room, but the baby's hungry sounds in the night often did not wake him; Leo slept like the teenager he was, greedily, obliviously, his body accustomed to taking for granted his mother's vigilance. Hannah, by contrast, woke at the first rustle, the first minor squeak; she would never not be a mother, she deduced, standing at the microwave, heating the bottle before Baby P even realized it was hunger that had pulled him from sleep. It was a pleasure to know something so surely, to do a job so well. After they moved the crib to her bedroom, Leo knocked before he came in, visiting every morning to say good-bye as he headed to school.

"Grandpa Chuck" brought over diapers and jars of mashed food, stuffed toys, and other haphazard supplies. He and Hannah stood at the crib, staring down at the boy, neither of them too old to be his parents—they might have conceived him right over there, on Hannah's bed. On its bedpost hung her nightgown, limp satin rag. There was no way not to think of sex in such a situation, and she knew Chuck was aware of it, too. And in some other lifetime, they might actually have gone that route, found each other in this curious circuitous way through their children and grandchild, reverse incest—a prospect her poor exhusband might never successfully assimilate. But fortunately, he wouldn't have to. Not in this lifetime, Hannah decided.

"Niffer isn't getting any better," Chuck chose to say. "Her doctor says postpartum's a bitch. It's sure kicking my ass." He sighed. "You should see our medicine cabinet. I never knew there were so many happy pills."

"Yet so little happiness."

"Amen." He squinted down at his grandson. "It's fucked up to say so, but I wish he hadn't happened. You know?"

"Yes."

"I mean, having a kid gave *me* a reason not to kill myself, but that's not working for Niffer. I don't know *what's* gonna work for Niffer."

The girl's misery descended momentarily between them, over the sleeping child, like a bleak, black miasma. And then was abruptly dissipated by Baby P's swinging fist and toothless yawn. Chuck cupped his own nicotine-tinged fingers around the baby's. "I don't wish you didn't happen, buddy," he apologized.

Hannah still drank wine, but only one glass a day. It was difficult to drink only one glass, maybe more difficult than not drinking at all. That initial infusion of alcohol prepared its drinker to let loose the reins. And though Hannah had always loved best the first drink—the sensation of ease with which it filled her, largesse, affection, gratitude—she had never been good at stopping while she was ahead. She likened this one drink to the hour it accompanied, when the air was oaky, just before dark, the benign warm light in which everyone looked lovely and life did not seem a useless and redundant pursuit. Every day, she closed her eyes under the wave of fulfilling calm. This abbreviated happy hour corresponded with Baby P's afternoon nap, and she had the additional luxury of toasting his sleeping peaceful face.

One afternoon in June, Hannah had just poured her ritual wine when she was surprised to find her other son Justin on the porch. He had not spoken to her for almost a year—and now he knocked at his own front door. These days, she knew of him only from what Thomas or Bea reported: he'd come out of the closet and landed himself not only a boyfriend and a job but an acting scholarship at the university. He was flourishing, suddenly at ease in a body he'd once loathed, a body he'd skulked about in as if to shrug it off and abandon it somewhere.

Justin had hurt Hannah's feelings when he moved away. Then, she would have bet her life he'd choose her rather than his father—and she would have lost that bet. Sometimes it seemed that she *had*. "What's wrong?" she asked him, opening the door.

"What isn't?" he answered, rolling his eyes. He thrust out a scholarship form that required his mother's signature.

"If you didn't need me to sign this, when would I have seen you again?"

"I don't know."

Since she held the form, he had to follow when she invited

him in. She led him to the kitchen, where Baby P slept crooked in his stroller. Surely the sight of the baby would melt his coldness? Hannah sat at the table and set her foot on the stroller's footrest, resuming the rocking metronomic activity that had become second nature to her. She and Baby P had recently returned from their afternoon walk. Every day they met up with dogs and other children and neighbors, Hannah touched by the goodwill the child afforded her. Home afterward, Baby P was always asleep, exhausted by ambassadorship.

"What happened to his skanky mom?" Justin asked.

Hannah appraised him. He had flung himself gracefully into a chair, one arm thrown over the back rung, one leg crossed over the knee of the other. He had always been a pretty boy, but now had adopted gestures that Hannah's father would have called "swishy." Hannah wouldn't have minded those, but his unabashed snottiness made her angry. Angry, and sad. Would he ever again be someone she understood?

"Aren't you worried he'll turn out as messed up as us?" Justin asked.

"I don't think you're messed up."

"You wouldn't." He nodded at her glass of wine. "Can I have some?"

"Okay." His portion finished the bottle, which Hannah laid gently in the garbage. Justin sipped, then winced.

"I prefer white zinfandel," he said, and Hannah couldn't help laughing. For that moment she missed Thomas, sharply: he was the only one who would have been properly amused and touched by their twenty-year-old son's preference for pink wine.

"What's so funny? At least I don't polish off a bottle or two a day. At least I have a job."

Hannah rose to find a pen. He'd come to have his form

signed, she'd sign his form. If he didn't care for her anymore, well, what could she do about that? Science, she reminded herself, concerning love. "Justin," she said, after scrawling her signature in the proper place, "Those things you mentioned are, more or less, victimless crimes. And in a way, I don't really think they're any of your business."

"This family is so my business!"

The baby jerked awake, so suddenly fierce was Justin's voice. But he did not cry. He blinked, looking from Hannah to the stranger. Justin was breathing heavily, his slender shoulders moving with his chest. He had always been sensitive, his feelings easily hurt, his emotions close to the surface. It had never seemed a useful trait, especially for a boy, but Hannah had cherished it, encouraged it, loved it about him.

"I can't believe you're in charge of that baby. I can't believe that's the best option available."

"I'm very good to that baby."

"He doesn't even have a name." Justin didn't look at her, but at Baby P, shaking his head disgustedly. His respiration was mechanical, like a machine. No, not like a machine. Like an injured animal, an inarticulate being whose life was at risk.

"What's wrong?" she asked him softly, reaching for his hand.

He snatched it out from under her touch. "You're so mean to him!"

"Who? Who am I mean to?"

"Dad. You're mean to him."

"Thomas?" she said, stunned. "I'm not mean to Thomas. I was never mean to Thomas." What had he told Justin? It wasn't like him to fabricate or dramatize.

"He loves you," Justin cried, making two fists before him as if to wring a garrote in them. "He fucking *loves* you!"

At this, Baby P's lower lip began to wobble. Hannah stood to unstrap him and put him to her shoulder, grateful to have somebody to hold, to comfort. "It's not mean not to love somebody," she told Justin, wondering if this was true. "It's kind of tragic, I guess, but it's not mean."

To this, her son had no answer. He jerked his gaze away, as if the sight of her was unbearable, as if she had slapped him, hard. But she saw him swallow, again and again, fighting tears. Twenty years wasn't very many, she reminded herself.

"I should go," he finally said. But he didn't get up.

"You want to hold him?" she asked, eventually.

He took the baby awkwardly, as if she were handing him a vase of too many flowers or a bulky parcel marked "Fragile!" treating the baby as if it were dangerous. Bomb threat, indeed, thought Hannah. "Leo knows how to do this?" he asked.

"Leo's pretty good at it." Leo, dad and dishwasher, off at Red Lobster earning a little more than minimum wage. He hadn't completely mended his ways, her boy Leo—his driver's license was suspended after he'd declined to pull over when an officer clocked him doing forty-five in a school zone—but when Hannah dropped him off at the restaurant every afternoon, he never failed to lean through the back window and kiss his son on the forehead.

Soon Justin deposited Baby P back with Hannah, eager to unburden himself. The room had grown dim, the baby was hungry, evening was upon them. It would be more difficult than usual not to pour another drink, tonight. Justin smoothed his shirt and sniffed, past his anguish.

He picked up the scholarship form and headed for the door. "You wouldn't have cared if I forged your signature, would you?"

"No, not really. It just seems like red tape, officious hoop jumping."

"Dad wouldn't let me do it. He made me come here and do the right thing. That's the kind of person he is."

"Yes, that's the kind of person he is." Hannah wasn't unhappy about agreeing, closing the door behind him. She, however, was a different kind.

PARTY OF ONE

P ARTY OF ONE?" the hostess greeted Emily. She caught
her breath. Everything was striking her in the solar plexus
these days. "Party of one" seemed the saddest phrase she could
imagine, so oxymoronic. Or like a code name for masturbation.
Or for death.

"No," she was glad to be able to say, "I'm meeting somebody."

The hostess might have been amused by the circumstances,
had she known them, or, just as easily, unimpressed. Emily
had come to meet her sister Mona's lover, who was breaking
Mona's heart. Who had no idea how big a break it was.

The Grapevine had gone trendy since high school, when
Emily and her friends used to come to the bar for lunch.
There hadn't been a hostess back then, dressed in black,
with spike heels, and there hadn't been linen tablecloths. Back
then, there'd been a useful absence of bright lights and strin-
gent requirements about valid ID. You came to the Grapevine
because anything went.

Tonight, she was here to meet Nicholas Dempsey. She
identified him easily: he was the most antsy man at the bar.

"You look like Mona," he said, standing up awkwardly around his barstool, which rocked on its four legs. In a suit, he looked disguised, a youngster trying to sucker someone into believing him grown up, although his hair was the dirty tousled blond of the bad seed, and his feet were alluringly big. He wore a wedding ring, gleaming and unscarred, a ring that had not yet fallen into the garbage disposal or got lost for days at a time in the backyard.

He extended the hand without a wedding ring for Emily to shake. And she thought what she always thought when she shook a man's hand: the last thing that hand had gripped, and in just this way, was his own dick at a urinal.

"You could be her twin," he said in disbelief. He was drinking a black-and-tan, which looked as rich as chocolate, molasses floating a layer of cream. He had a faint rim of foam on his thin upper lip.

Emily lifted her hip onto the barstool beside him, wiping her palm on a cocktail napkin. "Merlot," she told the bartender.

"Your sister always orders whatever I order," Nicholas Dempsey said.

"She's easy."

He shook his head, lips thoughtfully pinched as if to whistle. "She's not easy. That's just the problem."

Emily had to agree; it was why she had come.

The signature trellises still lined the bar's walls, plastic grapes hung from dusty synthetic leaves. Once, she and her friends had celebrated a birthday here—whose?—an extended lunch, pitchers of golden beer in the afternoon sunlight, a blood-colored chocolate cake called Red Velvet. Their hands and lips were brilliant with crimson dye when they returned— as if from a crime scene—stoned and sated, ribs sore from laughter, to honors fifth hour. Emily missed her youth with a sharp pang, as if it were a beautiful dream on the verge of dissolving: Come back!

Nicholas Dempsey's loose-hinged knee knocked suddenly into hers, forcing their eyes to meet, the present to descend. Like his wedding ring, he was unmarked by experience, party-boy pretty, someone who in later years would trade his smug slimness for a paunch, his rosy glowing cheeks for gin blossoms. Emily sighed. She had intimated blackmail to get him here. But all she really wanted to do was to instruct him on how to break up with Mona well, so that she wouldn't try to kill herself again, the way she had on her last breakup from a married man with children.

Emily had watched that chain of events with a kind of horror, and most horrifying of all had been her part in setting it off. The man had been her husband, and she'd discovered his affair with Mona in the tiniest of mistakes. In the large areas—rendezvous, phone calls, love notes—they'd been scrupulously discreet, but at the micro level they'd failed. One evening, Emily had watched Mona simply lift Barry's cup and sip his coffee. Just that small moment, that piece of thoughtless intimacy, and Emily knew that they were sleeping together. She gave Barry a blow job that night and told him that he had to end his affair, pronto, naming no names, citing no evidence. He was in the habit of being wowed by her; and he complied with her wish immediately, as if afraid of her abilities, as if he might otherwise be transformed into a toad.

That same night, Mona had ingested as many pharmaceuticals as she could lay her hands on, and not two weeks later Emily found herself shrieking at her sister to take her antidepressants, pulling her into and out of the back seat of a car for her therapy sessions. Somehow Emily's own right as an injured party had been pushed aside for the larger issue of her sister's life. You could get nowhere trying to assign blame in such a circumstance—everyone seemed both victim and perpetrator. But Mona, it could not be disputed, had been the loser. Barry had won, taken so much from her that she was left empty. Now Barry was Emily's ex, and Mona still believed that the affair had been secret.

Emily thought of herself as an amazing repository, a holder of secrets, and she was now harboring a new one of her own: a cancer that smoldered deep inside her, ready to ignite her from the inside out. Neither Mona nor Barry knew about that, either.

Emily had heard that Nicholas Dempsey had two children, the ages, more or less, of her own children. He did not seem qualified to be a parent, but who was she to judge, given her own inadequate ex-husband?

"How's Mona?" he said finally, his tone weary.

Emily pictured her sister on the bathroom floor just the evening before. She'd opened the door after knocking and not getting an answer, pushing into the room while unzipping her jeans, and the door caught on what turned out to be Mona's feet. Mona lay on the bath mat, half dressed, fists at her eyes, sobbing silently, in a tableau that bore the appearance of insanity: tub full of water, its still surface broken every few seconds by a slow drip, lights off, razor nicks on Mona's calves and knees, as if she'd been attacked by a rosebush.

"Mona!" Emily had cried. "What's wrong?"

"Bluh," her sister said.

"Bluh?"

"How come everybody knows how to act, anyway?" Mona asked. "How'd you get so confident?"

Emily stepped around Mona to sit on the toilet. "Do you

mind? I have to pee." Her need to urinate was twice as frequent now. Often when she laughed she leaked, like an old
person, the way she had during pregnancy. Her female parts
were betraying her, sending her to a new specialist, the one
called a "gyno onco."

"Pee freely," Mona said dispassionately.

Emily flushed, then spread a bath towel over her sister and
knelt down by her head. Emily's job, always, was to ferry her
sister from despairing, drifting sea to solid land. But what had
put Mona at sea this time?

"What happened?" Emily asked.

And so the story of Nicholas Dempsey had come out. Emily
listened, unsurprised. Was there any lesson more often reiterated than that history repeats itself? That people have a will
to live and not learn? Her married boyfriend had stopped
calling her. Mona expected the worst. She pleaded with her
sister for an explanation. "I don't get it. I can't get it. He just
stopped caring. Where was I when they were handing out
that particular gift?"

That this man beside Emily at the bar, this random
breathing organism named Nicholas Dempsey, could be responsible for such devastation seemed like a cruel hoax. He'd
asked about her sister, and Emily did not know how honest
to be.

"Mona is confused," she said, which seemed safe, something you could say of anyone worth her salt.

"So am I," he said quickly.

"I bet Mona is more confused."

"Well, I don't want to get into one-upping misery."

Emily appraised him, recalling her sister's misery, which
hung on her like a lead apron. On the bathroom floor, Mona

had accepted toilet paper to blow her nose. "How could he just stop?" she asked again.

"It's self-protective," Emily guessed. Didn't men do that, the preemptive strike?

"Would *you* be able to just stop? Let's say you'd been having a raging, obsessive romance for about six months, every waking minute spent thinking about each other, calling each other, leaving messages, meeting in parking lots and weird motels out in Augusta and Kingman. I mean, I *know* it was reciprocal. I don't have any doubt about it. So how does he just pull the plug on that? Could you?" Her open, wounded face made her look like she was a four-year-old again, appealing to Emily for an explanation of the cruel world, the boy who'd sucker-punched her and stolen her candy. Innocence like that was stunningly dangerous.

"I could," she confessed. She had. "Although I sort of wish that I couldn't, if you want to know the truth."

"Why?" Mona cried. "Why would you want to suffer like this?"

Because it was pure, and because it meant that its inspiration had been just as powerful. This kind of distilled pain could only have come from sublime pleasure; Emily pictured a huge shade tree, under which grew a root system as knotty and veiny and vast as the tree above, mirrored there in the subterranean dark, inhabited by slick eyeless centipedes instead of songbirds. Was that not some definition of perversion?

What was difficult was reconciling Mona's response with the figure beside her at the Grapevine. Nicholas Dempsey sipped his creamy drink. Emily wanted to push him off his stool and kick him, repeatedly, in the groin, where his reckless penis hid, and in the ribs that housed his tiny, tiny heart. Instead, she said, "You kind of have the upper hand right now."

He sighed mightily. He seemed to enjoy the adult quality of the situation, the disposal of his first mistress. There would be others, it was clear. "My favorite thing about Mona is how, when she wakes up, she stretches," Nicholas Dempsey said, trying a new tack. "I love how she makes her hands into fists, and there's her belly button, and her face is a little hedge apple, all squeezed up. You know?" He stared into Emily's impassive eyes. So what if he could speak metaphorically? She was trying to figure out if he was a sweet person or not. These days, she had more skepticism than usual concerning sweetness. She couldn't afford to be fooled. She had no time for games, however intricately fashioned they revealed their player to be. Talking about her sister in bed seemed unappealingly intimate, like some strange come-on line. Or perhaps he was merely naive. Was he flirting? Or simply eager to talk about his secret life? Besides, the last time Emily had seen Mona's fists, they'd been grinding into her weeping eye sockets.

"I just can't manage having an affair anymore," he said abruptly. Emily felt some shift in him, some veil of coolness slip off.

"Because?"

"She's too intense. She was messing with my home life." He licked his lips. *Too intense*: Here they went again. Barry couldn't handle her intensity, either. Intensity frightened cowards like Emily's ex-husband and this jerk. Moreover, how had Mona manufactured intensity for Nicholas Dempsey? Like Barry, there seemed to be little to attach to in Nicholas Dempsey; his charm was utterly elusive, or had yet to develop. But of course that was beside the point. Love was all about creating the beloved, concocting from whole cloth the object of one's affection. Mona's version of Nicholas Dempsey resided in her mind and body and heart, and it was a character Emily couldn't begin to understand or know. She'd heard all about their long conversations, their secret assignations, heard in Mona's voice the man she had made up—who bore little resemblance to the man before Emily now.

"I mean, it seems like she changed the rules," the real Nicholas Dempsey said.

"Her feelings changed," Emily said. "She likes you more than she thought."

"But the deal is I told her right up front that I was married, and I wasn't going to get unmarried. I have been in no way leading her on."

He was a letter-of-the-law sort, she thought. "Sometimes people fall in love," she told him. Emily knew Mona fell. Fell hard, and hurt herself, and then felt in every important way that the rejection was justified. Sure enough: she was unworthy. Every one of Mona's relationships ended without her permission. That she would let herself fall in love over and over—open herself like a flayed animal—seemed to Emily both beautiful and insane.

The way Nicholas Dempsey stared into Emily's face told her that this wasn't his first drink, that he'd been here for a while, fortifying himself. She had the sudden wild impression that, if she wanted to, she could go with him to wherever it was he went for these sorts of things and make love.

"You look so much like Mona it's scary," he said, blinking deliberately.

"I'm five years older and an inch taller, and my head is smaller. She's got this great heart-shaped face." Emily prattled on some more about the differences between her and her sister, but Nicholas Dempsey was peering into her in a familiar and unsettling manner. If she resembled her sister, and if he had undressed her sister, then he was capable of seeing inside her clothing. Nothing she'd heard in high-school forensics applied; her audience had a complete understanding of not only her underwear but what it covered. Nicholas Dempsey's frank expression of longing was flattering, there was no denying it. A body wanted to be loved, wanted to respond to desire. She sighed, feeling she was getting far ahead of herself. Sleeping with her sister's lover would make her and Mona even in some way, yet Emily didn't sense that revenge was necessary. Barry and Mona had both seemed to need to punish her for her sheer competence in being an adult, and it was oddly elegant—economical—that they'd done so together. Emily had forgiven them long ago, she realized, so sleeping with Nicholas Dempsey would not be revenge but something else, a fresh joust, a new wounding of her sister. She could afford it because a cancer was growing inside her. Once Mona knew about it, she would have to forgive almost anything.

Nicholas Dempsey had ordered another black-and-tan before he'd finished the one on the bar. He was the kind of drinker who doesn't like to be left empty-handed. This made him more interesting to Emily, put a dent in his generic demeanor. He was becoming distinct to her now, someone with personality, and though it was a personality she disliked, at least it had edges and angles.

"Wine?" he asked, raising his eyebrows at her half-full glass.

"Sure."

"Here's the thing that clinched it," he said. "My daughter— she's eleven months old—she crawled over to me a few weeks ago, after I got home, the last time I was out with Mona, 'working late.'" He used both hands to make bunny ears around his euphemism. "Anyhow, so I get home, all glowing and smug, and there's little Ella, doing her thing with the furniture. She can't walk yet, just goes around from one piece of furniture to another, like a drunk. Way cute. So she crawls into my lap and starts patting my face, like she forgot what I looked like, I'd been gone so long. I can't tell you how"—he searched for the word, the future crow's-feet at his eyes appearing briefly—"*despicable* I felt. How low and repulsive, how I'd been looking into Mona's face when I should have been at home with my daughter."

"Uh-huh," Emily said blandly. He'd patted his own face when he imitated his daughter, and she couldn't help thinking about Petra, *her* toddler, who might have to get along without her mother. This made Nicholas Dempsey's problem seem so mild to Emily, so self-indulgent and ridiculous, that she wanted to punch him. Fuck you, you little punk, getting all angsted out by a love affair.

Emily drained her first glass, setting it down so sharply that the stem snapped. Nicholas Dempsey looked alarmed. "What's the matter?"

"Oh, nothing."

The bartender swept away the two pieces of the glass without expression. All in a day's work. "I don't know why wineglasses have to be so delicate, do you?" A worthier man would have known to comfort her then, but Nicholas Dempsey, hopelessly young and self-absorbed, grew afraid, and addressed the issue of stemware instead of the forceful hand that had brought it down.

"Hush," Emily said to him finally. He bristled, but he closed his mouth. "My sister is fragile, even though you think she's tough." Emily did not want to disclose Mona's suicide attempt; if Mona hadn't told him, then he oughtn't to know. "Do you think you could possibly work this out so that she thinks she broke up with you?" She had to restrain herself from going into a rant about his ability to pull off such a trick, because she knew that he wasn't likely to be good at this kind of orchestration. He did not want to be the one who got dumped. He was not someone who got his heart broken. And it was Emily's job to persuade him how truly manly it was to commit such a thing, to fabricate a broken heart. It was true that he had the most to lose—his wife, his children—but Mona had no one to cushion her fall, no one. Parents and siblings and even a cute niece and nephew were not the same, not nearly. And, so far, Petra wasn't really that cute.

Emily drank her second glass of wine quickly, felt it take up glowing residence. "Okay," she said. "The deal is you can do this really easily. Just go make yourself miserable in front of Mona, suffer some guilt, tell her the story about the baby patting your face. That's a really good story. And you have a son, right? He probably talks and could say some things about missing you? Maybe your wife could get sick?"

Nicholas Dempsey stared at her, no doubt thinking, This woman looks a lot like Mona but she is totally not Mona. Emily waited.

"What kind of sick?" he asked.

"I don't know. Uterine cancer?"

He made a face. Emily swallowed something bitter, trying not to squint unkindly at his youth, at the arrogance that had revealed itself. *His* wife would never have uterine cancer.

"Mono? Anemia? Give one of the kids strep—that'll keep you home for a few days, then you can get it yourself. Let your immune system run down, get some bags under your eyes." He would be vastly improved with bags under his eyes, Emily realized. With bags, he might turn into something. "Start looking bedraggled and hopeless, and let Mona take the initiative. Let Mona rescue you by ending the deception." When he didn't respond, Emily said, "The deception that is eating away at you."

"Right."

"Are you patronizing me?"

"No," he said, throwing his head back, swallowing the last of his black-and-tan, his Adam's apple working in an ugly fashion. "No, you're patronizing *me* is what's going on here."

"Another?" the bartender said, unhurried, familiar with scenes. Would it be interesting to tend bar? Would it make you wise? Or just jaded? Were the two the same?

"Mona's sister," she'd told his snotty secretary that morning, when a name had been demanded. He came instantly to the phone then, agreed readily to their meeting. Now Emily leveled the same threat. "If you don't at least try to do what I've suggested, I'm going to call your wife and tell her all about Mona. And I might give you a few other girlfriends." She stood up and nearly fainted, so quickly did the blood leave her head. She bent over, took a deep breath. "You seem like someone who needs to have a whole stable of girlfriends."

"Fuck you."

For some reason, this made Emily laugh. The last person to say "Fuck you" to her had been Barry. It was his favorite phrase; he said it all day long, could inflect it in a hundred different ways, give it a whole continuum of shadings. He could say it like Nicholas Dempsey, in anger, and wholly unlike him, as in the middle of sex: "*Fuck . . . you*," with longing and release and pure animal pleasure. Emily missed Barry just now— young and useless as he was, he was still preferable to Nicholas Dempsey. How had she ended up having Nicholas Dempsey say "Fuck you" to her in this cold, mean manner?

"She's way too good for you," Emily couldn't help telling him, and feeling the truth of what she'd said swell in her made her want to slap him. Her love for Mona was bigger than him, better than him, and it couldn't help matters in the least—a fat impotent fact, a gun loaded with blanks.

"Yeah?" he said, like a bully. "Well, you're nothing like her, not one thing."

OBO

Fʀᴏᴍ ᴛʜᴇ ꜰʟɪɢʜᴛ'ꜱ ᴏʀɪɢɪɴꜱ in LAX through the change of planes in Dallas, Abby Mills followed the kind stranger, a grandmother, a midwestern matron whose final destination was also Wichita. Abby trailed her gently bobbing gray bun into the small jet. Their seats were not assigned together on this leg of the journey, but Abby sensed the woman's continued goodwill, three rows behind, radiating like the heat from a potbellied stove. On the first flight, Abby had not initially noticed her as she surveyed her compatriots, the hip and pretty, amused by the way, when there was turbulence, all the women's breasts jiggled in unison. But when the plane wobbled earthward like a doomed balsa glider, Nana from the Bible Belt had put aside the thick paperback bodice-ripper romance she'd been reading and covered Abby's moist hand with her own steady dry one. Lurching descent, those crazy rubber tires Abby had watched countless times from airport bars and waiting areas throwing off their black mist of tread when they hit the ground, the explosive reverse back-thrust, the popping racket in one's own inner ear, the rattle of gear and shudder of abrupt cessation. "It's perfectly fine, honey," the woman assured her, blinking clueless blue eyes inside folds of skin, unconcerned about chin hairs or neck wattles, wearing a cherry red holiday sweat suit. Patting, patting, a confident kindness beyond any reasonable expectation.

In return for this kindness, Abby had lied. Told the woman that her visit was to her fiancé's home in Wichita, the edgy first meeting with the future in-laws. They were the Bonatellos, in the oldest neighborhood with the grand but fading houses of former oil men, cattle kings, war plane manufacturers. Nana knew the neighborhood. Was this Dr. Bonatello, the psychiatrist, whose wife had recently passed? Nana believed she had been a nurse. Quite likely, Abby realized, panicking. She did not know if her host had a son of marriageable age. The lie produced a film of sweat across her brow. She'd exaggerated the degree of her anxiety, attaching it to the flight, told a few other half-truths concerning near-disasters in the air. In fact, she was coming to Christmas with her English professor's wife's family. She'd been invited on account of the lie she'd told Dr. Shapiro—professor of Romantic literature—which was that her own family had disowned her. She had nowhere to go for the holidays, she said. She was feeling very depressed—this much was true, a recent love debacle—but her parents held nothing against her and, back in Claremont, were hurt that she'd opted against them. Dr. Shapiro conducted his Blake seminar in his home on Thursday evenings, and there Abby had made acquaintance with his wife, Lucia Shapiro, née Bonatello. It was Lucia who had inspired the lie, Lucia with her two small children and exhausted beauty—hair pushed away from her face, dark wells of fatigue floating her eyes. The way she skirted the dining room table and its Thursday-evening fervency, her baby clutched against her chest,

the toddler trailing—supplanted, morose, thumb in mouth—
and being hushed, as if her husband were conducting a religious ceremony, as if she were his servant. Lucia, who brought
in a warm pastry, cheese, little spreading knives with ceramic
pineapples for handles, a bottle of red wine and real stemware.
Wedding gifts, Abby guessed; students were rarely served so
graciously. And, too, the way Dr. Michael Shapiro palmed
Lucia's rump as she passed his end of the large oval table.
That calculated thoughtless proprietary hand on her. Abby
had at first liked Dr. Shapiro, his wit, his quick dismissal of
his dull colleagues, those cowboy boots he wore, the way,
when you visited his office, he put his feet up on the desk and
stretched out to talk to you, twiddling his earring, grinning.
But she grew to adore Lucia, the truly romantic woman married to the callow Romantic scholar. The more Abby learned
about William Blake, the less she respected him; Dr. Shapiro—
"Michael," he insisted his students call him—emphasized the
poet's decadence and gluttony. Yet she'd stayed in Michael's
good graces in order to finagle an invitation to Christmas at
Lucia's family's home; they almost always invited a grad student along. She'd cried in Dr. Shapiro's office. She'd bussed
the dining room table at his home, when the crumb-laden
china plates and smudgy glasses had been pushed aside by her
pointy-headed peers. She was always the last to leave. She
feigned an interest in those whiny little children.

"My fiancé," she told Nana sniffily on the plane, "he's afraid
his family will not approve." She was acquiring for some reason a German accent to go along with her story.

As promised by Dr. Shapiro back in his office, Lucia's family
home was immense, the weather dreadful, the city bedecked
with tinsel and lights as if to hide its preponderant grayness.
L.A. seemed a remote planetary distance away. A Bonatello

teenage nephew had been sent to the airport to retrieve Abby. She told him the airline had lost her luggage, when in fact she had not brought any. She wanted to borrow Lucia's clothing while pretending to wait for the airline to deliver hers.

To Abby's chirping inquiry on the ride, the nephew said nothing, concentrating on the gearshift of his Mustang. Finally he informed her that he was a practicing nihilist. He swung into the driveway like someone who didn't care if he lived or died, screeching to a stop behind a logjam of automobiles, and had already slammed his door before Abby could catch her breath. She followed him out of the low-slung vehicle and into one of several back entrances.

A table full of faces looked up at her blankly as she stepped into the kitchen, five sets of eyes exactly like Lucia's. Yet Lucia wasn't among them. "I'm Abby," she said. "A student of Dr. Shapiro?"

At this the youngest occupant of the table, a teenage girl stretching melted cheese between two corn chips, laughed. "You call him *doctor?*" These were indisputably Lucia's kin, the scornful girl, a niece perhaps, three men who must be Lucia's brothers, versions of the same aging handsome man, each more dejected-seeming than the one before, and the prototype—the desiccated gray face, eyes behind his spectacles scowling at Abby: Who was she, exactly, and what was she doing here?

"My luggage got lost," Abby said. "I love your house."

Fortunately, Lucia appeared then, her children attached per usual. She wore house slippers, and a bed jacket, an outfit that could have signaled illness or languor. A person wearing this could have just gotten up, or given up. All four men followed her with their eyes, straightened in their seats, smiled weakly. She was their favorite, their darling.

"Abby," Lucia said vaguely, shifting her baby to her hip to give Abby a hug. The child had a hand inside Lucia's satin jacket and shirt, holding on to a breast. "Let go Mommy's booby," she said to the baby, who violently averted her face as if to make Abby disappear. Lucia's neck was damp where her hair was falling from two chopsticks she'd jammed in a thick roiling knot.

"Anthony will show you your room," said Lucia. This was the nihilist's father, Lucia's oldest brother. But he had to move his car first, and when Abby looked out the kitchen window a few minutes later she saw him and his son smoking on the driveway, stomping their feet and hunching their shoulders, suffering but stoic. Eventually, the bedroom she was led to was in the servants' old quarters, two floors up. The room was a former kitchen, with books now stored in the ancient stove and a nest of stuffed animals in the sink. The single bed was wedged beneath a dormer window, from which Abby could see the downtown skyline. A metal floor radiator with claw feet put out a cozy heat. She never wanted to leave this garret; she would close the door and open the cardboard boxes that had Lucia's name written on them. High school memorabilia, she guessed, letters and pictures and trinkets.

"I wish *I* could sleep up here," said Anthony's wife. "It's quiet, and there's only room for one in the bed." Abby didn't want to be in league with this malcontent, so she merely smiled, as if she didn't speak English well enough to follow the insinuation. "Cocktail hour in fifteen minutes," the woman called as she trundled back down the stairs. "You won't want to miss that."

The other two bedrooms in the attic were waiting for a cousin and an uncle. Each room was commodious, comfortable, full of the stuff of the family: a dressmaker's dummy and a functioning train set in one, a collection of dismantled fish tanks and equipment in the other, more boxes with names markered on them. The window over the narrow steps rattled with a burst of cold air, and Abby shivered as she descended to the second floor. This was where the immediate family re-occupied their old rooms along with their new families, cots and cushions and couches everywhere adorned with pillows and comforters. Abby investigated, the ample evidence of *plenty* behind every door she tentatively tapped upon and then opened: the closet full of Christmas gifts that Santa would bring to the little children, the linen cupboard, currently depleted as sheets and towels had been distributed throughout the house, and in each of the five children's bedrooms the same-yet-different clutter, the way all of them had sprung open their luggage and left their intimate articles everywhere—jewelry, pajamas, makeup, pharmaceuticals. The last, largest bedroom belonged to the patriarch; it alone was orderly, chilly as a tomb. On the mantel a clock ticked, and the air smelled of soot from the fireplace, of camphor and dust and the cool steam of a humidifier. A bathrobe hung from each of the footboard posts, two ghosts, and a large wooden cross was propped menacingly in a corner. In the top drawer of the dresser Abby found a stack of mint-fresh twenty-dollar bills—stocking stuffers, she wagered, slipping one in her pocket. She'd taken less obvious things from the other rooms, pills and an earring and a pair of pantyhose. But from the generation that occupied this room she wanted nothing but cash.

Downstairs, more people arrived. Cars rumbled into the driveway, voices rose in greeting, hoarse masculine laughter barked out, cupboard doors squeaked and slammed. The phone rang and rang. Abby felt she'd stepped like a spy into an important drama, its cast of characters in medias res within an elaborate set. Children chased past her as she made her way to the kitchen, which was crowded and steamy. Several conversations went on at once; Abby was offered many drinks and settled on a red wine after seeing Lucia's glass of the same. The nihilist had been sent to pick up some fossil named Agnes from the nursing home, and then to the Safeway for this evening's provisions; he had only recently received a driver's license, which seemed to provide a reason for continuing to live. Errands: the salvation of the hopeless.

Abby could imagine how her presence had been sold to the family; she'd sold the same bill of goods in Dr. Shapiro's office. Sad-sack suicidal student, nowhere to go on Christmas, the one who'd volunteered to babysit for her professor and his wife, her patience with their children, her dedication, the way she tidied up the house. She could help while Michael went to the MLA meeting after Christmas.

Now she was introduced to Lane, Lucia's big sister, and her teenage girls, the fifteen-year-old she'd already encountered and her eighteen-year-old sibling. They reminded Abby of magpies, operating as a team, baiting their mother in front of her family. The eighteen-year-old was holding a pink drink in a martini glass.

"She sets us up," the other said to the group at large, "sending me into Walgreens to make a point. The point is this: I can buy a pregnancy test but not condoms."

"Mom was all pissed because she got carded there the day before buying tonic water."

"That'll teach her to go out without her license."

"All it taught her was to argue with the clerk."

"No one drinks tonic water who doesn't drink alcohol. Hence, the carding."

"Mom kept telling the woman she was two times legal, forty-two."

"Then she comes raging in after us to dick around on the condom issue. Same clerk from yesterday."

"So *bunk*!" the girls chorus.

Their mother listened with a strained smile. Her daughters possessed the general family looks—olive skin, dark hair, luminous black eyes—but none of the graceful gestures that made Lucia lovely to watch. The three of them, Lane and the magpies, lived in Chicago, which had upped their tempo. Lane, angular and suspicious, cast her glance around the room like a surveillance camera. Abby avoided looking directly at her, afraid of what she would intuit. Instead, like the men, Abby focused on Lucia, who poured drinks and satisfied the general need for snacks. She was helped by the wife of one brother and the girlfriend of another, these women who didn't seem to mind their auxiliary status in the house, while Anthony's wife sat slack at the table with a stein of beer and a bowl of peanuts before her. Children ran in and out, demanding food, tattling on one another, tearful, defiant, ecstatic, each causing a noticeable flinch in the face of their grandfather. The adults were nervous on his behalf, Abby saw; he'd lost his wife since last Christmas, and she had apparently taken some crucial part of him with her.

"Come *play*!" exhorted one of the cousins. But Lucia's children wouldn't, the baby safe above the fray in her mother's arms while her brother, the mama's boy, held on to her knees. Nobody, not even their father Dr. Shapiro, could persuade them to unlock their grips.

Abby eased her chair farther into the corner, preparing to be the house's spectator. In one pocket she worked the twenty-dollar bill into a tube; in the other she repeatedly poked the tip

58

of her finger with the sharp back of an earring. These were charms for luck, or something like it.

Among his in-laws, Michael found himself checking clocks and calendars, calculating the moment he could begin to drink, the number of days until he would depart for his conference in New York. "Why do you drink?" his wife had asked him once. She had been pregnant at the time, so not drinking at all. Sobriety had turned her more pensive than she already was. She blinked so slowly.

"I drink to calm down," he answered; without it, he arrived at evening with a short temper and a racing heart, poised as if to fight or yell, as if he'd spent the day being primed for some challenge that would never arise. He had a few other reasons. He drank to blunt his persistent disappointment in people, to keep himself from the great paradoxical state of restless boredom. Drinking, he was tolerant, resigned, benumbed. Drinking provided a personable face for the world, an accepting nature.

When he came home from his teaching days, he would be greeted by a cluttered house and the remaining odors of breakfast. Lucia often would still be wearing what she'd slept in, a soft all-purpose outfit, breasts harnessed in a nursing bra beneath. Though he knew that his wife and children went out— to the grocery, to the park, to play groups—they all three seemed in suspended animation, posed exactly as when he'd left them. Lollygagging around, no feel for the satisfying rituals of a passing day. Dog hair swirling on the tiled floor in ever-growing abundance. Meanwhile, he'd fulfilled a host of chores, meetings and classes and all manner of social encounters around campus. He'd brought a coffee cake for the secretaries, written reports and commented on files, thrown into the trash a gratifying amount of junk mail, even paid bills during his office hours; he'd spent a half hour at the gym hefting weights. Check off enough daily obligations, and you earn your right to come home.

"What have you been doing?" he asked each evening after he'd poured his first drink, keeping accusation out of his voice by an act of will.

Lucia would smile sleepily, a little sardonically, as if he ought to know how she'd spent her day, how it had been relentless labor. It was he who'd requested children, and she had agreed, as was her nature. Michael often felt he had not really known her when he married her. He had adored her, that much was true, but he had also made a lot of assumptions about her, something she encouraged by not being a particularly definite person. Thoughtful, he'd thought. She'd grown up last in a house of opinionated elders, and her nature was to assume their points of view, conform like a chameleon to the dominant mood, follow instructions without questioning the wisdom, to thrive and depend on being prized, the amenable baby of a big family. Now she had her own children to provide adoration. They wore her out with it. Michael knew, from having stayed home with them himself, that it needn't be this way at the end of the day. There didn't have to be no particular meal plan—waffles? for dinner?—nor did the toys have to cover every floor. The boy, three, ought to be working on toilet training; the baby, nearly one, could be weaned. These gestures would pave the way for other growing up. The children, too, could begin thinking of their own daily checklists, obligations other than hanging on to their mother like marsupials.

But a recycling bin full of wine bottles helped Michael not make that complaint. Drunk, the loading and unloading of the dishwasher wasn't so terribly unpleasant. Time, under the influence of alcohol, passed smoothly enough. Drunk, he could enjoy watching some inane cartoon with Will, stack up blocks and knock them down, stack and knock. Drunk, he could remove sleeping Cecily from beside his sleeping wife and take her to her own bed, then climb in, ignore the damp spot the baby had left for him there, and pass out.

This was the only time Cecily could be easily withdrawn from Lucia. He had tried to win his daughter's affection, to become her favorite. He'd thought the family might balance out with her arrival, that a daughter would be different from a son. But she, like her brother, didn't care for anyone except her mother. The two children competed for Lucia to such an extent that Michael had given up, bored, disappointed—the same feelings he had for most people. The last time he and Lucia had made love she fell asleep in the middle.

She must encourage their clinginess, Michael believed. Yet Lucia seemed vaguely indifferent toward most of her entanglements. She smiled wanly at her children; she patted Michael gently when he hugged her; she phoned her father and siblings weekly to check in. She never lost her temper, she allowed one and all to love her, but she had a permanently distracted expression on her face, as if she had lost something long ago that she could never reclaim. Like Gabriel's wife Greta in "The Dead," pining for old Michael Furey, stuck instead with Michael Shapiro.

At the MLA convention, he would meet his mistress, who was another frustrating person. She was, thankfully, nobody his wife knew. He'd made the fatal mistake of inviting his last mistress to Christmas with his in-laws; what had he been thinking? Once she had spent the week with Lucia and her family—carols at the piano, tree-trimming, midnight mass with the mother, a Rorschach session with the father, cinnamon rolls and hot toddies and log fires, wandering the house in pajamas and slippers with a toddler in her arms—she could no longer sleep with Michael.

Over the years, he'd made his peace with the way he loved. He loved Lucia—he had loved her for twelve years now, never flagging—and he loved his children, but he also was in possession of another love, a secret sort. As long ago as adolescence, he'd had a public love and then another smoldering type—the girl he pursued outright and the one he kept to himself. What seemed most baffling to him was that he had yet to meet a woman who required exactly what he did. Given how much one heard about extramarital affairs, how rampant the impulse, how long its history, he'd thought he could find a partner in crime, somebody who wished for a fierce, passionate, utterly private attachment—a tragic attachment, in some ways; a romantic one, in others. Where was the woman who felt its urgency, who would plow headlong into its incendiary kamikaze terms?

Well, Christine Paulsen was in Houston at the moment. She, like his wife, was a lapsed Catholic. But Christine's lapse was not as complete as Lucia's, and although she hadn't lived with her husband for the last five years, she had not divorced him, either. He had left the marriage because he had decided he was gay. That's how Christine presented him to Michael, as somebody who had made a decision about his sexuality, not a discovery. Michael had begun with great hopes for Christine precisely because she *was* married. The circumstance seemed closer to his own, although Christine had no spare affection for her husband. The man used her as a last resort, moving back in when his boyfriends broke his heart, emptying her refrigerator, keeping her up at night with his weepy stories.

"Do you sleep together?" Michael asked, curious, worried. Would he really risk having sex with a woman who slept with a gay man?

Christine had made a noticeable bristling sound over the phone; he had offended her. "I don't want to talk about my husband," she said stiffly.

"I tell you about my wife."

"Not because I want to hear about her." They hadn't spoken on the telephone since. In these and other ways, she held a peculiar power. He never knew when he was going to upset her; it was her pious background, he concluded, that accounted for her tender sensibility. Intimacy pained her. But wasn't that what people having an affair did, exchange their romantic histories? She was more comfortable with superficial conversation about books or politics or their colleagues, anecdotes from childhood that didn't lead to intimate revelations about adulthood, tedious briefings on daily activities. If he pushed—sent a sexy e-mail, shared a fantasy—she retreated, fell into silence, and he was left floundering, feeling he'd done something coarse. She was a strange woman for him to love, he thought, remembering her shy run from beneath the bedsheets to behind the bathroom door, scurrying as if to keep him from seeing her. Shame prevented her from ever saying one thing about their lovemaking. She wasn't very good at it, as if she'd had extremely limited experience. Michael suspected the gay husband was all she had ever known. She and Michael had spent just two weekends together, one last year at the MLA where they'd met, one last spring at another conference in Montreal. It had been eight months since he'd seen her; six months since their last actual conversation over the phone. He was trying to hold on to her image, the way she blushed so thoroughly as to inflame the part in her scalp, the quick smile she always covered with her hand, the aspect of orphan she exuded, of someone early and damagingly abandoned, although she was emphatically unorphaned, full of exasperated stories about her family—her needy parents and her siblings she was more than willing to tell him about, and that needy husband she only occasionally alluded to with a fed-up sigh. What was it about her that obsessed him? Her willingness to join him in New York had taken a semester of pleading. If it weren't for her daily messages on his office phone, he would have abandoned the whole effort; it was shading toward humiliation. But she called his office early every morning, on her way to Rice, where she taught, or out to the suburbs to see her parents, stopped at a light or waiting in the Starbucks line. Houston was not a city for the impatient, she let him know. "It's like living with an old person," she told him. "An old slow person you're really fond of but you've forgotten why." In an especially brazen moment, as they parted at the Montreal airport last spring, she had told Michael she loved him. This was the only time she'd said so, just blurted out the words, and Michael was touched to realize how much it cost her, clumsy as it was, delivered as her face burned red, buried in his neck. All of her messages began with "I'm sorry," because she couldn't bring herself to actually speak with him; she phoned, knowing he wouldn't be there to answer, and ended with "I miss you," which was, he chose to think, her euphemistic way of repeating what she'd said in Montreal. She wasn't as pretty as his wife. She wasn't as bright. Her habit of calling him was more like a daily confessional than a love affair. But she had held on to him at the airport as if he alone could save her. When he thought of it, something tangible moved in his chest. It was what he recognized as love, secret love, flame-red and invisible, love for no good reason.

He would meet her at LaGuardia four days from now.

Until then he was stuck in Kansas with his in-laws. Because Lucia's mother had died, Michael's status had further depreciated, his and the other non-Bonatellos, the two wives, and the new girlfriend with her three shell-shocked children; they were not in the inner family circle, the one with the right to grieve. Extraneous, he was free to roam the big dank house, read, take runs around the park, drive children to the movies or mall—those escapes from the frigid gray of Kansas. Pass by, on occasion, the chair of old Agnes, the crazy ex-wife of his father-in-law, who joined them every Christmas to play her peculiar role. He drank, of course; in a house this size, with a larder this replete—wine cellar, fully stocked bar—you could drink from morning to night and never really attract anyone's attention. The only person who seemed to be watching him was Abby Mills, his suicidal graduate student. He hadn't wanted to bring her to Christmas—she was a mope, a leech, a brown-noser—but she had been necessary as a decoy. Two years ago he'd brought his mistress here; Abby's presence this season would serve to defuse Constance's, to undermine the instincts of someone canny like his sister-in-law Lane, or his father-in-law the former shrink. Sometimes he thought he still loved Constance. She had yet to obtain her Ph.D.; he was still on her committee, and she dropped chapters off in his mailbox at school, carefully orchestrating her hours not to coincide with his. This pained him, to know that she avoided him. The last time they'd kissed had been in her attic bedroom here at his in-laws'. The very room that Abby now occupied. That kiss could also make his chest ache, lost love a slightly different twinge.

Occasionally he would recall that he'd had a hard time choosing between Constance and her friend Dina, the two of them with similar looks, joining the program the same year, best friends immediately and catching the eye of all the male faculty and student body. What did it say about him that he might just as easily have pursued Dina? That it could have been she he had seen through some circumscribed love affair?

His nieces, Lane's two kids, were the least tedious of the Bonatellos. Michael liked to hear them badmouth their mother. In the basement, playing pool, having procured drinks for them both, he heard about Lane's online personal ad.

"She'd *die* if she knew we knew."

"We wouldn't except she always uses the same password."

"Flavia," they both recited. It was their dead grandmother's name.

"She posted a picture of herself from like ten years ago. She makes herself sound completely different from what she is."

"You should see what comes looking for her."

"Holy shit are they awful."

"This one guy, oh my God, this one guy who was just such a feeb. Here's what he was: a DWM, ISO LTR, *OBO.*"

"OBO?" Michael burst out laughing. They joined him, the three of them hanging onto their pool cues in hysterics. Poor Lane, he thought. But Lucia's stories of growing up in Lane's shadow had made him dislike the woman long before he met her. His wife didn't seem to realize that her sister was a stick: cold, jealous, bitter.

And rich, now, since she'd married and divorced well. She looked at Michael as if she could see right through him, as if she knew exactly what, and who, he was thinking about. She'd led a calculating, presumptuous life, and her own desperate foray into romance—the exposure, the tremendous vulnerability—seemed the perfect fate for her. Michael realized, later, awake and sober and squeezed out of bed by both his children, that part of what amused him so thoroughly about Lane's quest for love was that it was more pathetic than his own.

Abby had thought she would borrow Lucia's clothing in the absence of her own, but instead she was handed the outfits of Lucia's dead mother and the local cousin Jennifer. There was no shortage of female attire to borrow, and it became a daily ritual to model for the family her latest pieced-together ensemble.

Sometimes the senior Mr. Bonatello would blink blissfully at her from behind his glasses, then abruptly frown, as if Abby had intentionally fooled him into thinking his wife were still around.

Scouting about, Abby had located the house's true heart and then set up camp. Not an obvious place, the butler's pantry, but a perfect one. An inauspicious location adjacent to the kitchen, a small square room with five different doors into it, something like the switchyard of a railroad. From it you could descend to the basement, pass through to the kitchen or dining room or general hallway, and, finally, up the narrow back stairs to the third floor, where the help had once-upon-a-time lived. Ten feet by ten feet, the room was the size of a prison cell, adorned by two generations of children's pictures taped to its wainscoting, fluttering faintly when anyone passed. Contained in this small clever room were many necessary objects, each in its own place. Up high hung two cupboards; behind one door a medicine chest, full of prescription pills and salves; beside it, the bountiful liquor. Below, on a countertop, sat an antique rotary telephone with a variety of beauty aids strewn about it—hair dryer, lipsticks, combs, lotions. Tethered to this spot by the immovable phone, you could at least improve your appearance. Behind this countertop the wall was mirrored. Down below, where you wagged your foot while you primped and made phone calls, were three shelves of toys. Every day the younger children pulled out all the toys and deposited them on the room's colored linoleum floor. A heater ran up the opposite wall, making a cozy atmosphere. Beside it was a blighted black grease spot where the dog had lain for ages. Like the grandfather, the dog was startled and tormented by the children; he would sigh mightily when forced to abandon his niche. The room's lighting was very poor, but that only meant that the mirror seemed forgiving. And how well did you need to see to fish a Band-Aid from a box, assemble a drink, answer the phone, or dump toys onto the floor?

Maybe it would have been nice to have been able to read the pill bottle labels clearly.

Beyond, in the kitchen, the light was bright, and there was always grander action, an elaborate stage with a shifting cast, its players exiting and entering all day and night in different costumes. Pajamas, winter wear, princess gowns, work clothes. A skinny boy wearing nothing but boxer shorts and a hula hoop. There was always someone studying the interior of the refrigerator or washing his hands or waiting expectantly for something to happen. Groceries came in; trash went out. The round wooden table in the center held the newspaper and pancakes early in the day, syrup a condition of its surface, then the mid-morning snacks—yogurt, strawberries, dry cereal—next the lunch detritus, everything microwaved, served on a potholder; later the crayons and clay and paint and scissors of children's projects, sparkling glitter that stuck in the syrup, then the mail and bills and doctor reminders and snapshots and a road atlas, nail polish remover and cotton balls; later, drinks and adult snacks for cocktail hour—salmon mousse,

Brie and slivered almonds, mushrooms stuffed with pesto—
then the children's dinner table, spilled milk draining through
the cracks, applesauce, clove-studded pork, rejected cauliflower;
afterward ice-cream cones for the very young and the very old,
then the disappearance of everyone to prepare for night—dog-
walking, cigarette-smoking, bath-taking, phone-call-making,
Internet-checking, news-watching—an interlude where the
dishwasher reigned, moistening the atmosphere, noisy wet
motor and sucking drain, then, during the dry cycle, the children returned pink-cheeked in pajamas to be kissed good
night. A green felt cloth was spread upon the table because it
was time to play bridge, crack the ice trays, mix the drinks, find
the saltines; then later, when the patriarch was overwhelmed
by shuffling and counting, exhausted by his offspring and their
offspring, then came the peanuts and poker chips and whiskey,
an ashtray when their father was soundly asleep, the younger
men finally unleashed, loud and profane. The cool breeze of an
open winter window, an illicit chill to carry off odors.

At three in the morning, when the two sisters arrived for
their nightly bout of insomnia, they slammed shut the window,
grumbled at clearing the wreckage, making way for teacups,
novels, hidden expensive chocolate, gossip about their family.
Maybe they would start a batch of cinnamon rolls rising on the
stove, to turn the day toward morning and light.

"We go through a pound of butter and bacon every day,"
one of them noted.

"Cocktail shrimp," said the other, making a list. "Clemen-
tines."

They discussed everybody, but it always came back to the
loss of their mother. This was the season's center. They fret-
ted over their father, who was frail and perhaps losing his
mind. His shrewd, inestimable mind. And then there were

the brothers—Anthony, whose garage business was on the skids, whose son was on probation, and whose wife was on lithium; Leon, from Vegas, who missed their mother most, who'd lost a great deal of money gambling, as if he might buy back her life by hemorrhaging cash. The teenagers had taken to calling him "Wine Cure." Red-eyed, he'd told them that a glass of wine first thing in the morning would keep him from getting infected by one of these numerous snot-nosed children; he was so sick of getting sick at Christmas. Every morning you'd find him with a juice glass of last night's wine, sipping at it over the sports page. Then there was Manny, who'd both divorced his wife and adopted a whole new family this year. The sisters couldn't believe he'd brought not only a girlfriend but her—one, two, three!—children to Kansas. These, in addition to his other two kids, caravanned from Oklahoma in two cars.

Their mother's death was to blame, they agreed, every late night. It was ubiquitous, like the layer of dust covering everything in the house.

While Lucia and Lane murmured below, others slept above the kitchen and pantry and all the rest of the first floor. But not Abby. Abby had made her way down the hidden stairway, stealthy as a cat into the pantry, where she now crouched, listening in. It was the day after Christmas. The gifts had been opened, the novelty of seeing one another had faded, the holiday seemed used up, worn out. It was also the day that Michael Shapiro was leaving for New York. This day was the one Abby had been waiting for. This was *her* Christmas morning.

"Best to be a widow," Lane was saying about her own divorce of several seasons ago. "Nobody blames the widow for a failed marriage. Nobody goes second-guessing the widow."

Lucia murmured in seeming agreement; agreeability was

the same relationship she had with her professor husband; perhaps she'd learned it growing up with her bossy sister. How Abby admired Lucia's goodness, her patience and placid cheer, her easy alluring smile. The baby was at her breast, as usual; she was listening to her sister the way one might a radio. Lane didn't like Michael Shapiro and felt free to explain why; two nights ago she'd wagered he was having an affair, and Abby had since been speculating about which woman in the English department it might be. Tonight, Lane declared Michael a racist. When offering his opinion of his Chicano colleague's prose style, he claimed the man couldn't write his way out of a wet paper bag. "A wet paper *brown* bag," he amended. Scandalous! And although Abby herself had happily stored away his comment to use against him at some undetermined future date, she felt now the bad manners of Lane's badgering.

Lucia said, "Will you put another lump in this?"

"How do you tolerate him?" Lane demanded, clattering at the sugar bowl. "As soon as you wean Cecily, you should have your own affair."

Lucia laughed, saying, "I think another person in my life would just about kill me."

"Person," she'd said; Abby's heart thrilled. Maybe Lucia's affair would be with her. They would proceed slowly. Abby would never pressure her. Despite not being handed her clothing to wear, Abby had been pleased to see that Lucia was reading the book she had recommended to her. "What part are you at now?" she could ask her, and Lucia would smile guiltily, apologetically tell her that she'd only had time to read a few pages, that she was more or less stuck somewhere in the first third of the thing.

"But I'm *really* liking it," Lucia said.

71

"I thought you would," Abby responded. "I really liked it, too. I *loved* it."

"Uh-hmm," Lucia had hummed, concurring.

"Dad didn't love her enough," Lane was saying, of their parents.

"She was the one who cared more," Lucia agreed. "Is it always that way, do you think? One who loves, one who's loved?"

"Yes," Lane said. No, Abby thought.

"Which would you rather be?"

"The object," Lane quickly responded. "Always better to be the beloved."

"Really?"

"God, yes. Think how sad Mom would have been if Dad had died first. It would've been a sea of tears, here."

"You don't think he's sad about her?"

"He's scared, not sad. He's remorseful, he's anxious, he's full of regret, but he's not sad. It's different. You don't have to defend him. He wasn't faithful to her, you know."

"I know. But so what?"

"This is why your husband is having an affair, because you don't care."

"I've never understood why everybody makes such a big deal. I mean, it's not a competition." In the pantry, Abby breathed in enviously; only someone who'd never had to compete could make such a declaration.

"If he left you for another woman, you wouldn't think of that as losing?"

"If he left me, then we would be divorced, like you. Having an affair is different. Some people have a taste for it, they can't help it."

"Your naïveté is exasperating. You make me want to scream."

"Oh, please don't scream," Lucia said, and they laughed. Was that what Abby wanted? A sister?

She had learned to move when she heard their chairs scrape, when they rinsed their cups to return to bed, their nightly consultation over. Abby would quickly take herself up the back steps to her garret on the third floor. The cousin and elderly uncle in the other rooms up there both snored; she hated having to share the bathroom with them, imagining their naked bodies sitting and standing where hers did.

In the public kitchen hours, the next day, Abby sat enraptured as Lucia performed the ordinary miracle of coming into the room, preparing a snack, feeding herself and her baby and son. She wore a long white nightgown and matching robe, a cotton just thin enough to suggest her black underpants, her breasts, open to expose the bones of her clavicle. Her hair was tied in a sloppy knot. One of her pierced earlobes had grown infected, swollen pink—Abby longed to hold it, like a berry between her fingers. Lucia's high cheekbones made pretty hollows beneath. She looked like a tragic Victorian figure, someone straight out of Dickens. She set the baby on the counter and propped her there with one hand while rummaging through the fridge with the other. The robe billowed open as she swung the fridge door shut. The baby made fists and threatened to jump off the counter. "Oh, no, you don't," Lucia told her, sweeping Cecily onto her hip, meanwhile slathering mayonnaise on a slice of bread, then trading sides as she carried the food to the table. Transfixed, Abby hadn't thought to offer assistance. Lucia's teeth bit beautifully into the white bread with its white filling, turkey, mayonnaise, Muenster. A tiny morsel was offered the baby, who sat now on Lucia's lap at the table, mother and child cross-eyed evaluating the exchange. Abby wished for a photograph of this, the pink skin and fine white fabric, the child's plump little fingers meeting her mother's long graceful ones, the way Lucia's mouth opened reflexively as the baby's did, her smile when the child looked vexed over the flavor in her mouth. The way she instantly demanded more, snatching as Lucia turned her face away to take another bite. Abby felt rapturous, as with a painting, some other piece of great art.

And then Michael, crashing in with his suitcase, the black suit he wore seeming to move on its own, the whiff of mothballs he brought into the room. "Aren't you dressed?" he said to his wife. "I have to get to the airport, you have to take me. No, no, bratty, I don't want you anyway." The baby had gripped her mother's robe lapels as her father swooped down upon them. At the sink he swallowed pills, shot his cuff to check his watch, frowned at the window thermometer and complained.

"It'll be colder in New York," Lucia told him.

"Hence all of this foul-smelling wool. Get dressed," he repeated. This was a voice he must reserve for private moments, Abby thought, which meant she had been demoted. A pet: invisible, underfoot, loyal to a fault. But not loyal to him.

"I'll take you," she volunteered. "You can drive out, I'll drive back. I'm dressed." She wore the mother's corduroy pants and the niece's sweater set. Socks she'd found in a basket of linty orphans on the dryer. "I know where the airport is." She watched Lucia rather than Michael, and was pleased to see Lucia's face uncloud, relieved. She smiled when her husband kissed her cheek. His pats to his children were perfunctory; already he seemed en route to another world.

In the car, he apologized for his in-laws, but it wasn't sincere, merely prattling monologue opportunity. Abby was learning to keep her mouth shut. She wouldn't have made such a fool of herself with her last lover if she'd been mysteriously silent instead of righteously demanding. Honestly, Abby had enjoyed her bereavement, the ten pounds she wept away, the circles beneath her eyes she enhanced with gray eye-shadow.

Michael asked, "What did you think of *Ag-nes*?" Everyone inflected her name this way, as if it were an assumed identity. The form nesting in the living room seemed an installation there, one with the stuffed and stained chair. This old woman, Mr. Bonatello's first wife, was a family responsibility. She was indulged every Christmas—chattering, murmuring, making noise from her seat—because she'd been doing it for so long, prepared by her keepers at the nursing home for whatever driver the family dispensed—the newly licensed nihilist on probation, this year—and then navigated into her place in the living room, her chair. A broad floral affair, filthy with ancient food spills, sprung and lumpy, tailored by abuse to her particular proportions. She stared from its depths with small, clouded eyes, giving the impression she could see no farther than the ends of her fingertips, and that it was an act of faith that the people surrounding her were kindhearted and therefore unlikely to harm her, in fact perhaps willing to listen to her wax British as they delivered tidbits and drinks.

"'Figger'?" the scornful teenagers might quote. "'Shed-yule'? What the fuck?"

"She thinks she's from England."

"She thinks she's the queen, on her truly disgusting throne."

"It's better she can't move. This way, we always know where she is."

Abby chose to say to Michael, "I feel sorry for her." Her, and her former husband, people who'd once made love with each other, now like old neutered house pets, looking for a quiet place to curl up.

"Don't bother," Michael said. "She's a snob. 'Air Capital,'" he then scoffed at the Wichita motto emblazoned on the airport sign, swerving off the highway. "Air Capital, my ass. I'm flying in a prop job out of here."

"Safe trip," Abby responded blithely, trading places with him, scooting the seat closer to the wheel and turning on the radio.

He'd checked his office phone every morning from Kansas, savoring the ritual, looking forward to it. Christine Paulsen left her usual news. She was spending the holidays with her parents, who lived just outside Houston in a place called Katy. She talked about them, their ailments, their cantankerousness. Michael listened impatiently, waiting hungrily for the brief thought of hers that had to do with him, with the two of them. Her flight was due to arrive only an hour after his; he'd wait, and they'd take a cab together. His plane connection was through Dallas, and he half expected to run into her on the crowded walkways or waiting areas, as if simply being in the same state would dictate a meeting.

He promised Christine that he would tell no one about her; he thought he'd begun to appreciate the true sanctuary of his love, its hermetic enclosure. Before, he'd confided in a few people about Constance. She had done the same, and Michael understood—too late—that others' knowledge diluted the power of their affair. He'd promised Christine, he'd promised himself, but he'd broken that vow and told his oldest friend, his mentor and colleague back in L.A. After Michael and Frederick Bernier had given their panel at the Montreal conference last spring, Michael had pointed out Christine to him. She sat in the back of the sparsely attended session, clapping enthusiastically when they concluded. Bernier had listened as Michael giddily explained who she was, how he felt about her.

Bernier studied the woman, then turned a look of pure mystification on his protégé, friend, co-worker. It was the same look he gave Michael a few weeks later in L.A. at the end-of-semester barbecue at the chair's house, where Lucia, minus the children, circulated. She had lost her pregnancy weight yet retained the swollen breasts, the fabric of her halter dress straining to hold them, the bright apricot material snug at her hips, skimming her knee knobs, its knotted loops at her neck, where her hair was wrapped in a loose bun but threatened to burst free and spill over her bare shoulders. Frederick Bernier ogled Lucia, then turned his bewildered face to Michael in frank and total perplexity. His thought bubble said: *What the hell are you thinking?*

Michael now was thinking he regretted telling his colleague anything, exposing Christine to him. A flare of protectiveness went off in him—her lack of experience, her awkward ways (when they embraced, she nearly always jerked her head into his jaw or got her arms stuck in some ridiculous contortion, as if she had extra ones hanging from her shoulders). She provoked in Michael a tenderness he felt proud of, reverent toward, as if he'd done something pure, made a charitable donation, say, and not bragged, or as if he'd jimmied open some ugly clenched shell of self to reveal—surprise!—a pearl. He was deeply sorry he'd confided in Frederick Bernier. At the party, he fantasized that Bernier would try—and fail—to seduce Lucia; Bernier would feel permission for this outrage by virtue of knowing Michael's secret. Then later Lucia laughed when she reported that Bernier, drunk, *had* given her a wet kiss good-bye. And Michael vowed never to speak to him again.

Also, he had vowed never to tell another soul about Christine. And then, drunk last night, he'd confessed to *Ag-nes* in her chair. Family lore held that she'd never gotten over losing Dr. Bonatello to the second wife; she'd gone mad, affected an accent and new identity, wandered Wichita homeless until she could be caught and contained in the institution where she'd now lived for many years, speaking out of a delusional world that held few clear signposts. The temptation was to tell her things—human repository, unjudging witness—toss in your own madness, your secrets and desires, like pennies in a wishing well.

In New York it took Michael nearly an hour to retrieve his suitcase and then locate the baggage claim area for Christine's flight; his efficiency pleased him, the way he'd planned so well. The plane from Houston was due in fifteen minutes, according to the monitor, then on time, and then safely landed. At the bottom of the escalator he watched, aware that he would see her before she saw him, which excited him, the moments she would not know she was being watched, being consumed by his hungry eyes. All these people, the thousands he'd been among today, and she was the one he waited for, unfooled by the other women's feet and legs that rolled endlessly toward him.

They continued coming down the escalator, these hundreds who were not Christine, and he continued waiting. Waiting and waiting. Eventually he asked. And then he phoned his office to hear her apologize, which she did repeatedly, because she just couldn't do it, she couldn't come to New York, she didn't know why. His eyes began to tear as he heard her crying. That movement in his chest, it wouldn't stop, a flare that had no physical source but was felt nonetheless, sparking and sparking and sparking—with nothing to ignite, a sudden pocket of soot inside his ribs. He loved her. He believed she loved him. But she was afraid.

Already, Michael could feel the thin trickle of self-pity

begin. Love and heartbreak were two sensations he could access like songs on a jukebox, subjects in a book index, separate yet related, situated there in his body, each with its own visceral side effect. It was going to be bad, knowing he wouldn't see Christine again. She might continue to call him, but she wouldn't come to him, wouldn't allow him to come to her. For the next three days he would sit in his hotel room interviewing candidates for his department's open Cultural Studies line. A parade of women would pass through, and he and his two colleagues would arrange themselves awkwardly on the beds while each woman took the only chair, still warm from its last occupant, and they would have polite, intellectual, lively conversations. These well-dressed, well-educated women would want to impress him; they would be actively in pursuit of his approval. They would laugh, ask questions, flatter, shake his hand, thank him profusely. They would look forward to hearing from him, would be overjoyed at having been invited into his room, would no doubt be happy to join him for drinks or a meal in the hotel lounge. In Kansas, his wife would welcome him home, pleased enough to have him back, quiz him intelligently about the conference. On New Year's Eve she would finally put on some real clothes and give him a deep kiss at midnight, her mouth sweet with champagne, her hair at last tumbled from its bun over his arm. They would make love quietly in the room with their children sleeping nearby.

Yes, there were a host of women in his life. And there was devout and mousy Christine Paulsen. "I miss you," she closed her message to him, miserable. "I really do *miss* you," she pleaded, through her tears.

Abby had begun drinking early in the day, alternating Diet Coke with alcohol so as to keep herself awake, yet also relaxed.

She and Lucia had cooked dinner together, those impossible children of hers literally underfoot, while the metallic Midwest light rusted away in the sky.

They had made ravioli—great wide strips of pasta dough dangling over the dish rack and chair backs, bowls of meat filling, bowls of cheese and spinach, garlic and olive oil in the air, red wine in their glasses, the quaint machines used for the process covered in flour, Abby and Lucia also powdery and sticky, at once. Family members had passed through to exclaim, pitch in for a little while, then wander off. At one point, Lucia's father had stood suddenly in the doorway, hair wild, face alarmed, belt unbuckled, pants unzipped: as if he'd come to urinate there.

"Dad, you need your glasses," Lucia called out. "Glasses and your hearing aids." Lane had swept in then, leading him away. "He misses Mom," Lucia told Abby. "She kept him presentable."

"He seems lost."

"He didn't know how much he needed her. They were like a single organism."

"I don't know anybody like that," Abby said, suffering for an instant the sting of her lie: her own parents were like that. She and Lucia looked at each other, mirrored blank expressions.

"Marriage," Lucia said, as if it were a full sentence. Abby took the opportunity to avoid tripping over the children by now bumping into their mother. She wanted desperately to put her hand on Lucia's cheek, her lips on Lucia's lips. She wanted to undo that abstracted empty face. She felt both brave and clumsy, in the kitchen, her chance before her, proximity and drunkenness, the strange charge that the children's presence created, even the fact of the book she'd recommended to Lucia lying flapped open on the table. Lucia had almost finished it; she'd told Abby that she too loved it, she had lost precious sleep devouring its pages.

Abby had smiled, gratified and high, bent over the dimpled metal press, fitting together the two halves of the instrument, sealing twelve pockets of sweet sausage between soft flaps of dough. When she handed them to Lucia, their fingers had touched, over and over, these little pillows being fed into the steamy contents of a kettle of boiling water. On impulse Abby grabbed Lucia's hand, and Lucia returned the squeeze; at the table, with Lucia's family, Abby had been bashful but proud, accepting their praise and exchanging knowing glances with Lucia.

"If I was on death row," the brother nicknamed Wine Cure declared, "if I was gonna be executed in the morning, *this* is the meal I would order!"

Everybody had laughed, even sour Lane, even those magpie girls of hers. Abby and Lucia had made this happen. Lucia smiled dreamily at Abby, as if nobody else were in the room, as if Lucia were thanking her for helping serve up this familial bliss. Was it a coincidence that they all seemed more relaxed without Michael Shapiro here? Wasn't Lucia happier—wasn't it clear to everyone?—without him? After dinner the two of them—and of course those children, and the senior Mr. Bonatello with his peculiar first wife *Ag-nes*—were disallowed from helping to clean up. "Relax, relax!" the family cried, waving them away. Lucia and Abby had left an extravagant mess in the kitchen; it would take the rest of the Bonatellos an hour or more to dispense with it. "Worth it," they all agreed, well worth it.

While the old people settled stunned before the television, Lucia and Abby sat together on the sofa, the only light that of the Christmas tree, its bottom half now bereft of gifts, a stark, still-blinking monument. The after-dinner drink in the Bonatello house was amaretto on ice. Lucia leaned her head back, her throat moving with her last swallow.

"Lucia," Abby said. She loved this name. It was almost enough just to say it.

"Hmm?"

"Lucia, I'm . . ." Abby stalled. How could she still not be drunk enough? She'd done nothing but fill herself with alcohol, courage, and bravado, yet still this sober fear, this clarity, uncertainty.

"What, hon?" Lucia patted Abby's hand, smiled ruefully. And Abby made her fatal error then, without letting herself think any longer.

Lucia pulled away from the kiss elegantly, but firmly. "No," she said, shaking her head, her hair loosening as she did so. "No, Abby, I'm sorry." She looked sorry, too, but not as if she'd been tempted, like a Catholic, not sorry because she was married and didn't believe in infidelity, nor because it was strange to her, a kiss from a woman, yet an idea she might take a shine to. No, she was sorry for something much more painful, sorry for Abby's unrequited, completely unrequitable, love, sorry because she pitied Abby, sorry the way she'd be if her children had fallen down or, not even that proximate, sorry the way she'd be if some stranger sitting next to her—on an airplane, say—was in sudden pain. It was a sorry that had nothing of Lucia herself in it at all.

Abby had leaped from the couch, hurried to the kitchen and shoved through these Bonatellos and the other hangers-on to snatch up the splayed novel from the table, then grabbed the first bottle of pills she could from the butler's pantry cupboard, and fled up the stairs to the attic, slamming her door behind her.

What had she seen on Lane's face, that sharp sentient glance from the sink, where she hand-washed the carving knives?

Abby sat now on her single bed at the top of the house, humiliated, horrified, and filled with a futile rage. Look how she had thrown herself into this trap—in distant Kansas, holed up in a house of strangers, wearing the clothes of a dead woman, her overwhelming love rebuffed. The pills she'd grabbed were diuretics, nothing more—did she think she could urinate herself to death? She had flung them across the room, then had turned to the book in her other hand. It was a wonderful novel now ruined for her. She sat down on the bed, and the day's alcohol finally caught up with her, as if it alone had chased her upstairs to lay her flat. Drunk, she tore out the book's final pages, then methodically began shredding them into a thousand little pieces, making confetti of the beautiful ending. Lucia said she had lost sleep to read ahead, following the amazing course of events that Abby had recommended to her. Lucia loved this novel, she said, Abby could still hear her saying so, *loved* it. "Too bad," Abby murmured, tearing and tearing, crying, too, "just too fucking bad." Now she was never going to know how it all turned out.

FALSETTO

A LL YOUR FRIENDS ARE weird," Michelle's little brother Ellton had said to her that morning. It was a statement with staying power. She would be thinking of it for years to come. She thought of it now, this evening, as her boyfriend gave her brother a playful sock on the shoulder. The resigned look he turned on his sister said, "See?" He seemed then like the most mature person in the room, although he was only eleven; she was eighteen years older, old enough to be his mother, and her boyfriend was in between, twenty-two.

Plus, Michelle was accustomed to thinking the opposite: that her *family* was weird.

Ellton realigned his video camera, a sleek little unit cupped in his palm, replete with secret abilities. Far too complicated for their elderly parents, the device—a gift from their sister— had been handed over like a bomb to the boy for defusing. It made him seem sneaky, unpopular, destined to some day be accused of a crime he hadn't committed.

Her brother was the opposite of Teacher's Pet, Michelle thought: Teacher's Bane. The clever kid who never failed to name the emperor naked. With him you got away with exactly nothing, although he took no smug pleasure in correcting people—he just liked to have the facts straight. Things could be got right.

"Yo Elton John," said Michelle's boyfriend Max, still in sparring position. He looked to Michelle for affirmation of his Whimsical Tendency. It was the dinner hour, for which Michelle had prepared by drinking a lot of beer during the cocktail hour. Now Max tied an apron over his polo shirt and stuffed his feet into his sheepskin scuffs. He enjoyed cooking, even though his repertoire included just the one dish, a green-flecked, chunky, orange-colored vegetarian sauce; part chili, part marinara, part sloppy joe, you could pour it over pasta or rice or beans or a bun, depending.

"Why is that funny?" Ellton responded, aiming the camera away from his tabletop drama and into Max's face, capturing the gape-mouthed, faux-innocent prankster's expression Max put on when he thought he was being endearing. He wasn't used to not being liked. Everybody liked him, with his lazy Georgia accent and his bundle of homey bromides handed down from some grandmother. At Ellton's fingertip a red light blinked, accompanied by the electronic whirring. "*Ellton* is a family name," the boy explained for the tenth time in as many days, his voice tolerant yet fatigued. Max couldn't know that Ellton was showing admirable restraint, not mentioning that *Max* was a name his and Michelle's family had once chosen for their rooster.

They'd eaten Max for dinner one day, fed up with his early-morning antics.

Ellton did say, "And why must you keep hitting me?"

"*Hitting* you?" Max looked to Michelle as to a kind of referee. What sort of sissy was her brother, anyway? The camera followed. In its lens, Michelle corrected her posture. She told Ellton that Max was just playing.

"Playing what?" the boy asked. And Michelle wondered too why Max thought that making fun of a person's name and cuffing him on the shoulder was somehow evidence of good sportsmanship. "It's like he thinks I'm Leroy," Ellton said. Leroy was the dog. He was a dog who invited getting kicked, stubborn, stinky, self-absorbed. *All your friends are weird.* Her brother's thin arms and unmuscled body afflicted Michelle; he was so fearless, yet so unprotected. He'd hung around in his mother's womb for ten months and still only weighed six pounds when he finally came out. He had no defense except the one he'd just employed: weary inquiry. He'd been raised by adults as if he were an adult himself. It was her parents' nature, as a caretaking pair, not to apply much pressure, to more often sit back and observe. Their tolerant philosophy, this entropy-in-action, yielded mixed results, Michelle thought. Her brother was extraordinary, in her opinion, but the dog she could envision euthanizing.

Her boyfriend, if he hadn't been a southern gentleman, would have expressed the opposite opinion. "Lighten up," he told the boy now, his mush-mouth accent softening the command.

In the greasy glass of the tall kitchen window Michelle saw the three of them—herself, Max, Ellton; woman, man, child—reflected against a dark mass of approaching clouds. The sky *was* bigger in Montana; she never remembered this until she had left and then returned. Trails of steam wandered like tears down the glass, while outside the storm front rushed over the Bitterroot Valley and Rock Creek toward them. Their home sat on a hill, and weather could be anticipated for hours before arriving. She felt poor and pitiful, watching the clouds, like an orphan, undeniably bereft. Just that quick, she quit loving her boyfriend. He did not belong in the window reflection: the oncoming storm, two sad siblings. The sensation came as a relief, as if she'd taken the advice Max had offered Ellton and lightened up herself, opened a hatch in her heart, at last relinquishing its contents, the confusing and crowded affections like caged birds, set free in a burst of wind.

"Hey, Ellton," Max had said days earlier, "you ever seen anything as weird as a fennel bulb?" He held the object up by its hairy stem. Yes, Ellton had said, yes he had seen many things as weird as, if not weirder than, a fennel bulb. Undaunted, Max asked how Ellton felt about cottage cheese. The reply to this was that the stuff made Ellton's tongue retreat. Tough audience, Michelle thought, forcing Max into Trying Too Hard: kids could sense it a mile away, especially this kid.

And now Michelle no longer had to love Max. She thought he had been kind to come with her, but maybe he was guilty of trying too hard with her, too. They'd only been dating for a couple of months. He hadn't met her parents, so it did not naturally follow that he should join her. That his eyes should have filled with tears when she told him what had happened. She'd been touched, back in Houston, but now she was skeptical. He was adopting her family, glomming onto their grief. It had real substance, grief, unlike the ethereal contents of their college classes. "Us," he said, often; the word made her avert her eyes as from a disfigurement. "We." From Houston to Missoula, with a gloppy layover in Salt Lake, he had thrown himself into the role of "support system" in her "time of need."

It was Ellton who had phoned to tell Michelle about the

car accident. "They aren't dead," he'd said, right off. He'd always had a masculine voice, husky, unsentimental. "Mom and Dad were in a crash," he said with this voice. In the background, the shadowy concerned conversation of the neighbors whose house he'd gone to after school that afternoon. His mother and father were driving home from Missoula, where they'd been purchasing sprinkler pipes and mulch and seeds and saplings: the hopefulness of spring that would lead to a summer garden. They didn't often leave Portersburg; they preferred pleasures that cost nothing and did not require going anywhere. This had been their annual pilgrimage to the garden center, where Michelle could imagine the quiet coupled contentedness they shared, something she both envied and resented. They didn't mean to exclude. They didn't realize how insular their marriage seemed, how it had not really required children in order for it to feel like a family.

Only later did she admire her little brother's sequencing of information: "They aren't dead," he'd known to tell her first.

His videotape was a re-creation of the accident. Max, who was studying elementary education, found the project disturbing. His reaction was to chide the child, nudge and tease him into some other, acceptable, sort of person. Didn't he want to help cook, grate some odoriferous cheese? But Ellton was a detail freak. For him, facts offered consolation. He was using toys and rocks and twigs to simulate the pileup in Antelope Canyon; the cop who'd attended at the scene had drawn up a quick diagram on a yellow pad that Ellton consulted like an instruction manual. He'd never been an ordinary boy. He was so thin that people grew angry when he wouldn't eat. When tickled, he didn't laugh so much as suffer a sort of spasm. His solemnity frightened most adults; it was as if they understood he could not be embarrassed himself, but he could embarrass them. Constantly, aggressively, people were insisting that he *smile*.

He made Michelle's heart hurt.

Finished with Max, Ellton swung his camera back to the tabletop. "This guy swerved to miss an animal. Or something."

"A UFO," Max suggested. "Sasquatch."

"Whatever," Ellton said. The red Matchbox convertible that represented the first driver dodged the Scooby-Doo figurine and left the lines of the braided place mat that was the road. "The log truck was coming downhill and couldn't stop." Lincoln Logs made for the spill of lumber that had forced their parents' car, a little Matchbox Wonder Bread van, off the kitchen table. Their car had hung suspended upside down in a ridgepole pine before falling finally to the ground

Every day, on the drive to Missoula, they passed that broken tree. It looked as if it had been struck not once but twice by lightning.

"The police told me Mom wasn't wearing her seat belt." He reiterated this daily, as if it might eventually make sense to him, spoken enough.

Michelle responded with her lines: "She was napping." Late every afternoon her mother napped. A creature of habit. A creature, Michelle thought, subject to her instincts, respectful of those of others. "She doesn't like how the shoulder part cuts into her face." Her mother's sleeping form came to mind— on her chenille bedspread at dusk, hands palm-to-palm beneath her cheek as if in prayer—supplanting, briefly, the stiff comatose one faceup in the hospital bed.

"They say," said Max, gesturing with a wooden spoon, "that sometimes a seat belt can kill you. Sometimes, they say, wearing a seat belt is the worst thing you can do." He had taken it upon himself to be their cook, their captain, their bossy cow, and plunged the spoon back into the onions spitting in oil at the stove while Michelle and Ellton studied the tableau on the table. It was a large round wooden table, sticky with many meals, the table that had always sat here collecting the most important of the family matter. Max had tried to remove that stickiness, spraying grease cutter, rubbing with sandpaper. For ten days the siblings waited while Max, shirtsleeves metaphorically, literally rolled, busied himself at the stove, at the sink, at the washer and clothesline. His teeth were straight and white, his hair thick, his clothing fresh: shipshape. At each station he remarked on the improvements he foresaw: brighter lighting, handy shelves, Lysol, fumigation, flat-out gutting. He'd spent a long time rattling the kitchen drawers searching out a knife, only to discover its rusty dullness. Then he began the rattling quest for a sharpener. In lieu of that, he used the rough bottom of a ceramic plate, swiping the blade back and forth till it gleamed, till it could nick an arm hair from his arm, a piece of legitimate ingenuity Michelle was impressed by, despite herself. Tidy, handy, gallant, comely: what more did she want? Or maybe it was *less*?

"Splatter cover?" Max asked. "Colander?" These had long ago become rhetorical inquiries; theirs was the most poorly stocked household Max had ever encountered. And he couldn't have found a worse town for fresh produce, nor a more lackluster audience for tonight's vegetarian lasagna. Ellton loved meat, and Michelle seemed to have lost the capacity to taste anything besides grief and fear. The flavor was wretched; it occasionally choked her.

She put her fourth beer to her lips and closed her eyes, letting the warm sweet fluid fizz in her mouth, all texture, no taste. This was her father's brand, dark and thick. He drank it at room temperature. Neither she nor her brother bothered to interrupt Max as he nattered on, adding garlic, herbs, a couple of cans of tomatoes. Their mother stocked a lot of tomato products because the dog was always getting skunked. Leroy was a profoundly self-indulgent dog, Michelle thought; the habits her parents allowed him to acquire and keep were dreadful. Unlike the children, Leroy had had no peers or teachers or friends to instruct him how to fill the gaps, behave in a civilized manner. For the last week and a half, he'd been holed up behind their father's easy chair, growling if anyone dared come close. If he needed some basic necessity—water, kibble, a trip outside—he climbed stiffly out of his cave, grizzled and blinking, and approached the door with his gray head sternly lowered, as if he would butt right through it, given provocation.

Just before the phone rang, Michelle could feel its jangle coming toward her; you always could, in this house. Ellton said, without looking up from his cinematography, "That'll be Roxanne."

And of course it was.

"Hi Roxanne!" chimed out Max, who'd never met her.

"Who was that?" Roxanne asked.

"Max," Michelle answered.

"Doo Wop?"

"The one and only." Michelle had broken Max of his annoying habit of saying "Do *wha*'?" It was a tic, something he'd picked up in Georgia and brought to Rice University. "Do *wha*'?" he responded, no matter what you had just said to him. At first she thought he had a hearing problem.

"I can't wait to meet Doo Wop."

"Yes you can." *All your friends are weird.*

Roxanne and Michelle were identical twins. Enough work for any two parents, especially parents who didn't seem to particularly want or need children, merely to accept them, the occasional byproducts of sex. Twins: surprise, surprise. Michelle could imagine her mother's pregnancy, the rising bulk of her girls beneath her dress, the way she and their father must have looked down, alarmed at what was happening. Her parents loved all growing things—animals, flowers, weeds. Yet overseeing their own offspring had not come naturally to them. They were unconfident parents, daunted. Michelle and Roxanne were wild children, left quite often to their own devices, driven home by neighbors, looked after by shopkeepers and teachers. Portersburg itself had raised them. Then, the year the girls graduated from high school, their mother had another baby, a bigger surprise. Why had she waited so long, the sisters complained? Why, now that they were leaving home for college, had their parents finally gotten around to delivering their brother? There was no answer but a pair of sincerely perplexed shrugs.

It was Ellton's arrival that had most likely accounted for Michelle's dropping out after a semester and moving back home. No doubt her baby brother was responsible for her remaining in her old bedroom for another five years, thereby permanently separating her life's path from her twin's. It was probably Ellton Michelle could thank for what her current professors named "life experience," that commodity that was serving her so well as a "nontraditional" undergraduate right now. Junior year, at age twenty-nine and a half.

Her sister Roxanne had been a sparky, daring girl but was a busy, irritated woman. She seemed to believe that their parents had perpetrated a terrible injustice on their children, raising them the way they had. Away from Portersburg, when she'd discovered how freaky she was, she'd made big changes. Mother of a five-year-old and pregnant again, she cut immediately to the chase. "What's going on with them?"

"Mom's still unconscious. Dad's stable." In traction, in a full body cast, he couldn't be any more stable, Michelle thought.

"Mom's eyelids were twitching," Ellton reminded her. He had run upstairs to ransack his room for a more suitable-size animal figure, returning with a lifelike big-shouldered bison to take the place of Scooby-Doo.

"What'd he say?"

"He said her eyelids were twitching," Michelle repeated. Her sister's daughter was shouting in the background, hundreds of miles away in Seattle. She was spoiled in the most pedestrian and uninteresting ways. Roxanne's household operated with the child as the centerpiece, like the sun; Michelle wondered if every home had its most radiant member. If so, theirs was their mother. Their slumbering mother, a mild cool star, undemanding, a little unobtrusive, as far as heavenly bodies went, yet the nucleus, nonetheless.

"I can't fly out there because of the fucking baby," Roxanne said. "And Bobby won't let me drive by myself." Her husband grumbled, reasonable arguments being laid out like bullet points, Michelle could tell by the intonation. Roxanne's husband Bobby was a manager at Boeing and wore a suit over his pear-shaped body; his closet resembled a rack at a dull department store, dozens of white shirts hanging ironed in a line, gray pants creased beneath, red and blue neckties hanging above the row of black dress shoes. Their house, which Michelle had visited just once, was part of a subdivision named after the trees it had obliterated, a house brightly lit like a catalog display, everything new and smelling of recent manufacture, the floors golden oak, the rooms painted creamy ivory, the appliances silent and tucked into the walls. There were shelves and baskets and drawers designated for all of their belongings, a peculiar and alien tricky neatness to it all. The girls had not grown up this way. Their home was dark, filled with, oh, birds' nests and shucked antlers, dated magazines and obsolete kitchen tools, broken mantel clocks that their father collected, dried flowers their mother pressed between the pages of all of the heavy encyclopedia volumes, rust rings and shed hair everywhere, piles and piles of books like pieces of furniture, a cloud of enveloping dust when you sat down in a stuffed chair. Serious sedimented strata on every surface, history, mystery. "So we'll all come on Friday," Roxanne was saying, "just as soon as Bobby gets off work." A door closed in Seattle, and there was sudden silence, Roxanne's breathing. "I have to go to the damn potty to get any privacy around here. I'm gonna tinkle, sorry."

"That's okay." Michelle would have liked to find some privacy, too, but there was only one phone in the house, and it was attached to the wall.

Roxanne and Michelle had frequently confused their mother over the phone, when they were young, but Roxanne's adult voice was flat, imperious, loud with assurance—potty? tinkle?!—while Michelle's remained tentative. Their mother never mistook them when they called home nowadays.

What if, Michelle panicked, her mother could never answer a phone again? A sudden strange heat fell upon her, like a flood of molten wax flowing from her skull to her knees. This heat wave ambushed her several times a day, leaving her afterward in a film of sweat, dizzy and disoriented. Meanwhile her sister was lauding a Seattle neurologist, recounting the phone calls and fact-finding activities she'd been engaged in since last they spoke. In these anecdotes, Roxanne always played the bully who would not take no for an answer. As soon as it was possible, her mother would be airlifted to the university hospital in Washington. Then Roxanne would be the one who visited daily. She would bring flowers and a nightgown and fragrance. She would know what to ask the doctors, nurses, therapists, and orderlies. And even though they all dressed exactly alike in their scrubs, she would know how to tell them apart.

Maybe if Ellton hadn't been born, Michelle would have finished college when Roxanne did and met and married a man in graduate school, as Roxanne had, and become a young presumptuous matron with a mortgage and a minivan and a cigarette smoker's mature, knowing voice, even though she didn't smoke. The acquisition of these things seemed to ensure the compliance of officials and professionals. You could sense her belligerent expertise even over the phone, even big as a house with a baby.

"I didn't want to alarm Chelsea," Roxanne said. "I haven't told her Ma'am and Pop-pop are in the hospital. She's going to spaz." The toilet flushed, in Seattle.

"You know what?" Michelle said, under the sedating influence of her father's beer, looking at the back of her little brother's head as he bent over the table. "Ellton is closer to Chelsea's age than to ours." Her sister's silence let her know that this was no brainstorm. Roxanne frequently allowed a deep pause to convey her disappointment in Michelle. Michelle, the undergraduate. "I mean, I know he's closer to her age, but, like, these are his *parents*. Not his grandparents," she added, in case Roxanne wasn't following. Max, she noticed, was shaking his head in sorrow at the sink as he sluiced water off another thick wet noodle.

"I know that," Roxanne said. "I am well aware of that. What are you, stoned?"

Ellton said, "Can I talk to her?" holding out his hand for the phone. Michelle passed it over after saying, "No, I am not stoned."

"Roxanne?" Ellton said, "Will you bring back that Lego guy Chelsea took at Christmas? I said she could *borrow* it, not *have* it." He described the missing figure in detail, down to the expression on its tiny plastic face. By now Chelsea would have lost it—she would have lost it in the car, swallowed it, or flung it out the window the first five minutes of their drive back to Seattle in December—and Roxanne wouldn't have known to return it even if she'd been aware that the girl had taken it. Ellton had two personality traits that would now battle inside him: one was that he loved particular things, studied them carefully, remembered them, used them, needed them. The other was that he was generous, unconsciously so, giving his beloved things to other people, sharing.

He handed the phone back to Michelle. "You have a million Legos," Roxanne was saying. "You've got crates—"

"That's not the point," Michelle said.

"Oh, it's exactly the point, it's just heartbreaking how he's fixated on that thing, and I wish I knew where the hell it was, but I don't, and really, the point is that Mom and Dad are in the hospital and I feel so frustrated I can't just get there right now. I feel like a turtle on its back, just waving my legs waiting for somebody to put me right. Tell him I'm sorry, I'll buy him a dozen of his goddamn little Lego men. Is he bathing?"

"As we speak?" But Michelle hunched uncomfortably as if Roxanne could see her and their ripe little brother. In fact, Ellton had not, to her knowledge, bathed recently. She hoped Roxanne wasn't going to ask if he had returned to school yet. "And did you see her eyes twitch, or did you just hear about it?"

Again she flashed on her mother sleeping here at home, on the butter-colored chenille spread in a block of autumn light from the window upstairs. Outside the window tall aspens quaked and their leaves cast a flickering shadow like water, shimmering over her in the late afternoon. It took an effort to superimpose the true sleeping form of their mother. The no-season gray light of the hospital, the inky bruise where an IV needle had been inserted, the dark hairs on her chin. It almost seemed that you should be able to make her eyes open by sitting her up, like a doll. The nurse—doctor? candy striper?—had stood behind Ellton when they visited, ready to catch him if he fainted, though it was Michelle who'd felt woozy. Max had decided that his role was Rock, and he kept kissing Michelle's cheek and squeezing her shoulders, as if he had the power to bolster her. Michelle was sorely tempted to throw an elbow into his torso. The nurse had mistaken the three of them, thinking Max was Michelle's husband, Michelle Ellton's mother, Ellton the grandson of the injured woman. You couldn't blame people for jumping to the obvious conclusions, could you?

"I guess there was a kind of flinch, if you can call that movement." Seventy-five miles away, their parents slept in two different parts of Saint Pat's. Their father, who'd broken a great many bones, was expected to live. Their mother's damage was of the internal and hidden sort, shrouded by coma. This was considered a mercy, a gift her body had given itself, a cocoon inside which no one knew what transpired.

"This is going to sound awful," Roxanne said, "but I wish it was Dad who was in the coma. I mean, we love him, of course, and maybe it's different for a boy, you know, to grow up without his dad, but I can't help thinking that Ellton needs Mom." Now her strong, capable sister was crying. "I get contractions when I cry," Roxanne complained. "I can't cry, or I get contractions." But she didn't stop. "Think how much we needed Mom. You know?"

"I know," Michelle agreed. "I know exactly what you mean."

"You are one odd little dude," Max said to Ellton as they climbed into the car later. His southern accent made him sound so golly-gee, like Gomer Pyle.

"That's the way he's always buckled," Michelle explained. Ellton had long ago devised his own seat-belt arrangement, two of them crisscrossed over him as he sat in the middle of the back. Statistically, he'd let you know, this was the safest place to travel. Last year he'd taken to wearing a helmet whenever he left the house. It was only logical.

"You don't have to mention it every time we get in the car, you know," Ellton said. Not angrily, just observantly. "It's not like I'm going to stop doing this just because you talk about it a lot."

"Do *wha'*?" Max said abstractedly, pulling away from the curb.

Given a choice, Ellton would stay at home. Permanently. But Max wanted to go scout for animals on the roads around Portersburg, and Michelle knew she couldn't leave her brother home alone. Max wanted to visit the ghost town up the hill. Michelle had made the mistake of telling him about the annual litter of fox pups that cavorted in the empty fields just north of the town limits. The bears, the elk, the moose, the owls, the bighorn sheep—all of the Montana wonders. He wanted to experience everything, as if he were notching a belt or earning scout badges; he also wanted to help distract them from their uneasy sorrow and the queer dark house that contained it. He was a practical man, Michelle thought. Excited by flora and fauna, kind, helpful. Why couldn't she love him anymore? Until tonight, she had gone through each of the ten days they'd been here understanding what would come next and how she would respond, as if the routine were a twenty-four-hour repeat performance she had merely to act her part in, as if there were an end to the show's run somewhere in sight. Each evening Max would finish washing dishes, fold the apron away over the towel rack, and clap his hands to rally his mopey cohorts as he promoted "taking a little spin." Michelle brought along a beer—no one in Montana was going to get fussy about drinking and riding—and Ellton his helmet and Game Boy. The dog followed them as far as the front door as if nervous to be left alone, but could not be enticed to join them, retreating once more as they slammed the screen. Max drove slowly along the dirt roads of town, small rocks pinging off the underside of the rental car. Only Main Street was paved; most of its shops were closed or vacant. The three bars were lit; the Elk Café was open. Soon they traveled into the hills and along the river, past the closed mill, past the abandoned mine, beyond the dilapidated barns and outbuildings of ranches that had failed. It was defeated terrain, under that famous big sky. Max would narrate blandly, querying about every brown lump, which Michelle would peer at and name: horse, rock, stump. The season of rampant wildlife was at least a month away.

"Don't they have animals in Texas?" Ellton had asked, the first night.

"Sure," Max replied. "But I like to get the lay of the land wherever I go. And we got unlimited miles."

"People must think they can do anything, in a rental car," Ellton said. "This road is four-wheel drive, usually."

"How 'bout you turn the sound off that Game Boy," Max

said, "and listen to Mother Nature?" Ellton sighed, complying. Michelle poured more beer down her throat, grateful for its muffling effect. Outside this amniotic sac of ale awaited panic, a peripheral force poised to strike. She thought she might never feel safe in a car again.

The first driver was dead, the boy who'd apparently swerved to miss the unknown animal. The trucker was dead, the one who'd come upon the little sports car and then braked crazily, unleashing his load of enormous logs. His hitchhiker was dead, as was the hitchhiker's dog, but Michelle's parents, they who'd come last to the scene and skidded over the mountainside, dangled briefly in the tree, then fallen to the ground, lived, each in a separate wing of the Missoula hospital.

Michelle and Ellton visited every day. After the first day, Max waited in the cafeteria. They began with their father's room. Although he looked ghastly—like the Invisible Man, swaddled in bandages in some sort of torture device—he could now speak. It would have been funny, if it were in a movie, a man-shaped cast, a mummy in traction, weights and levers and hoists elevating legs and arms in suspension, waiting to be puppeted about. "I can't hear a thing," he said loudly from inside this plaster form, cutting off Michelle's greeting. "You'll just have to bear with me, my hearing is temporarily gone. Kaput. And I've got the most odious melody running in my head, it would just figure that I'd get stuck with this song that I absolutely cannot stand but which I know every single damn lyric to. I wake up, can't hear a thing but Neil blasted Diamond." He breathed audibly through the two holes that were his nostrils. They had to lean over his face so that he could see them through his eye holes. "'Song Sung Blue,'" he sang. One of his hands was free from the wrap, bruised, scratched, but there, and that's what Ellton held, gently stroking his father's swollen fingers. They looked purple beside the brilliant white, flesh like fat sausage links, dirt beneath the nails. "Son," said their father, "Son, squeeze my thumb if your mother is all right." Ellton looked to Michelle, who nodded automatically. Let him receive simple, hopeful messages. Ellton squeezed as if making a wish. "Ahh," said their father.

"He's got a morphine drip," the nurse told Michelle, "and he knows how to use it! He's in no pain, is what I mean." He hummed his tune and laughed. "The deafness is temporary," she went on. "We expect he'll be fully conversant in a day or so." His room was like a hotel room—TV, easy chair, reading lamp, window unit, art bolted to the wall.

"Now Mom," Ellton said, once they were outside the door in the hall.

In the ICU he stood close to his mother's head. Unlike their father, their mother they could see and touch completely— arms, face, black eyelashes, slender body beneath the covers— yet make no contact. Ellton swallowed, pale, his clothes looking to Michelle suddenly filthy, ill-chosen. When a boy stood beside his mother in a coma, nothing could look right. Their mother was diminished by her environs, at its mercy. She slept, it seemed; the tube in her arm was transparent, her new food source clear and pure. Aside from the bright light, the various monitors, the attendant who always sat at a console, the paging calls over the public address system, the bing-bonging of elevator door bells, aside from all of that mechanical racket and asperity, their mother looked normal. Simply as if she had decided to lie down in this active and acrid-smelling institution to take a very public nap. Ellton leaned in close to her face as if to whisper in her ear and instead pulled out a hair from her forehead. Then another.

"What are you doing?" Michelle asked.

"Watch her eyes," he said, pulling again. The eyelids barely moved as the hair gave. "She always wants me to get rid of her gray hairs for her. She can't see them so well."

Later, back in Portersburg, Michelle had stood in front of the bathroom mirror and wrapped a strand of hair from her temple around her finger. The yanking sensation made her eyes fill. The hair had a tiny bit of white flesh on the end, and the sight of that made her cry in earnest, great heaving sobs of despair. Despair, she had thought, watching her afflicted face contort in the mirror. It was rare, like a miracle, and real, like a law of nature.

"What's that?" Max shouted, pointing beyond the windshield into the gathering dark of the hillside, braking abruptly. A few grazing deer had stopped, still as lawn statues. Three were pregnant but extremely thin does. With them, a large buck, behaving as if he could protect them. Like everything else in these last ten days, they seemed no longer harmless nor beautiful to Michelle. It was one of their ilk who'd forced the first car off the roadway, an animal that no doubt still roamed about the forest, unscathed. A momentary heightened heartbeat, the spur of screeching brakes, and away it had bounded, whatever it was. These deer darted away suddenly, too, terrified, the buck last, as if making some point.

"Deer," Ellton answered Max's question, back to his Game Boy. "Haven't you ever seen deer before?"

"Of course I have," Max said, gunning the engine as he lurched forward.

"He didn't mean it sarcastically," Michelle explained. "He just didn't understand why you didn't recognize them."

"I did recognize them."

"Then why did you ask what they were?" Ellton asked.

This nitpicky argument—an argument that one of its partici-
pants didn't understand was an argument—felt at a numbed distance from Michelle. She would have to keep drinking beer, she
thought. When she woke up tonight in a panic, rather than lie
stricken and sweating, she would go straight away to the kitchen
and wedge open another beer. This would be what Max would
call her "coping mechanism." Another Guinness, or perhaps a
Grolsch. Grolsch, with its elegant masculine bottle and pretty
lid apparatus. Her father probably preferred it for the ceramic
cork and wire fastener. He liked old-fashioned things—wind-
up clocks, typewriters, push mowers, his own long marriage.

"You should get back to school," Michelle told Max when he
cut the engine in front of her parents' house. She put her fingers to his lips to stop his Doo Wop. Once more they'd forgotten to leave on the porch light. The place looked haunted.
They'd never gone for typical upkeep, her parents. Instead,
they did things like install bat habitats under the eaves or
make a dog pen out of used tires, a greenhouse from reclaimed
storm windows. The birdbath was a former sink basin sitting
on a former engine block. As soon as the car had stopped,
Ellton had unstrapped himself and hurried inside. "You don't
want to screw up your semester," Michelle said vaguely.

Max didn't want to leave her—he didn't appear to want to
get out of the car—but Michelle held firm. "I really appreciate
your coming with me, but there's no reason for you to miss
classes. And your plants will die."

"I will do whatever you need for me to do," he said sincerely. He was so keen to please her that Michelle wanted to
hurt his feelings. None of his habits had bothered her—in
fact, she'd been toying with the notion that she might marry

him—until he had walked into her family's home. Suddenly he had come clear, like the solid human artifact placed in an otherwise unfathomable photographic image—the vast expanse of the moon, for instance, or the highly magnified body of a flea. Coming home had provided undeniable and inescapable scale. His handsomeness and his attraction to Michelle had blinded her to his essential missing qualities. Now she was sending him away on an airplane, back to Houston to finish the semester without her. To never see her again. In her mind she was busy saying good-bye to his apartment, wandering its rooms for the last time, leaving the tiny stovetop and the Murphy bed and the chair by the bare closet light where she read books when she couldn't sleep. That had been her previous insomnia, waking and then furtively reading in a crack of closet light while Max snored peacefully in bed. That had made her happy, his sleeping while she read. They'd had a pleasant domestic situation, she thought, recalling Max's elaborate collection of essential spices on the sill over the sink. Now she was packing away him and his life, as if in a box with a lid.

"I want to help," Max insisted. "Nothing is a higher priority than you, right now." Michelle patted his knee and climbed out of the rental car's bucket seat, staggering slightly. Inside the house, she flapped at the panel of light switches by the front door; only a few functioned, and she always forgot which. Ellton, long accustomed, had raced in ahead of her and gone upstairs in the dark. The dog's tail thumped from behind the chair. Michelle had to first call the hospital to see if there had been any changes. Her parents did not own an answering machine, and she made this phone call every evening after their ride just to make sure no one had been trying to reach her. Next she needed to pee; so far as she could tell, that was the only drawback of her beer remedy.

Max was still working to convince her that he ought to stay. Outside the bathroom door he asked, Who would cook, clean, drive? To hell with college, he claimed, while Michelle washed her hands. She stepped out of the bathroom to catch his noble sweeping gesture: with it, he smote the whole of higher education.

Michelle smiled; bladder empty, she still felt full up to her skull, wobbly and afloat on something turbid as molasses. "You have to go," she said thickly, patting his arm. He had been burrowing into her life, her family, her tragedy, with an enthusiasm that made her queasy. She knew he would go—he wasn't secure enough in his duty to her to stay—but she also knew she would have to have sex with him tonight. It was an unspoken part of the deal she was proposing.

He snuggled close when they got into bed.

"Are you sure you want me to go?" he said, kneading her breasts.

She found it difficult to feel erotic in this house, in the place where she'd grown up, in the bedroom and the very bed where her parents each night, until in a fit of peevishness at age fourteen she asked them not to, had come to tuck her in, to murmur shyly their love for her. Her father was a wry person, droll, analytical, typically prickly in matters parental. He was such an oddball, he'd always claimed, that he couldn't believe his luck in finding another oddball to marry. His wife, he understood. But his children continued to confound him. He assumed that they knew without requiring spoken proof that he of course loved them. Yet when he leaned over Michelle in her bed, ran his large rough hand over her cheek, all restraint and mockery fled, leaving his eyes damp with surprise at the feeling he had for his children. Every night he gathered the force of his gratitude and kissed Michelle squarely on the forehead as if to infuse her slumber with it. Then he traded places with her mother, who had been saying good night to Roxanne across the hall.

In her bed with the rosebuds and winding vines hand-painted along the iron headboard Michelle had waited. Her mother rested her weight gently beside her in the dark and began her nightly performance of folk songs. Max would have found these alarming—the winking lass wandering the hills selling barley, the maiden whose virginity was wagered for five hundred pounds, the tree in the forest where the rifles were stored—but these were the songs Michelle sang to herself when she courted sleep, the ones guaranteed to turn her mindless. Sleepy limp amnesia.

She'd not shared her childhood bed with any man before Max. "You have to go," she told him gently. "Really, I insist."

A shadow, like death, standing mutely at her side as she woke suddenly that night. She rolled quietly from beneath Max's hot possessive arm and followed Ellton down the hall.

They climbed into their parents' bed, which was cool and smelled like hand cream, her brother on their father's side, Michelle on their mother's. "This is cozy," Michelle whispered, having felt tears on her brother's cheeks. *Cozy* was his favorite word. That was how he described the cave he'd made of his own lower bunk bed, blankets and flashlights and a drawing pad at hand. Stuffed toys and a box of crackers. A small television at the foot, a smoke alarm at the head. "Bunker bed," her parents had named it. When Michelle had lived at home, she'd taken turns with her parents beside Ellton in the dark until he fell asleep, assuring him that all was well, humming to him the songs she'd once been sung. Every night he had dangerous propositions to explore before he drifted off, crafting them in the stuffy space between his face and the bottom of the bed above. The plight of the ozone layer. Sharks. Toxic mine tailings. Escaped felons. The wail of a rare siren, the rumble of thunder, the screaming headlines of the evening news. His child's mind, that genie in a bottle, turned toward spectacular, wide-ranging disaster. This disposition might suggest he'd be prepared for his parents' car crash, the accident he'd been anticipating all his life. But no.

Michelle held his hand, which was the size of her own, and they looked out the window at the moon, which shone through the bare branches of the aspens and broke into faint elongated quadrants on the blanket pulled over them. Chenille, old as Michelle, older, no doubt.

"Isn't it weird that the moon is mostly shadow?" Ellton said.

"Yes," Michelle said. Was it mostly shadow? Was it weird?

"When I can't sleep, I pull these little dots off my pajamas."

"People call those 'pills.'"

"Pills bother me."

She heard something. They both sat up.

"That's Leroy," Ellton said. "Coming up the stairs. Do you remember BoBo?"

"Of course." BoBo was the dog before Leroy, the one who'd died when Ellton was three or four, buried now under a brick out back.

"No one was nice to BoBo until he got sick. Then everybody started being nice and quit yelling at him."

Like Leroy, BoBo hadn't been a dog you'd feel charitable toward. It was true, what Ellton said. No one was good to a bad dog until he was dying.

"Leroy hasn't come upstairs since I got here," Michelle said. The dog moved slowly, one step after another, and then clicked limpily, as if three-legged, down the hall into the room where they lay. "Hey Leroy," Ellton said. The dog ignored the greeting, simply sighing in disgust as he crawled under the bed, moving in a circle beneath them, settling, wheezing once more very deeply, as if he'd been waiting for a long while to have reason to do so. "That's where he usually spends the night," Ellton explained. "Here close to Mom."

"Poor dumb dog."

"He's eighty-four, in people years. Actually, eighty-six or so, if you count half years." Michelle guessed it was just about time to start being nice to him. Ellton went on, "Maybe there has to be someone *in* the bed before he'll crawl under it?"

"That could be," Michelle agreed.

Ellton fell finally to sleep, his hand balled beside his cheek, and Michelle waited for dawn. This was her mother's view; day or night she lay appraising this square, divided exposure to the world. She looked at it over her husband's sleeping form, she viewed it alone, she listened to her old dog sighing beneath the bed. She thought her thoughts, here, watching the trees grow larger, sway in the wind, fill with leaves, lose them, the moon beyond getting fat and thin as the world spun itself between it and the sun. Michelle attempted some version of her mother's voice, recalling the cuckolded characters and the virginal ones, all the euphemistic Irish songs, wondering if she could sing herself to sleep, but she couldn't. Her mother's deep slumber, seventy-five miles away, was vast enough for them both, she supposed. Instead, Michelle would lie awake, holding her mother's place, under the window, wrapped in the chenille spread, next to the boy, above the dog.

She lay there as daylight broke, as she heard Max rising, his sounds and the house's as he moved through it: his elaborate honking nose-blowing, the clanking blustery shower, his solid thunking feet as he sought her out in her parents' room, where she pretended sleep, and of his next taking the creaking stair treads two at a time, running water in the kitchen to fill the ancient percolator on the stovetop, and then the ringing bell of the phone call that she had been awaiting. Like the rest, it felt predictable, the second—or was it the third?—act of this strange drama she'd been living for ten days. Eleven, now.

She had to leave her parents' bed to take the call, since there was no other telephone in the house.

"*The hospital*," Max mouthed.

"I'm sorry," the doctor said, speaking his part as Michelle's inner organs began dissolving, slipping formless inside her assemblage of bones, messy, confused. "Is there someone with you?" the doctor asked.

"Yes," she said, thinking not of Max, before her, studying her with his slow-moving big brown eyes, but Ellton, upstairs asleep, still dreaming, still under the spell of hope and a happy ending.

"We're waiting to notify your father," he said. "His hearing remains compromised. I don't know if we want to risk further strain, at this point."

"I don't know either," Michelle said. Now her bones were going, entitled to also succumb, given that she'd been drained of vital substance through the soles of her feet. Even her breathing seemed affected, as if someone had snipped the wires and left her powerless. Powerless but not mindless. She was imagining how to break this news to her brother. If only Max would disappear. She should have sent him away days ago. He would refuse to go, if he knew her mother had died. "Passed," he would say. He'd brought home yellow-frosted cake from the grocery yesterday. "Yellow is the color of friendship," he'd told Ellton.

"Yellow is the color of urine," said Ellton.

FALSETTO

"Do *wha'*?" Max said.

"Thank you," Michelle told the doctor, who had expressed his sympathy repeatedly during her long silences. She hung up the receiver and sat at the sticky kitchen table. Fortunately, her shock was profound enough that she did not think Max could guess what was wrong.

"My flight's at eleven," he said, bringing her coffee. "If you still think you'll be all right?"

"Fine," she said.

"'Cause I can definitely stay. I can stay indefinitely." But his bags were packed, she noticed. "You okay?" He reached to push her hair back from her cheek.

"Tired. Ellton had nightmares."

When Max pulled open the kitchen curtains, he exclaimed; it had snowed and the ground was an alarming bright white, reflecting in the sunlight for miles and miles. The heater, Michelle noticed, had kicked on, providing a dusty dry warmth. A burst of wind made the shutters creak and a gate outside slammed. Some time between the clouds rolling in yesterday afternoon and the moon beaming down late last night, a load of spring snow had been deposited onto the hills.

"Wow," Max said, staring in wonder. "That is just about blinding. What'd the hospital have to say?"

"Nothing," Michelle said, burning her mouth with a hot swallow of coffee.

"Just a wakeup call? Weather here is *nothing* like Houston, is it? Geez Louise. So, we should leave pretty quick." He was always cheerful the morning after sex. Cheerful and industrious, two more character flaws. His bags stood already at the front door, lined up in descending order of size: one duffel for clothes, one for toiletries, one for his laptop. "You think old Ellton would lend me a computer game for the flight?"

"Sure." Ellton would hand over the disc without thinking twice. And Max would forget to return it.

Leroy's feeble descent down the stairs now began, the skitter and hop and pause, and behind him the patient sound of Ellton, who would wait for the dog to take the steps as slowly as he needed to. In between depositing Max at the airport and their visit to the hospital, she would tell her brother what she had to tell him. It would be far, far worse than receiving the news herself, having to hand it to him. He was special, she knew that. But however special he was, however peculiar Michelle felt her upbringing had been, despite how oddly shameful and wonderful her family seemed to her, and no matter the resplendent bizarre morning in its dizzying white ground and radiant blue sky—no matter how extraordinary this day and how it had arrived seemed—she was soon going to have to bear some very ordinary bad news. Every day somebody's mother died.

Max began singing a silly song, putting on a sappy falsetto voice, rocking his head and shaking his fists as if they held maracas. "Ellton Ellton fo fellton, be bop bo-bellton, tree top tellton . . . ," and Michelle's brother ignored him, rubbing his eyes and leading Leroy to the door to let him go pee, tapping his rear end gently with his foot to hurry him along. Why, when the cold wind blew in, the snow so bright she could make out as if in an X-ray her brother's thin limbs through the light pajamas, did Michelle think of fences?

Those falling-down fences that you saw all over Montana, those crude elementary dividers crisscrossing the land. They required no hardware, no nails or post holes or wire or notching, that was supposed to be the beauty of them. Along every road and river, up and down the hills, ran the pine pole fences, structures that looked like tent skeletons, great long rows of them, sturdy triangles set one after another and in constant need of repair. One of the pieces of timber was always crooked or down or busted or missing; livestock was forever wandering off, stepping through or over, unaware of their own escape. These fences tempted you to stop and park your car, jump out, and set them right. They seemed just that obviously and simply broken.

KANSAS

THE GIRLS DROVE OFF early, the three-year-old being delivered to Montessori by her seventeen-year-old cousin. Three of their four parents lay in bed hung over; the fourth had risen unsteadily to fix breakfast, nauseated by a new pregnancy. Standing dazed at the stove, Anna had felt grateful to her niece for her morning cheer, her willingness to dress little Cherry Sue, tuck her in at the table, wash her face and hands—one of them bound in a bright green cast—and then carry her away to school. Cherry Sue had been singing about babies this morning, waving her bandaged fist like a maraca. She sang about everything, gesturing wildly, as if her life were a musical.

"Don't forget her plug," Anna said, meaning the pacifier.

"My plug," Cherry Sue chorused.

Anna was in despair about her second pregnancy, and at a low burn with her husband for announcing it. Now, she had no choice. In her daughter's songs the new baby had a name—No White or Toto—and everyone at Montessori had congratulated Anna. Another child with her husband meant she was further delayed from leaving him. She was still exhausted from Cherry Sue, who had only this month finally been weaned—by force. Just when Anna thought she might possess her body all alone—hers, and no one else's—here she was hostage again.

"Bye Aunt Anna," her niece Kay-Kay had said, leaning down to put her cheek next to Anna's—her cheek that smelled of syrup and sunscreen—little Cherry Sue hoisted on her opposite hip, riding her cousin like a horse. The girls were the only two people in the house who got along one hundred percent of the time. Often mistaken for sisters (even, alarmingly, for mother and daughter), fair and freckled, light-eyed, plump in the way of healthiness, they both chanted as if they felt sorry for Anna: "Bye-bye, Ma Ma," sang out Cherry Sue. "Don't cry, Ma Ma."

"Don't cry," joined in Kay-Kay, smiling brightly. Four years ago her adolescence had descended upon the household like a lit match in a powder keg. Now the disaster had passed. Gone were the frightening clothes, angry music, Sharpie-marker makeup. Restored was the pretty child who bathed every day and made conversation with her family. Anna sniffed sentimentally. She didn't love her husband, but she loved these girls. Her own little one had been a factor in the survival of the other. Another baby might wrest another worthy thing from the shipwreck of her marriage; she might once again help aid the greater good. Without Cherry Sue, she and her husband would have gone their separate ways, but now their fates seemed impossibly knotted. He refused to use condoms and failed to withdraw because he *wanted* her pregnant, a weapon he could plant like a bomb. Cherry Sue loved him, and so would the new baby; children didn't know any better. He was like the devil, Anna thought: somebody whose deceits were not clear until it was too late, until you were implicated.

"Good-bye." She sighed, waving at the girls, wishing to be driven away herself. She would remember that desire later, and not mention it. Kansas was sunny today, birds poured their hearts out in trees just beginning to bud, and Anna fell asleep in the backyard hammock, waking later with a sunburn, the skin on her thighs imprinted with hemp netting like a rump roast.

The family cell-phone plan had seven subscribers, their numbers all one digit apart. Kay-Kay's was the simplest to remember, 246-2468, and she was the one most frequently called.

Her father forgot to turn on his phone or to charge it; he left it places, restaurants or jacket pockets (Cherry Sue carried around one of his models that had gone through the wash). He was the oldest parent, fifty-eight, a psychiatrist, a mild man who let life happen to him, let the people he loved talk him into things—like cell phones or children or trampolines. This was his third marriage, and Kay-Kay's mother was a generation younger than he. He kept marrying women in their twenties, having a single daughter with them, then divorcing. Probably this would be his last marriage and daughter; he'd stayed here longest, seeing Kay-Kay into puberty and beyond. The other girls he'd left when they were in grade school, two half sisters Kay-Kay hardly knew. One had married a cop. One was a lesbian whose lover had been a patient of her father's. Wichita was just that size, big enough for lesbians and psychoanalysis, small enough for impractical, coincidental cross-pollination.

Kay-Kay's maternal grandmother remembered to carry her cell phone with her, but mistook it for other objects: the TV remote, a radio, her glasses case. Nana lived across town in a condo she only left on Tuesdays, when she made her "rounds": hairdresser, physician, bridge club, grocery. Every now and then she had a minor accident, and there would be talk about taking away her car. But she always had a pretty good explanation, and so far nobody had been injured. She forgot things, but nothing fatal. True, she'd recently served her dog a bowl of creme rinse instead of milk. Occasionally, Kay-Kay stayed over at her grandmother's. That had been one of her dodges, during the time of trouble, saying she was with Nana when she was simply at large. She had also thrown parties at Nana's, Tuesday-afternoon blowouts, sharing with her friends the old woman's pharmaceuticals and liquor, some late nights sneaking off with her car. For Christmas this year, however, Kay-Kay had embroidered a set of pillowcases for her grandmother, bluebells and daisies and sheep and a shepherdess, script that read "I Love Nana" in rose-colored thread. The family was still taking in this revised self, this hellion turned hausfrau.

Kay-Kay's mother, Emily, and her aunt Anna had programmed into their cell phones the identical ring tone for Kay-Kay's calls, an assaulting electronic jangle that ended on a sour interrogative. Recently they had discussed changing it, since it no longer seemed to suit Kay-Kay. She had become somebody more dulcet, they said. They had yet to settle on the new Kay-Kay ring tone, although they were reminded of the need every time the girl called, the noise that never failed to startle.

Anna's husband Ian's phone had a lock on its functions. Because he violated others' privacy, he assumed others would violate his. He'd pulled off the phone's housing to toughen its appearance, then mended the removal with duct tape. He had his phone in his possession at all hours, in his palm like a gun. It was set to vibrate so that he alone would know he'd been summoned. When Kay-Kay stole his cocaine stash, Ian had been frustratingly unable to report the theft to anyone but his wife. In debt himself—to Anna and her family, to his boss, to all of his friends—he felt especially outraged. He was *owed*—by somebody: an apology, a sum of money, carte blanche.

The seventh phone belonged to Kay-Kay's ex-boyfriend Wesley. Of course Kay-Kay had outgrown him—did they really expect her to marry her first boyfriend?—but nonetheless the family missed him. For two years he had lived with them, an eighteen-year-old, yet not in any way an adult—at fifteen, Kay-Kay had seemed more mature. Wesley's parents were divorced, living in different states; he had no real home of his own, no address or phone. Including him on the family cell plan cost an extra $9.99 a month; nothing, really. Kay-Kay's father paid the bills without giving them much thought. He was generous by nature. And as a therapist, he made a lot of money, his life financed by other people's troubles. Why shouldn't he contribute to the welfare of his daughter's boyfriend? When Wesley needed a root canal, it was Kay-Kay's mother who'd made the appointment. The family coached him on his ACTs, and he still stopped by to consult about perplexing pieces of the grown-up world, student loans and car insurance. He had a new girlfriend, Lucy, who was exactly—*exactly*—like the Kay-Kay they'd known three years ago. The family sometimes accidentally dialed Wesley, and sometimes it was the new girlfriend who answered. She even sounded like the old Kay-Kay, sullen, stoned, suicidal. For just a second, you could be fooled, suddenly jerked back into the nightmare.

Mid-morning, Kay-Kay's mother Emily rolled out of bed. Her hangover was from red wine. A bottle only held four glasses' worth, which was why you needed more than a bottle.

She had turned forty last week, and evidently she minded, although she hadn't thought she would. In the kitchen she found the usual mess: her sister Anna's sloppy breakfast makings, eggshells, milk left out to spoil, as well as the residue of last night's drinking, empty bottles and glasses, crusty bowl of salsa, the tart odor of pickle juice, desiccated cheese rinds. Emily muttered as she ran hot water. She had been forever in this role: mother—first to her little sister, through their childhood and beyond, and then to her husband, and of course to her daughter, Kay-Kay. Then, when they'd declared bankruptcy and moved in with her, to her sister's husband and their little girl. Naturally, her sister would have more children— Anna got pregnant at the drop of a hat, while Emily had had no luck after Kay-Kay. And then there was her mother, hers and Anna's, who seemed more and more often in need of mothering—unpleasant mothering, the variety that now involved wheedling and deception, and that would soon enough include feeding and diapering.

When sixteen-year-old Kay-Kay had turned up pregnant last year, Emily had delivered her immediately for an abortion, forbidding even the briefest fantasy of another baby (why couldn't it have been *Emily* who was pregnant? Why everybody in the house but her?), yet one more person to become Emily's responsibility.

And another of her responsibilities? Keeping the abortion secret from Kay-Kay's father, Henry.

Responsibility was plaguing. Sometimes it drove Emily to drinking too much, to letting loose—which required an act of *ir*responsibility. The bright *pup* of the wine bottle relinquishing its cork. The gentle bell of stemware leaving the rack. The silly conversation over snacks, over music, her brother-in-law proving his most tolerable self in service to a party, careful sound track selection, finger food, refilling the glass; her husband, just so happy to see everybody get along.

Emily drank cold water, then hot coffee. Some days, there was nothing but fluid.

Her daughter had forgotten her school binder; it was stuck in syrup to the kitchen table. Emily pried it off and carried it upstairs to Kay-Kay's bedroom, where she stood at the door. For years she'd snooped in her daughter's life, read her diary, slit open the seams of her coat, turned over the dresser drawers, shoved her hand between the mattress and box springs. She didn't want to do that anymore. Suspiciousness was soul-killing, and it was never satisfied until it found what it was looking for. She told herself that Kay-Kay deserved her trust. She tossed the binder on the bed and shut the door.

Sometimes at noon Kay-Kay came home from school. For a while, last fall, on the upswing of her adolescent sentence, she'd brought friends with her for lunch. She'd been proud of her communal life, then, just beginning her climb out of rage and wretchedness, proud of her rambling old house with its many airy rooms, a place where you might find her aunt Anna sunbathing nude on the porch or her father brandishing a civilized glass of merlot midday. "For my heart," he would say, "purely medicinal." At noon, her boyfriend Wesley would be rising, zipping himself into his coveralls, ready for his shift at the lube pit. Cute Cherry Sue, humming in her high chair, Kay-Kay's mother serving up lasagna or soup. It was a capacious kitchen, dining table made from an ancient farmhouse door, eight expectant chairs. Flowers in vases, fruit in bowls, cursing in the conversation.

But these days Kay-Kay came home alone. She was getting ready to leave: high school; those starstruck friends; this hospitable house. Senior. Her future, Emily hoped, held college, Europe, Africa; what else had they been prepping—as well as preserving—her for but departure? While Kay-Kay paged through catalogs and brochures, eating yogurt or toast, Emily imagined her as a volunteer in another country, barefoot on terra incognita, or wrapped in a raincoat, in the frame of a window on a train, pensively eyeing an ocean—Pacific, Atlantic—cutting through a city on either edge of her own continent. Emily had believed she'd do those things herself, once upon a time: attend Harvard, adopt orphans, observe the world from the basket of a hot air balloon. But then she'd fallen in love with Henry—scandalously her elder, and married, to boot—and then with this funky old house, and then there'd been the birth of her daughter . . .

Today, Kay-Kay didn't come home for lunch.

Indulging his hangover, Kay-Kay's father rose from bed only long enough to cancel appointments with his lunatics and lumber back, crawl between the warm sheets littered with his shed hair. Fridays were half days anyway. Between bed and phone, Emily doubted he'd even opened his eyes. He was their bear, gruff, kind, loyal to a fault. Sometimes she believed that Kay-Kay's misbehavior would have killed him had it gone on much longer, either him or their marriage.

Tender today with her own wooziness, Emily decided to join him, nudging herself against his furry chest. He had grown soft in their nineteen years together; she was his last wife, he always said, last and best. He'd had a starter wife for practice, and another for refining his skills. He performed with forbearance, faith, patience, permitting Emily to be the hotheaded one, while he stood by, complementary extinguisher.

"Admit it!" Emily had accused him crazily on her fortieth birthday. "I'm the oldest woman you ever slept with! Old women are *witches*! No one even *notices* them, let alone finds them attractive. *You* don't find old women attractive, admit it!"

"Not yet," he'd confessed mildly.

They lay together into the afternoon, bound in a cocoon of indolence: it was spring again, and they had arrived here with their girl after a long, treacherous journey, and it only seemed now, just now, that they were safely out of the woods. To celebrate, they'd do this: nothing. Henry slept, wheezing, and Emily lay in his arms, and it wasn't until three o'clock, when Anna borrowed her sister's car in order to drive to Montessori to pick up Cherry Sue, that anyone realized something was wrong.

"You phoned this morning," said Miss Juliet, proving it by producing the form with the time, Anna's name, the fact that Cherry Sue wouldn't be coming to school today. All the Misses at Montessori had the identical voice, blameless and assured. If Cherry Sue wasn't there, it wasn't their fault.

Kay-Kay's cell phone sent all calls immediately to voice mail. Like her ring tone, the message was a leftover. "Kay-Kay says shut up and *fuck off*!" a boy yelled, Sid Vicious–ly. He wasn't even her ex-boyfriend Wesley, but a stranger, Kay-Kay's slurred laughter in the background.

The next number Anna hit was her husband Ian's. Like Kay-Kay, he was sending callers to voice mail. Shaking, Anna phoned her sister, and Emily (who always answered) advised driving to East High. "School's not out, yet. Maybe she took Cherry Sue with?"

"Maybe."

"Show and tell."

"Sure."

At the house, Emily hung up and closed her eyes, thrown instantly into the grim fright of last year, and the year before, and the year before that: her daughter, that force of nature, out wreaking havoc. Rising from a bed made of relief—smugness, Emily thought, presumption—into a sudden landscape of lava. She had the sensation of wind—as if being blown backward— or of something hurtling toward her. "Goddamnit, Henry!" He sat up blurrily, face imprinted with his own palm, as if he'd been slapped. She called their daughter and listened to her message, hating the familiar chill it gave her. She clapped shut the phone and threw it at Henry, fear leading directly to rage, and her husband, right there, ready to receive it.

Two miles away, high school was letting out when Anna arrived. The wind had picked up, and dirt filled the air, trash flattened into the chain link. She drove against the current of muscle cars and trucks surging around her, unnerved by the exuberance with which the teenagers handled their vehicles, their lives. They yelled and honked and screeched their tires, lighting cigarettes and popping up through sunroofs, out back windows, some riding on hoods, dust and exhaust whirling as they revved their engines. Anna eased over speed bumps, praying, the lump on her lap already announcing itself as a solid presence against her rib cage with each tire roll. She scanned desperately for her niece's gold Celica, willing to forgive Kay-Kay for taking Cherry Sue to high school. Plenty of students came to school with their babies, or with their big embarrassing bellies held before them like basketballs. Anna guessed that Kay-Kay wasn't beyond vying for some attention, some better attention than she'd been accustomed to getting these last few years, when she'd been warned and suspended and flunked and arrested, handed poor marks not only in performance and attendance but in attitude and appearance, as well—in *personality*, it seemed.

Often, Anna had defended her niece, even envied her—as if on behalf of her own former self, both patriotic and nostalgic about a lost homeland.

Now she searched with growing pessimism the thinning trickle of cars and pedestrians. Cherry Sue wasn't here.

"They're not here," she told Emily on the phone, driving home. She began to sob, cramping as she did.

"Where's Ian?" Emily demanded.

"*I* don't know." Anna had no idea what her husband did with himself; borrowing her sister's car had become a daily necessity.

"We ought to find Ian." Ian had been helpful on a few occasions. He'd located tolerable community service for Kay-Kay after her possession conviction. He'd stayed up all night talking to the speedy girl when the other adults were utterly worn out. Once, when she declared that she'd be fine with being a prostitute, he took her to the seedy side of Wichita, to some strip clubs he knew, just to get a taste.

"You call him," Anna said of her husband. "He won't answer me."

Sure enough, Ian took Emily's call. The noise on his end of the line suggested a submarine. "Where are you?" she asked.

"Work," he said flatly. "What do you want?"

"I wonder if you've seen Kay-Kay. She took Cherry Sue this morning, but they didn't go to school." On his end she could hear a door close, an echoing clatter as he dropped his push broom. Racquetball court, she guessed. He practically lived at the club, hanging out in the seating area of the juice bar, disguising himself as a healthy handyman/bodybuilder type person when in fact he made most of his income dealing drugs in the parking lot and men's locker room. His uniform was a warm-up suit. Sport bottle full of vodka. Of particular appeal was that he had an excuse to exit his in-laws' house every morning, leaving his killjoy wife and her stuck-up family to themselves.

Or at least that's what Emily believed. She had no idea what really went on in her brother-in-law's head. He'd been hanging around in her life since he was a bratty neighbor boy ten years her junior. Often she imagined the two words he'd most like to say to her: *Whatever, bitch.* Now she couldn't tell if his lack of reaction meant he was thinking, or merely stunned, or concocting a story.

"So I'm wondering if you know anything?" Emily finally said. His silence was hermetic, like the room he stood in, and it made her impatient, tempted to hang up. But Kay-Kay sometimes confided in Ian—he had the tactical advantage of being the other acknowledged delinquent in the house. Drunk, he could be very endearing. Last night, for example, he'd done hilarious imitations of all four principals, and a few extras, in *The Wizard of Oz* as if they'd been pulled over for DUI.

Straight, however, he defaulted to paranoia. "I know what you're thinking," he said.

"No, you don't," she assured him. Emily was thinking of Kay-Kay's car crashed in a rural ditch, its interior vivid with blood. She ordered the image away; indulging it felt too close to inviting it.

Ian said, "Let me get back with you," and hung up.

"'Get back' with me?" Emily said to Anna, who was coming through the mud room door. "He said he'll *get back* with me."

Anna jumped as the wind slammed the door shut behind her. "He's an asshole," she said for at least the hundredth time.

She turned her pleading, tear-streaked little-sister face to her big sister: "Where *are* they?"

Meanwhile, Henry had pulled himself from bed to perform his ritual: driving around. He had done this whenever Kay-Kay disappeared. Same with the missing pets. It never paid off, but it seemed necessary, a biological imperative. He was confirming that the obvious explanation didn't prevail. The dog wasn't chasing tail at the park or lying like a rug in the road; the girls weren't parked down at Dairy Queen or visiting any of Kay-Kay's known acquaintances.

Last time she'd run away, she'd taken a bus to Burning Man; the time before that, she'd hitchhiked to Ohio. She'd never before had her own getaway vehicle. It was Henry who had insisted on buying Kay-Kay a car, even though Emily was opposed. They'd argued for weeks. The girl had totaled two—*two*—of the family cars in a single year! although later Emily had grudgingly acknowledged that he had seemed right: Kay-Kay got a job to pay for gas, had not one ticket or wreck, and volunteered for trips to the grocery or to drop off Cherry Sue.

But now look what had happened. Wait around long enough, Emily thought sourly, and you can win any argument.

Henry slapped at his jacket pocket before he left, showing her he had remembered his phone.

"Pointless," Emily said, of his errand. "Complete waste of time."

"I hate how all we can do is wait," Anna said.

"We just have to wait."

Anna began to cry again. "I'm being punished!" she said to Emily.

"For what?"

"Bellyaching about Cherry Sue! Being pissy about being pregnant!"

"Oh, please, Anna. You're not being punished."

"Why can't I learn to keep my big mouth shut? Just count my fucking blessings?" Anna threw herself into a kitchen chair.

"Stop it, stop it. You're hungry." Emily was already pulling open the cupboard doors. "You need to eat."

"I *hate* how it's an obligation to eat!" Like a petulant child, Anna took the cookie Emily offered. "And I *hate* how hard it is to swallow when you're crying!"

That evening, the usual emergency vehicle sirens seemed especially frequent and jarringly loud; the wind blew so hard it whistled in all the old home's many cracks. Tornado season was upon them again; possibly they'd end up in the basement tonight. Their three cell phones lay on the scarred kitchen table while Emily microwaved leftovers for her husband and her pregnant sister. She herself had taken a Valium. It was Anna who noticed the wall calendar. "Today is Friday the thir*teenth*!" she wailed.

"Kay-Kay doesn't know that," Emily said. "She loses track of what month it is, let alone the day or date."

"I probably should have met my people today," Henry said reflectively, napkin tucked like a bib into his collar. "Some of them are definitely superstitious." He had gone to the police station while he was driving around, ascertaining there'd been no accidents involving a gold Celica, no ambulance summons for a teenager and toddler. His oldest daughter's husband Buzz was a cop; he promised to keep an eye out. "The desk sergeant asked if I wanted to report a *kidnapping*," Henry told Emily and Anna. "I mean, really." He rocked his head in disbelief; he'd never grown accustomed to thinking of Kay-Kay as a criminal, even when she'd been arrested and charged, found guilty and made to pay. Teenage Kay-Kay had over-taxed him—this despite the fact that he made his living hearing how people were routinely failed by their loved ones, and how relentlessly they failed themselves. In the office, he used the when-did-you-stop-beating-your-wife approach, asking not if but how often they fell short. With his daughter, however, he was as blustering and dumbfounded as a stereotype from a sitcom, a dad handicapped by blind love.

Having been a devious teenage girl herself, Emily experienced no real surprise when Kay-Kay misbehaved—it was more like confirmation.

Tonight, Henry kept positing the same fuzzy scenario. "She's doing something for somebody," he said. "Somebody in crisis, who called her on her way to school. And then it was more complicated than she thought, it snowballed."

"If somebody lured Kay-Kay with a phone call," Emily said, "it wasn't about salvation."

"But why take Cherry Sue?" asked Anna. "Why run away *with* a three-year-old? I'm always trying to run away *from* her." She didn't mention what *she* imagined: an alluring young pirate commandeering her niece's vehicle, Kay-Kay demoted, willingly, to the passenger's side. *Let's go*, he said, in Anna's imagination. Then, just before they took off in a whirlwind, he would notice the toddler in the back seat. Cherry Sue would greet the handsome rogue with a new verse in her on-going song: "*Hello you guy!*" she might belt out.

"She would never let anything happen to Cherry Sue," Henry assured his sister-in-law.

"Not on purpose," Emily amended.

Henry gave his wife the familiar disappointed look. "Please, Em," he said, not wanting to believe her heartless.

"I didn't mean what I said about running away from Cherry Sue," Anna said, pleadingly. "She's a lot of work, but she's awfully good company. Always in a good mood. *Much* better company than her dad." Nobody disagreed. Nonetheless, why wasn't Ian here?

The house phone rang, and Emily answered, then held it up so they could all listen to the high school attendance office recording letting them know that their *"son—or daughter— missed one—or more—classes today."*

"Oh, fuck you," they chimed in unison while the voice went on in its flat scolding way about what steps should next be taken. They'd heard it many, many times before. Yet Kay-Kay's trouble, however often it involved officials—rules, and the rule makers, and the rule enforcers—had never been solved by them.

The mud room door slammed open, but yielded only Wesley, the ex. "Find her?" he asked. He wore dirty garage coveralls with his name on the pocket, long-sleeved because his boss couldn't abide tattoos. He was a working boy who'd loved Kay-Kay dearly, who, when he lived with them, had tolerated Kay-Kay's teasing about her status as minor and his as statutory rapist. "I drove by Nana's, just to see if her car was there, but it wasn't . . ." Wesley trailed off. "It smells good in here."

Emily offered him food, but he declined, gesturing toward the driveway, where the new girlfriend Lucy was smoking a cigarette, flicking her head as if snapping her teeth. Wesley had made it clear he would return to Kay-Kay, given any sign she wanted him back. He would leave Lucy, easily. Or maybe not so easily, Emily thought, watching the girl pace in a tight smoldering ring.

"I'll stop by the hookah bar," Wesley volunteered. "And maybe Java the Hut. I've got my cell."

"Good man," said Henry.

"Thanks, Wes," said Emily, smiling wanly at him. She'd always thought he was too nice for the likes of Kay-Kay, who Emily believed required a little wickedness.

WHERE R U?? Anna text-messaged Ian at midnight. It embarrassed her not to know where her husband was, not to know for sure that he wasn't somehow involved in the girls' disappearance. Her mother had named him a hoodlum, years ago; as a teenager, he'd stolen dogs in order to receive rewards. Anna herself had collected the cash, as she looked more like a savior than Ian. That's what he did, turn you into an accomplice. Another time, he'd shown her how easy it was to break into homes, summoning a locksmith and waltzing right into the neighbors' house, waving to Anna from the window. Ian had handed down to Kay-Kay his powerful black shirt with neon yellow SECURITY emblazoned on the back. In it, you could go anywhere, do anything.

Looking for girls, he texted back. Anna knew this was true; but *which* girls?

She glanced up to find her big sister glaring at her, giving her an order. "You should sleep." Pregnancy was insistent, that way. This new baby, no bigger than a plum, was overruling her ability to stay alert on behalf of her other baby. She left her phone with Emily, knowing its ring might not rouse her.

Emily sent Henry to bed, too. What good could he do, furry, worried, lost looking? He kissed her cheek (she wiped it off), leaving her on the couch, where, at one-hour intervals, she called Kay-Kay's number.

At four thirty, her daughter finally responded, the disturbing ring tone launching Emily into a heart-fluttering panic. A couple lines of text appeared: *We r fine Dont worry! Luv u*

The message proved Kay-Kay was in possession of her phone, her wits, her cousin. Nevertheless, Emily began crying, and, of course, this was when Ian arrived home, sneaking in like a thief.

"What?" he said, alarmed.

"She called," Emily said. "They're fine, she says."

He smelled of bar. She wanted to kill him—for being who he was and not someone else, for catching her in tears. He had never liked her, not even when he should have been in awe of her, when he was a child. Always he'd preferred Anna; always he'd chosen her over Emily. As a kid, he'd kept the neighborhood in supply of cigarettes and soda stolen from the local 7-Eleven. Emily could remember when he'd finally been banned from the store, the way he'd squinted at her, as if he knew it had been she who'd snitched, and he wouldn't forget it. Nowadays he was beholden to Emily and Henry, unhappy houseguest. He blinked his heavy-lidded eyes. "A couple of people have seen her today," he said, dropping into the easy chair.

"Really?"

"They think so. Cherry Sue is hard to miss, specially with that cast on her arm. They had breakfast at the IHOP by Nana's, then around noon they were out busking with a guitar in Old Towne."

"Where have you been?"

"Everywhere."

"Buzz knows to look for her."

"Buzz?"

"Henry's son-in-law, the cop."

Ian scowled now; Emily thought she could read his mind: What good was a cop to them? Hadn't Ian himself supplied the most useful information yet? "I talked to her earlier," he said, rising.

"What?"

"She said we really upset her last night. She's feeling disappointed in all of us, you and me and Anna and Henry, all of us. She said she—"

"She called *you*?"

His mouth snapped shut, and Emily knew he wouldn't open it again. *Whatever, bitch.* As he left the room, her sister's words echoed in Emily's ears: "You don't go to him," Anna had explained long ago. "He comes to you." Emily had stubbornly refused to believe that a neighborhood punk, *ten years* her junior, wielded that kind of power. Fuming, she listened as he made his way up the stairs and down the hall to the room he and Anna shared.

Emily read Kay-Kay's text message once more, critically this time. *Luv u!* Emily had not grown up saying "I love you"; her family wasn't like that. Now, she noticed that both she and Anna said it all the time to their girls, like an incantation. Even their mother, in her widowed, vulnerable old age, would close a conversation with those magic words. The one time Emily could remember telling her parents she loved them had been when she was a teenager, coming home past curfew, neck ringed with hickeys, delirious on Ecstasy. "I love you guys!" she'd said, brandishing the phrase like a deflecting weapon. She could still see their faces: too shocked to answer with suitable punishment.

On Saturday, the sky was murky, churning with a wind that seemed to want to tear the roof from the house. Henry called his son-in-law Buzz to confirm that nothing bad had happened overnight on the police radio band, on highways, in storms. Emily made herself turn Kay-Kay's room upside down, page through her journal, sniff at her jewelry box, open her closet and drawers and CD cases. But Emily knew that if Kay-Kay wanted to hide something these days, it would be in her car; owning it had given her a locking trunk.

"What else did she say to Ian?" Emily finally asked Anna. Pride had prevented her from asking him. Pride, and fear that he would tell her it was none of her fucking business. Like a teenager, he had the capacity to shame you—even as you understood him to be in the wrong.

"He said she said we were terrible role models." Anna was making bread, keeping busy. "I think I might have told Cherry Sue to shut up." She leaked a tear or two into the dough, continuing to knead.

"Terrible role models?" Emily and Henry said together. At the table, Henry looked up from his project. He was making a MISSING poster, with photographs—Cherry Sue in nothing but a diaper, Kay-Kay still sporting braces. He'd had to find a photo with her hair the proper color, not the flat black she'd worn until last Christmas.

"That's what he said she said." Anna wasn't sure she believed her husband. It would be like him, to try to punish his wife and her family, convince them Kay-Kay thought they were bad role models.

"I *was* telling stories about my patients," Henry said, chastened. "About the stalker, and a few of my chem deps—"

"You never said any names," Anna assured him. "You're always really careful to protect privacy."

"Still, I shouldn't have been talking—"

"I'm sure that wasn't it." Anna paused over the bread dough, fighting nausea. Being pregnant was like being possessed, she thought.

Emily sat across from Henry at the table, staring into her coffee, trying to reconstruct the evening, completely prepared to take responsibility. But for what, exactly? For being drunk enough not to remember, she supposed. She could recall Ian's making them all laugh. The cop pulling over the drunks on the yellow brick road: lion, scarecrow, tin man, even that wacky dwarf, representative of the Lollipop Guild—reciting the backward alphabet, swinging their fingers to their noses, walking with arms outstretched as if on a balance beam. Round-heeled, blasted Judy Garland, in her earnest full-throated way trying to seduce the officer, inviting him for a romp in the poppy field. It had seemed like a good evening, Kay-Kay joining them for dinner, sticking around as the hour grew late, rocking Cherry Sue on her hip, helping Anna fix snacks, changing CDs on the player when Ian complained about Henry's music . . . Emily had the impression that they had been trying to please the teenager, all four of the adults staging an impromptu production called *Life Is Worth Living,* right here at this very table. What Kay-Kay had taught them, during the last few years, was that she truly could not see the point, as if she did not care whether she lived or died. And if she did not care, what was to stop her from whatever impulse seized her? Sleep with a stranger? Why not. Inject an unknown drug? Okay. Hitchhike, wander the streets, invite outlaws into her life and hallucinations into her head—all of it without regard for what her family kept calling *consequence,* a future with her in it. They agreed that it had been Cherry Sue who saved her, Cherry Sue who'd been able to sufficiently light what otherwise seemed a dark void—by loving Kay-Kay as passionately as she did, by assigning Kay-Kay particular status as queen of her heart. Her name had been the second one Cherry Sue said, right after "Mama"; when she finally learned to walk, it was Kay-Kay's arms she aimed for and fell into.

"What do you think?" Henry asked, holding up his MISSING

poster. He put himself into motion before he learned what the sisters thought. He would photocopy it, and then drive around posting it: in Old Towne, on Douglas, by East and the other high schools, at Wal-Marts and gas stations and bars and grocery stores and truck stops and at both the big malls. "I'll have my cell," he assured Emily, patting his pocket.

"Absolutely futile," Emily told Anna when he was gone. "I'm going upstairs to take a bath. You mind the phones."

What had they done? she asked herself in the tub. She'd swallowed another Valium before plopping into the water; otherwise, it seemed she might simply burst into flame. The atmosphere was shifting; Emily felt now that Kay-Kay was not oblivious to how her family would respond but, rather, knew precisely how this would resonate, as if she were watching them through some cosmic portal, while none of them had a clue as to where she was, neither what she was doing nor why.

Downstairs, Anna was daydreaming, longing to leave, herself—flee this house and the people in it, abandon her relationships and the heartache they bred. Fly away without notifying a soul, free, alone on a cheerful road.

And then she remembered her pregnancy. Not free, not alone.

Out the window, tree branches ached to break in the wind. Below their flailing canopy was the trampoline, Ian's sole contribution to the household. He had brought it home the same way he did all of his dubious belongings, with the implicit instruction that no one ask questions; it was as if he had that motto etched on his forehead.

The trampoline vibrated, like a living thing. When it was first set up, Cherry Sue and Kay-Kay had climbed right on

and begun to bounce together, holding hands, Kay-Kay a perfect patient companion to the toddler, smiles on their faces so
big you couldn't help smiling in response. They danced on it
to Kay-Kay's boom-box music, they loped around its rubber
surface singing about the muffin man, they lay upon it in the
dark, after it had absorbed the sun all day, breathing heavily,
watching as the stars popped on. A trampoline wasn't as dangerous to either of the girls when partnered with the other.

Could driving away in the car be thought of the same way?
Less dangerous if they were both involved?

Anna jumped when the house phone rang; the cop on the
other end wanted to know what the girls were wearing. She
shrieked, and Emily, who'd leapt from the tub and thudded
down the stairs, dripping in a towel, snatched the receiver
from her.

"Did you find them?" she asked.

He assured her they hadn't; he was merely following up.
What had the girls been wearing? "You saw them," Emily ordered her sister. "What did they have on?"

Anna's lip quivered. "The cast," she began, "and that pink
kitty dress . . ."

"Pink dress," Emily said into the phone, "kitty appliqué.
The three-year-old has a cast on her wrist, green like a tennis
ball. The big one's dressed like a hippie, long skirt, flip-flops,
camisole—" She paused, listening. "No, like a *slip*, like the top
half of a petticoat."

"The turquoise one," Anna supplied.

"Turquoise," Emily told the cop. She hung up after he'd
noted everything. "Imbecile. Anyone with half a brain wouldn't
scare us like that. Somebody should have asked yesterday what
they were wearing."

"I'm going crazy," Anna said.

"Me, too," Emily said, woozy from the hot water and the blue pill.

"Remember them on the trampoline?"

Emily glanced outside. She had not wanted to accept the trampoline—not because it came from Ian, but because she had foreseen the broken limb or crushed skull. Somebody would be made to pay. Some bone would have to be offered up. The sacrifice was Cherry Sue's, her little left wrist. Off to the ER they'd raced, the three-year-old sobbing into Kay-Kay's neck while Emily weaved through traffic, Anna riding shot-gun, crying uselessly. Emily had met her daughter's eyes in the rearview mirror, a complicit glance between them, the level-headed ones. Emily had liked that moment.

Now, with her sister flour-dusted and sad before her, Emily recalled another piece of Thursday evening's conversation. This had concerned their childhood. When they were young, and shared a bedroom, it had been Emily's habit to lie on the bunk above Anna and cross-examine her. Every night, the same conversation: "Tell me what she looks like," Emily would insist.

"No." Anna had an imaginary friend, so she was never alone.

"What's she doing right now?"

"I am not telling." *Herself*, she would sometimes call this friend. *Herself* had naughty notions. Before Ian came along, it was Herself who got Anna into trouble.

Night after night Emily wheedled, by turns threatening and pleading. She was a bully, and she had to win. Finally: "If you tell me her name," she had pledged, "I'll name my first child after her." This promise she'd made at age nine. Down below, a long silence came from her four-year-old sister.

And then Anna had said, "Her name is Kay-Kay."

"*That's* why you named me Kay-Kay?" Kay-Kay had asked, Thursday evening.

"You knew that already," Emily said, tilting her empty wineglass once more into her mouth, not wanting to open a third bottle.

"I didn't."

"I didn't, either," claimed Anna.

"I've told you both, a thousand times." The thing about being Anna's sister was that, by the time Emily had made good on her end of the deal, Anna had forgotten it was owed—was totally nonplussed over the telephone when Emily called blissfully from the delivery room. But Anna had been a scornful teenager, then, repulsed by her sister's marriage to a man practically their father's age.

That had been a long time ago. Now, Anna knew all about the tender sentiment attached to babies and their names. Later, pregnant herself, she'd agreed to the name Ian chose; then, she wanted him to stick around. "Cherry Sue," he'd declared. "Just like my first Z car, may she RIP."

"I don't even remember *having* an imaginary friend," Anna now said to Emily, as if she, too, had been trying to reconstruct Thursday night. "Maybe I already knew that the imaginary ones worked out better than the real ones?"

Ian entered the kitchen then. "You got a problem with reality?" he said to Anna, meanwhile running his eyes over Emily in her towel. "I'm going out," he announced, as if somebody might try to stop him. On the table, one of the cells rang with Kay-Kay's awful tone. It was her aunt's phone, a text message: *How much Ch Sue wiegh?*

"Why is she asking me this?" Anna cried.

"*What* the *fuck*?" Ian said.

Emily took only a moment to process the request. "She's

giving her Tylenol," she deduced. "She wants to get the right dose."

"I don't *know* how much Cherry Sue weighs!" Anna burst into tears.

Ian said, "What could it be, like forty?" He was making fists, flexing his elbows as if hefting barbells.

"Twenty-five," Emily instructed. "Let me text her back." She remembered from the ER, when the bone had been set. Twenty-five. *Thanp*, was Kay-Kay's reply.

Saturday night was a repeat of Friday night, starring actors sick of their roles, stuck in the production. Ian had not come home, and Anna's new baby was urging her to bed. Henry had developed the dark circles beneath his eyes that could lead to migraine, and Emily was furious at the helpless way he looked out from their depths. "A hundred posters," he'd said, of his MISSING mission, accounting for his exhaustion. On his night table was a fleet of pill bottles, his age most evident there. "Go to bed," she snapped. "I'll stay here with the phones."

At two a.m., Wesley called. There was wind and static on his end. He was outside a party from which he had been banished, but he thought maybe Kay-Kay was there. "Lucy needs to chill," he explained, so he was going to drive her home, but he gave Emily the address.

It took Emily two seconds to decide to call Ian instead of wake either of the others; as usual with his sister-in-law, he took the call, albeit unhappily. "Yeah?" he said. At his end of the line, there was also wind. He, too, stood outside a party. He smelled of bonfire when he picked up Emily ten minutes later.

"This is a weird address," he noted. "You sure she'd be here?"

"No," said Emily. The address was a mansion in a new subdivision, not yet finished, a baby blue porta-potty tilting in the front yard, stakes and PVC pipes strewn about, the only lights coming from within the giant house itself.

To Ian's credit, he performed beautifully as party crasher. He nodded as they entered the massive front door, murmuring a few "How's it going?"s as they pushed through the crowded rooms, Emily following in his wake. The place was cavernous, echoing, warmed by body heat, smelling of sawdust. Men with string instruments played folk music in a corner. The people milling here, holding plastic cups and cigarettes, were older than Kay-Kay by a decade or more. Many wore cowboy hats; a yard-long sheet cake rested on a set of sawhorses.

Ian said, "This isn't a party, it's a hoedown."

"I'm looking for Kay-Kay," Emily said hopefully to the man tapping the keg in the kitchen.

"Hey, yeah," he said. "Where is that *chica*?" Everyone recognized the name and nodded, smiling fondly, but they hadn't seen her. Ian accepted a plastic cup of beer, then grimaced as he drank.

"I was picturing teenagers," Emily confided to him. Some bit of Kansas miscreance, a meth lab maybe.

"You were picturing a big-ass opium den of iniquity," Ian scoffed. "I guess I was, too."

Emily canvassed the first floor, just to make sure, and then headed upstairs, carefully since there was not yet a rail. Here were the future bedrooms, five of them, each white and blank, vacant bathrooms, the smell of new carpet in rolls. Out the windows, other hulking houses, dark like quiet ships. Was it mere sleeplessness that made everything seem strange to her? She dialed up Wesley. "Where did you think she might be, exactly?"

"I couldn't get to the upstairs."

"I'm there. It's totally empty."

"Huh. Hang on, Emily." Wesley was talking to somebody on his end. "I'm at Saint Francis," he said apologetically. "Lucy might have OD'd."

"Might have?"

"She turned blue. Now she looks better—her mom says she's hypoglycemic, so sometimes that happens—but we're already here . . ." He trailed off, sighing. Once more at the hospital, with paperwork: he'd performed a similar duty on Kay-Kay's behalf, and not that long ago ("If one is good," Kay-Kay had explained, "why wouldn't two be better?"). Wesley said, "I'm sorry, I thought Kay-Kay might have been staying in that place. She knows some of the guys working on it. I gotta go, Emily. We're up."

"Good luck, Wes," she said.

Emily returned downstairs to find Ian accepting a second beer from the man in the kitchen. "Coors?" he asked Emily. "Cake?"

"No, thanks. I was hoping somebody'd seen my daughter."

"She said she'd be here. I don't much care for that other girl Wesley brought. She's sure got a short fuse."

"Wesley likes the short fuse," Ian said, downing his beer in one wincing swallow. "They're not here," he said to Emily.

"Thanks for coming!" called a few people as they exited.

In the car, Ian snorted. "Yee-haw." Then he grabbed his thrumming phone. "I'll drop you off," he said, studying its screen.

In Anna's dream that night she birthed an apple. A green apple. The same green as Cherry Sue's cast. Last dream, she'd had a small black monkey, his chattering mouth full of teeth, his hair greasy. In another, she produced kittens, a litter of three, and one had died, just quit breathing right before her eyes. Still: kittens. You could take them to the pound, if you tired of them. People were so much harder. She wondered sometimes what her brother-in-law, the professional interpreter of dreams, would say about hers, what he would know about her if he heard what went on inside her busy sleeping head. Tonight the tornado warning siren swooped into Anna's dream but didn't wake her; it was Emily who pulled her to her feet and led her down to the basement, where the three of them leaned against each other on the moldering couch, waiting for the all clear.

Sarah, Henry's oldest daughter, arrived Sunday morning with the sun. Heavy, stoic Sarah with the hairdo, holding a hot casserole before her. Besides the oven mitts, she was dressed for church. Her greeting was a list of ingredients, egg, sausage, hash browns, cheese. "And cream of mushroom soup," she finished. Sarah always wore a sorrowful expression in her father's house, as if she saw them headed in that handbasket toward hell. At first, Emily had reciprocated, pitying Sarah back. Later, when Kay-Kay had gone wild, she simply refused to make eye contact.

The sky was blue, the air still: the famous calm after a storm. You could hear birds again, earnestly going at their song. Emily began thanking her stepdaughter perfunctorily. At this, Sarah gazed demurely out the kitchen window, saddened but not surprised at what had befallen this group of savages. Then her brow furrowed. Out there on the trampoline slept the two missing girls, plus another person. You could see the blond heads tipped together, little Cherry Sue's neon green cast atop the army green tarpaulin covering them, and a third shape, besides. "Thank you, Jesus," Sarah murmured, pointing for her father and stepmother. "There they are," she said.

"Ian said you were upset by us, Thursday night."

"Why did he say that?"

Emily glared at her brother-in-law, who glared back. *Whatever, bitch.* "You weren't?"

"I might have been." Kay-Kay shrugged. She had the air of someone to whom blame could not be attached, nor shame or repentance, either. "It's temporary," she said of the rainbow tattoo on her shoulder, before Emily could ask. Cherry Sue had a matching one on her thigh.

Ian said, "I thought you were on the run from the man."

Kay-Kay scoffed. "That's you, not me. Why weren't you all worried about poor Nana?" The third person sleeping on the trampoline was Anna and Emily's mother, also missing these last two days, yet unmissed by her only children. Her, and her little dirty-white dog. Unforgivable, according to Kay-Kay, who was also bemused.

"I thought you'd been carjacked," Henry confessed, wiping his eyes. "I thought you picked up hitchhikers and got stolen, a good deed gone bad." He kept laying his hand on Kay-Kay's shoulder, as if never to let her leave home again. Kay-Kay studied the MISSING poster. Although the photograph he'd used was several years old, Emily had to admit it more closely resembled Kay-Kay than she had thought. "I'll have to go take those down," he said.

Kay-Kay nodded. "I'll help."

Why weren't they angrier, Emily wondered? Why had the girls' return inspired so little besides relief in her and Anna and Henry and Ian? What were they guilty of, that this was their reaction, this indebtedness, as if Kay-Kay had performed a rescue rather than the reverse? Cherry Sue nuzzled at Anna's neck, absolutely fine, a faint sunburn on the bridge of her nose and her cheeks as if from healthful recreation.

"You never once dialed Nana's cell," Kay-Kay said. "We checked."

"I wasn't thinking of her," Emily admitted. "You okay, Mom?"

"Why wouldn't I be?" Nana sat at the table with her dog in her lap, no worse for the wear, unkempt in the usual way. She had enjoyed her trip with the girls; Medicine Lodge, a hundred miles southwest, was her hometown. She hadn't visited there in she didn't know how long. "We stood in the backyard of the old farmhouse."

"That's right, Nana. For our picture."

"That fellow with the cart full of cans took it for us."

"You gave him a dollar."

"And then Nipper ran off after a rabbit."

"That's right."

Nana looked relieved, as always, to have her memory confirmed. She wore her usual floral muumuu; her hair hardly existed anymore, a few white tufts. Her fingers twitched in her pet's fur, which was filled with twigs and burrs and mulberry fluff. She had not panicked, picked up by her granddaughter Friday morning; for all she knew, it was a plan. "They've always had the best pie at the Toot Sweet," she recalled, "and we slept in a motel." *Moe*-tel.

"I sleep with Kay-Kay," said Cherry Sue, smiling slyly.

"You drove to Medicine Lodge and checked into a motel?" asked Ian skeptically. There was a missing part. Wasn't there?

"That sounds kind of inviting," Anna said. But the trip to a motel she envisioned didn't include her mother or daughter, and it certainly wasn't set in Kansas. The dangerous stranger, the pirate at the wheel, wouldn't have tolerated those.

"Nana wanted to visit the old homestead," Kay-Kay said. "It's pretty out there. Some places, you can't even get phone reception."

Sarah had served everyone a glass of milk, though none of them except Cherry Sue ever drank the stuff. As soon as she'd seen the girls and their grandmother, Sarah phoned her husband the cop to say she would be missing church today. Called to a higher need, she'd tucked a dish towel into her waistband and begun spooning up her eggy casserole, the family sitting obediently. The blandness of the offering went with the blandness of the adventure being described. From the old woman and the baby they learned there'd been burgers along with the pie, Tylenol for teething, television, some jumping on the beds, games of Go Fish, a walk around Nana's old land and ruined house, the three of them holding hands, moving slowly, trailed by Nana's little dog, trotting along leashless.

Emily listened, marveling, exhausted: the most dramatic things had been happening here at home, in their heads. They'd wakened this morning from an experience precisely like a nightmare, Technicolor catastrophes, figments of imagination and suspicion, now totally erased in the light of an ordinary day. There hadn't even been storms in Medicine Lodge, the weather passing just north of there. "We should call Wesley," she noted absently. He'd no doubt had a bad dream or two himself.

"I texted him," Kay-Kay said. "He's still at Saint Francis with the freak."

"Nipper's a bad dog," Cherry Sue reported, pulling out her pacifier. "*You a bad dog*," she sang at the animal.

"Nipper tends to run away," Nana said, plucking at his nasty fur. "Just to scare us silly. Oh, we called and called, till we were blue in the face." But then she wasn't certain and turned uneasily to Kay-Kay.

"Hours, Nana," Kay-Kay assured her. Both Emily and Anna waited for the girl to make a meaningful ironic comment, letting them know that she, too, had run away for the thrill of scaring some people silly, taking their concern out for one last whirl. But Kay-Kay went back to forking up sausage and egg casserole, drinking milk. Apparently, she'd forsaken her decade-long strict vegetarianism. On the back of the hand holding the fork was a seven-leafed marijuana plant she'd carved into it in ninth grade, a faint, fading white. She'd removed the metal stud from her tongue and the ring from her lip, so silverware went in and out without clinking. And if she wasn't careful, Emily and Anna thought at the same time, she would run to fat, like Henry's other daughters.

She hadn't gone anywhere, she hadn't done anything. Could they be disappointed?

"Oh, hey, check out the picture," Kay-Kay said, wiping her mouth and flipping open her phone. She found the image.

Around the table went the cell phone, everyone squinting at the mini-picture of Nana, Kay-Kay, Cherry Sue, and Nipper. They stood beside a broken storm cellar door, beyond them, the bleached Kansas sky. Three big grins, and Nipper with his nose in the air, preparing to run. "I'm gonna get a print made for you, Nana," Kay-Kay told her grandmother. She took back her phone and gazed mesmerized into its tiny depths. "In black and white, don't you think? Wouldn't that be best?"

BIODEGRADABLE

Y OU REMIND ME OF somebody," she said to him, tilting
her head and narrowing her eyes. Déjà vu had come upon
her like a sudden alarming odor. Mimi Paine and Gary Silver
sat in a generic hotel bar in Pittsburg, Kansas, a place she had
no doubt visited before, yet the sensation that she had some
deep relationship with it could not be accurate. "Who do you
remind me of?" Soon everyone would remind her of somebody, she told herself; she had forty-two years of experience
in meeting people—how many new types could there be?

"Maybe I remind you of me?" He smiled guilelessly, not
like a flirt, not like a pickup artist. "We've met before."

"Here?"

"Right here."

"You were wearing that shirt." It was all coming back to
her . . .

He lowered his chin and appraised his chest. "Maybe. Could
be I was. That's the kind of thing I do, wear the same shirt."
His smile was a drunk's, betraying his lazy secret self, one that
disdained rigor. He succumbed to simple forces like gravity

and inertia and all the other inevitable slips on the slope. Mimi did not fully remember meeting him before, but she couldn't deny that he was familiar. It happened when he lifted his glass to his lips, the glance he gave her over its rim, red eyes and, between them, a reddening nose on which he bumped his tumbler of whiskey, bringing on a blush that included what she could see of his neck. These things in sequence charmed her, attracted her, made her feel returned to a dream, a dream set in this identical location but lifted from time, launched like a bubble, which just as instantly might burst.

"Last time you were worried about your son. He wasn't well, five years ago. You had to call home a few times." He had been attracted to her then, when they'd met, and she'd completely forgotten him. Yet here he was, still attracted, and now she was ready.

Later they lay in his bed, in a farmhouse that creaked with the spring wind, on the dark outskirts of the little town. Mimi pictured her own home, a couple hundred miles away, and her husband asleep there. It had been many years since she'd rested her head on a pillow beside a man other than him. She and Gary held hands, a big letter M. They had been wrestling around in this bed for hours now, yet could not quite give up touching one another.

She closed her eyes and rolled closer to him, furling herself up his arm and into his ribs. "You remind me of you, it's true, but you also remind me of somebody else. My friend Garrett." Already she had abandoned the royal "we" and "our" of her married life. Her husband and children, *their* neighbor Garrett, the friend of the plural family. "Maybe it's just the name," she pondered. "Gary. Garrett." Gary was breathing heavily, not to say snoring, near her ear. Men fell asleep after sex; it wasn't personal. Her habit was to lie wakeful, flush.

Gary's bedroom, here on the prairie, was a mystery to her. From the county road, his house had risen like so many old ones across the state, peaked roof, bleached paint, sagging porch, worthless picket fence, old trees clustered around as a windbreak. Unlit, it could have been abandoned, a perfect piece of Americana. He had eased his car slowly over a loose cattle grate, and when the engine died, the silence was complete. He leaned to kiss her, over the front seat, and then didn't lose hold of her. Up the broken front steps, across a treacherous porch, through a close hall and a cool pantry; it was like a trip through a haunted house at Halloween, the knowledge—the near knowledge—that nothing truly spooky would come of it. And yet Mimi had been thrilled by fear, by desire, equally.

They'd climbed into this bed in the dark while peeling off their clothes, still touching, the seeming singular rule of their game. The air was humid, chilly, and his skin was warm and dry. The premise had been a drink—they'd closed the Pittsburg Holiday Inn Express Bar—but he offered nothing but himself when they arrived. He loved her eagerly, gratefully, as if he hadn't had the opportunity in a long while. She trembled, and couldn't stop.

Now he breathed noisily, unquestionably asleep. If she moved even slightly, he responded by tightening his hold. What did she really know about the man with his lips at her ear? The man with whom she'd just had unprotected sex? The man to whom she could feel her heart opening?

She'd never done such a thing before. And still it failed to surprise her now that it had happened. In the six years she'd been on the road, dispersing research grants to small midwestern colleges, she'd not once met anybody like him. She'd been well hosted, but she'd not made friends, certainly not lovers. The grants had to do with maize and its byproducts, its potential; Gary's school was designing biodegradable water bottles. "Toss it out the window," Gary had said, "watch it melt back into the earth.

"Not the lids, however," he'd added, sadly, later, regretting a sticking point.

Mimi liked her traveling job; it had proved to her that she wasn't indispensable to the lives of her family. "Now I know I can die," she'd told her husband cheerfully, years ago, when she'd first left him with their son and daughters. Traveling—it wasn't just about leaving home. It was also about coming back, lying in that customary bed beside that customary man and being able to sail away. In Wichita, the next night, she would think of Gary, put herself in his bed, recall his moist dark room whose contents could only be assumed—the bed was iron, its thin bars cold to the touch, its sheets and quilt soft in the way of use. There was a window in which the moon had been centered for a while, white with a milky nimbus. The rural sky outside was a greenish tint, its stars a little blurred, one visibly twinkling like the diamond of the children's song.

Was it completely foolish to develop the fantasy she now effortlessly entertained? A life here in this old farmhouse with this man? Rising every morning from his iron bed, with him? He would consider himself lucky, she thought; she was exotic in some way to him that she wasn't to her husband or children, and when had she last been exotic?

She woke abruptly and in full daylight, prepared to defend herself against the night's facts and aftereffects. But she felt nothing but peace. There were birds, a weak blue sky. There was Gary, who lay smiling beside her, unguarded. Nothing more.

*　*　*

She returned to Wichita in possession of her guiltlessness. Her children did not expect gifts anymore; they were ten and twelve and fourteen years old—what did Pittsburg, Kansas, have to offer them? Her husband was only mildly surprised by her hunger for sex with him that first night home. She meant to compare notes, discover what it was that made Gary mean something to her. His general goodwill, she guessed. His ready smile, his desire to be happy. She wondered at her own phrasing: *desire to be happy*? As opposed to actually being happy? Yes, that seemed so. A willed pleasure—an active pursuit of it, cultivating it wherever he went. At the hotel he'd been generous with the bartender, friendly to the bitch at the front desk, held all the doors for Mimi, and continued to inquire if she was sure she wanted to come with him to his house. He would understand, he assured her, if she didn't. "I want you to come," he'd told her. "I really want you to, but I understand if you change your mind." This would be her friend Garrett's way, too, Mimi believed, mannerly to a fault. Behind the manners, a kind of despair he argued against all day long, hid from others. How had she seen through his plain neighborliness into the bleak fatalism? Gary had seemed like someone she knew, which had led them swiftly to bed. With a stranger, who knew how long it would have taken?

For a few days after returning home nothing happened, nothing obvious. It was like living with a low-grade fever, or being under the influence of a mild drug, the world at a certain distance, common activities performed with either heightened or befogged attention. She received no word from Gary; when she thought of him, she imagined first his house, the big cottonwoods tossing their limbs around the roofline, then the old-fashioned iron bed, then his peaceful face on its pillow. Frequently she shut her eyes and replayed their evening together: the rousing moment he put his lips to her ear to ask what she wanted from the bar. The second time they had sex, when he'd clutched her as if she alone could save him from some mortal threat. And then lying there in his arms while he slept, surrounded by the sweet moldering air of his home. On the fourth day, she received an official thank-you card from the little college in his town, and he'd added his own shy words, a penned bit of gratitude and his timid signature. This, too, gave her a tiny thrill.

Her happy illness, her strange bliss, was interrupted when Mimi ran into Garrett, the family friend. He alone seemed to sense that she was in possession of an important secret. He'd come over to borrow the plumber's snake. When she hugged him in what she believed was the usual way, he stepped back afterward, scanning her critically.

"How was your trip?" he asked.

"Good."

He nodded, scrutinizing. "Where were you, again?"

"Pittsburg," she said. "Kansas," she added.

He wasn't satisfied; her destination didn't explain what he had sniffed out about her. "And what were you doing there?"

"Corn funding, as usual. They're experimenting with biodegradable plastic," she added. Still he scowled, as if she were lying. "You know, for go-cups, for Cokes at 7-Eleven? Water bottles?"

"Huh," said Garrett, squinting. Like Gary, he was a bachelor, a man now in his forties still unmarried. The woman Garrett would have married had broken up with him just before the wedding. "Left me at the altar," he would say. It was almost literally true. This fiancée had scarred him deeply, turned him skeptical of women and their intentions. As a result, he'd chosen to date only young ones, ones he felt indisputably superior to, ones he could mix and match, managing them like players on a team, trading them out, putting them at bat, retiring them. In this way, he protected his heart.

"The snake's in the garage," Mimi said, ducking away from his gaze, leading him there although it was unnecessary. She wanted to hide from his acuity. He lived down the block; they'd met years ago when an ambulance woke the neighborhood in the middle of the night, the so-called Goiter Lady having a nonfatal emergency. Outside her house had assembled a group, Garrett striking up conversation with Mimi and her husband. The three of them (no children, yet) stood there in their pajamas, wondering aloud if the goiter was responsible for the ambulance and, furthermore, why the old woman hadn't ever had it removed.

"It's like another head growing on her neck," Garrett had said.

"Like her unborn twin," Mimi added.

"Something musta turned ugly between them tonight." They had snickered impolitely while their neighbors glowered.

"You remind me of somebody," Garrett had said to Mimi a few days later, squinting at her over beers in their backyard. Only years afterward did she learn that it was his fiancée, that harlot who'd abandoned him at the altar, that she reminded him of. As a trio—she and Garrett and her husband—they'd grown close fast. No doubt it was because she seemed familiar. And he didn't seem to hold it against her that she was like his enemy, the woman who had ruined his life. He'd loved her, after all, before he'd hated her.

Garrett's most recent visit, to borrow the snake, to give Mimi a hug, and to make her face turn red, sent her to e-mail,

where she composed a note to Gary Silver. "Hey there, remember me?" For a long while she paused, the flashing cursor
on the monitor pulsing like her heightened heartbeat. What
tone did she wish to take? What trouble did she wish to make?
"I miss you," she wrote, and sent the message before she could
reconsider. And before she could get up from the desk, an answer appeared. "I miss you, too. I've been thinking about you
a lot."

And then, not three seconds later, another incoming: "A
whole lot. xo"

Mimi had never employed an X or an O to express her feelings. She wondered how Gary meant them to resonate.
"Maybe I'll be out that way again," she wrote.

"I hope you will!"

"I'll let you know," she wrote and then, after synchronizing
her heart to the cursor, attached her own X and O.

Like her husband, Garrett worked at the local university. He
was in charge of the groundskeepers, however, while Mimi's
husband was a professor in the economics department. The
three of them would meet for lunch at the faculty club every
couple of weeks. Her husband liked the fact of waiters, linen,
a wine list. These were his requirements for dining out. When
he was busy, Mimi and Garrett would go to a burger or bar-
beque joint, eat off Styrofoam with plastic utensils. With her,
he would discuss his love life in more intimate detail than he
would with her husband around. The funny thing was, she
knew he liked her husband more than he did her. He respected him; that was why he wouldn't report on his dates, on
his dalliances with girls technically young enough to be his
offspring. He feared the professor's judgment, where he didn't
fear a thing about Mimi.

"Multiple orgasms," he was saying over chili dogs at an out-door stand. "That's a new one for me." His new girlfriend he'd met at the climbing wall on campus. He poured Mimi more beer from the plastic pitcher on their plastic table. Mimi's husband believed that plastic was immoral and that beer was for hillbillies.

"And those climbing outfits, especially as seen from below . . ." He grinned, and Mimi returned it. Although he dated a lot of women, he retained an undeniable aura of loneli-ness. Not loneliness for friends but for the right woman. It was why Mimi had long tolerated his parade of young girlfriends; they weren't what he was looking for, not really. They were like the thorny underbrush he had to thrash his way through before he reached the tower where She lived. And she knew he knew it. He was still working out some revenge against the fiancée, a revenge whose ultimate victim was himself.

"I've heard most women are multiply orgasmic," Mimi said. The construction workers at the plastic table beside them glanced briefly over. "Maybe it's your technique that's im-proved."

"And she's got this blond down on her thighs," he was say-ing, "just above her kneecaps." He would date her for a month or two, and then he'd grow bored, take her to lunch but not dinner, return her calls but not pick up when she rang, even-tually relegate her to the broad, bland category of "friend." He had many. Wherever Mimi went with him, they showed up, girls and women calling out to him, waving, being intro-duced to Mimi and her husband, Garrett never forgetting a name or occupation. This latest would be "Wendy, the rock climber."

Was Gary Silver like that, Mimi wondered? Did he, too, use the college as a place to pick up girls? Did he take them to his farmhouse and make love with them? She didn't think so; his lovemaking struck her as unpracticed, earnest. He differed from Garrett in that regard, but not in the other, the one where he needed the right woman, was waiting for her with an increasing fear of never finding her, of getting lost in the thicket. In that fear, its sad conviction, Mimi had absolute confidence.

"What's up with you?" Garrett asked her when he dropped her off at home, a toothpick wobbling between his teeth. "I swear, you've got something going on in there." He knocked at her forehead.

Her next trip was to Manhattan, Kansas. It was farther from Gary, from Pittsburg, than Wichita was, but she decided to visit him, regardless, add another day to her itinerary. He could have come to her, she supposed; he could have driven to a Wichita hotel and checked in. During the day, when her children and husband were at their schools, she could have joined him there. But she didn't want to see him in Wichita, nor in a hotel. She wanted to visit his farmhouse. He had inherited it from his grandmother. Its furnishings were the old woman's; she'd made the quilt on his bed, the rag rugs on the floors. Under those rugs: patterned linoleum, flowers and checkerboards, undulating over the planks. The spices in the kitchen cupboards were hers, metal containers from the seventies, still half full of dusty no-color powders and flakes. On the wooden red table sat a yellow ceramic beehive honeypot, a ceramic bee on its sticky lid.

She pulled into his rutted dirt drive and over the rattling cattle grate. He stood on his porch, smiling, leaning against a rail. Since last time, a lilac bush had bloomed beside the steps. His white shirt was new, still creased from having been in a package. Hugging him felt like a homecoming; she put her face into his neck and began to cry on his starched shoulder. He'd bought a new shirt. He'd had his hair cut. He led her inside and to his bed, where they lay on its quilt, Mimi crying, Gary stroking her back. To whom could she explain this feeling? Nobody, not even herself. She had fallen deeply in love with a man she hardly knew.

Gary's e-mails were brief, and always punctuated freely with X's and O's. He missed her, was the general theme.

"I'm falling in love with you," she wrote in mid-May, just six weeks after meeting him. She hesitated, studying the words, weighing the air in the house around her, the photographs of her children beside her on the desktop, the objects they'd made for her on Mother's Days, the chic lines of chrome and blond wood that her husband and she had chosen as their preferred aesthetic. Everything here belonged to her, was a result of her presence, solidly obligating her. Still she tapped send, obligating herself differently.

She waited then for a long while, staring at the blank inbox, her focus and investment so intense that blackness began to creep up peripherally. If he didn't respond, it seemed to her that the blackness might completely subsume her, send her into its voided heart, she felt that vulnerable. It cost him to write back "I love you, too"; she could sense the solemnity with which he had typed the words, as if each individual letter had offered extreme resistance. And she felt whatever it was between them intensify, like a song that abruptly dips into a more resonant, lower key, like a body of water that grows suddenly deeper, colder, stiller yet more treacherous.

* * *

Along with the usual bottle of wine, Garrett brought a new woman to the house when he came for his weekly Sunday meal with them. It took a while for Mimi's husband to catch on to what was different, but Mimi noticed right away. Lillian was older than Garrett, probably by five years. She wasn't a coed from the college but a physical therapist he'd gone to when he hurt his knee on the climbing wall. Good-bye, Wendy.

Lillian didn't laugh at everything Garrett said, nor did she get caught up in the children's video games. Neither did she sit at the table simply smiling, complimenting everything dizzily, indiscriminately. Instead, she told them about her husband, who had died in a bike accident ten years ago. Until then, she'd taught first grade. After the accident, she quit teaching. She couldn't endure being among children, knowing she wouldn't have any of her own. "I was thirty-eight. We'd been trying," she told them over the end of the meal, the wine in her glass swirling slowly. Her hands were very expressive, as if her experience in the world had distilled there, in them. She would have had to be awfully pragmatic, she said, to find a new man, to fall in love, marry, and produce children with him during her years of grief, which happened to coincide with the end of her fertility. "And I was too sad to be a mom, then." She wasn't sad now. Rueful, maybe, in addition to seeming kind and watchful and witty.

"She reminds me of you," her husband said later, when they lay in bed. "She even looks a little like you, but mostly it's the way she uses her hands when she talks, and the way her eyebrows move. Or maybe the way she says things under her breath. Slightly mean things." He poked Mimi in the ribs to let her know he was teasing.

Mimi had been uncharacteristically quiet during the evening, not uncomfortable with Lillian, but more careful. This one's opinion of her mattered, unlike the others Garrett had brought over.

"Just kidding," her husband said, since she'd not responded. "I know."

A trip to Kansas City wasn't unthinkable; the Maize Concepts Foundation was headquartered on the Kansas side of town, in the wealthy suburbs. School was out for the summer; Mimi proposed taking the children. The older ones, the girls, declined—slumber parties, horseback riding lessons—but the youngest, the boy who was Mimi's favorite, was pleased to join her. Unlike his sisters, he wouldn't notice that his mother didn't go to any meetings, that they drove straight through Winnetka to the heart of the Missouri side of Kansas City. She took him on a tour of the art museum, through the large department stores Wichita didn't have to the bulldozed, sanitized display of the city's jazz heritage. For two nights they slept in a fancy hotel and ordered room service and watched movies.

Then on their trip home they would take a swing through Pittsburg, stay at the Holiday Inn Express. In Mimi's imagination, she left her ten-year-old sleeping in the television's glow while she made a quick drive to Gary's farmhouse, where he would greet her from the porch, smiling his easy unironic smile, hold her in the supple air of summer, kiss her hair, murmur endearments, and then regret, along with her, that she had to hurry back to the motel. She couldn't stay overnight, but she could take with her his desire. She would wrap it around her like one of those quilts. In the morning, he could meet her and her son for breakfast, Gary a casual friend she'd made when she was here before.

She didn't call him until she was checked in. Her son didn't particularly care that this motel wasn't as swanky as the four-star establishment they'd left. He could jump on these beds just as happily, leap from one to the other and slap at the ceiling while Mimi held the ringing phone to her ear. Gary wasn't home, and he didn't possess an answering machine; in her mind's eye, she saw the black rotary model on its table, faintly shaken by its ringing bell. All day she phoned—after a paddle around the pool, after a mediocre dinner in the hotel restaurant, after the first movie they watched, after the second. When her son fell asleep, Mimi quietly put on her shoes, eased shut the room door, and drove to the farmhouse. The county road was dark and empty except for a multitude of flying insects. Rabbits darted across the headlight beams. In the west, lightning skittered, a series of green flashes and subsequent rumblings. Mimi sat in Gary's driveway with the car windows rolled down, letting the stormy air wash across her. If she'd let him know she was coming, he would have canceled his plans, whatever they were. A fishing trip? A Vegas weekend? As clearly as she could imagine him here, in his natural habitat, it was difficult to guess where he'd take himself when he left it.

On his porch, she tucked a note behind the banging screen door, into the leaded glass of the locked wooden door. More of those inadequate X's and O's. She hesitated at the top of the steps, the boards soft beneath her feet, trees overhead thrashing in the wind. Again that sense of déjà vu, of having lived through this precise sensation—a pending cloud-burst, a desire achingly delayed, some perfectly poised balance between wanting and having. Others had stood here, Mimi thought, a frenzy in the air and chaos in the heart, just about to drop down these very steps and into a storm.

By the end of July, Lillian had moved into Garrett's house with him. "When you're our age, why wait?" had been Garrett's line on the situation. He had found her, Mimi saw. He'd found the woman he needed, and, like magic, she'd erased that other one who'd nearly doomed him. He no longer felt vengeful; his streak of skeptical cruelty faded, that aspect of character he had revealed only to Mimi, never to her husband. He chose not to confide in Mimi the sexual habits of Lillian, nor regale her with the ways Lillian was alluring. His ribald intimacy with Mimi was over, as were their cheap luncheons. He also neglected to notice anything different about her anymore. Like her husband, he accepted her as she claimed to be, just fine, the same.

On e-mail she told Gary everything, her present days and her past ones fashioned in screen-sized anecdotes particularly for him. The night she'd driven to Pittsburg, he'd been at his family's cabin on the Ninnesqua River; if he'd known, he'd have made other arrangements. He couldn't believe the one weekend he'd gone away was the one she would choose to surprise him. He regretted it so much that Mimi was glad he'd not been there. His regret verged on remorse, powerful and afflicting, and yet was as intangible as her imagination, and just as incendiary. These forces held them together, an intricate invisible knit, a nest of secrecy that Mimi fell into when she closed her eyes, a pain that was pleasurable, an exquisite anticipation, a nothing that was something. Distance was protracting their passion; she couldn't have been the first to wonder if relationships lasted longer, this way, occurring in episodes, stop-action animation.

*   *   *

Her desire for Gary woke her one night in mid-August. Her husband slept solidly beside her, sometimes nudging away, his back to her. Even in sleep, he found her imperfect, she thought. Or perhaps she found herself imperfect and, gifted at giving things away, had bestowed the opinion upon him. Let it drift in his direction. Let him be the critical party.

Mimi took her restlessness out the back door, onto the driveway, where she sat staring dreamily into her yard, into the neighbors' behind her. For a while, she didn't realize what she saw. Then she rose from the steps and hurried toward Lillian, who was striding purposefully down the alley.

"What are you doing?" Mimi asked, passing over the warm dirt barefooted. Lillian wore pajamas, too.

"I'm sorry, Mimi," she said. "Did I wake you? Maybe I've been crying kind of loudly?"

"I don't think so. What's the matter?"

"Please don't tell Garrett," she said, wiping her nose with the back of her hand. The streetlight gave her facial features extreme shadows, revealing the shape of her skull, her aspect of skeleton. "I know he's working really hard at this thing between us, but sometimes I just miss my husband." The words appeared to strike her like lightning: suddenly she shook so hard, was seized by a feeling so powerful, that Mimi could only stand in awe. Lillian quaked under the force, momentarily lost to it. "What can I do?" she finally said, when it had passed. "What can anyone do? I have this longing, and sometimes I just have to let it knock me down, totally down. I don't want to hurt Garrett, I don't even want to explain it to him, so I came outside. There's nothing the matter," she said, giving Mimi a reassuring pat on the arm, sending her away, "I'm just missing my husband." She said it as if Mimi ought to understand better than Garrett what Lillian was going through, as if Mimi ought to be able to occupy these feelings easily. Mimi thought of her own husband, sleeping in perfect ignorance on his side of the bed. If he died, if he were dead, if he'd disappeared before they'd made their children, before they'd entered middle age . . . But her heart wasn't full of having lost him, of never having him.

"It's strange," she said to Lillian, "how big goneness can be, isn't it?"

"Very," Lillian agreed.

The reporter was accompanied by a photographer, and Mimi kept being distracted by him, by his camera and its clicking, by the way he took pictures of her without ever seeming to really look at her. The interviewer, on the other hand, was eager, obviously understanding that his companion had the allure of disinterest, and that he himself was competing for his subject's attention. Maize Concepts had been given a federal grant worth millions; Gary's college, with its biodegradable bottles, had drawn D.C.'s eye. Now Mimi would be in the news, around the state, around the country. The man interviewing her certainly seemed to feel the reflected glow of celebrity, but the man photographing her was unfazed by it all. Mimi took her cue from him, downplaying her role in the project, passing credit to Pittsburg and its engineers and scientists. To the administrator who'd pursued the grant, a certain Gary Silver, who would also be interviewed, across the state. They would appear in two different photos, one atop the other, in tomorrow's edition of the *Kansas City Star*, the *Wichita Eagle-Beacon*, and the *Lawrence Journal-World*. The photographer and reporter would drive to Gary's farmhouse after they finished with Mimi. She would recognize Gary's grandmother's hutch in the picture, the row of ceramic cream pitchers the old woman had collected.

Terrence Rider was the photographer. While the reporter took a cell phone call in Mimi's foyer, Terrence began to pack up his cameras and shades. Mimi's son, who was missing the first week of fifth grade with the flu, called to her from his bedroom. Terrence looked up when he heard the boy. It was the first time he really seemed to see Mimi. "Is she okay?"

"He. The flu. He's fine." She went to Toby, who wanted to know if he could come out of his room now, if the men were gone. She brought him back with her, her pale little boy in his pajamas and dirty hair. Terrence shook his hand, smiled for the first time.

"Feeling puny, bub?"

Toby nodded, leaning into Mimi, hot and sad. She held him against her. Terrence tilted his head at them, then took out his camera again. "You want a picture of the two of you? I'd like to take one." He sat on the floor, shooting casually. The day was muggy, ocher-colored through the curtains in the absence of the flash. Mimi and Toby drifted over to the couch to sit, her son easing his misery onto her lap, where she stroked his cheek and chin. "I have two little girls," Terrence said behind his camera.

"What's their names?" asked Toby without opening his eyes.

"Elizabeth and Charlotte." He kept taking pictures, scooting over the rug. "But you know what I call them?"

Toby shook his heavy head on Mimi's leg.

"Liza J and Charlie Q." Beyond the foyer door they could hear the reporter on the phone, his voice an irritant, a bad sound track to their sudden yellow-tinted tableau. "I also have a son," Terrence told them. "He died when he was a baby, a long time ago." He lowered the camera onto his crossed legs. "I always feel like I should mention him," he said apologetically, "when somebody asks about my children." He drank from his water bottle, comfortable on the floor with his tragedy the way Lillian had been in the middle of the night, in the middle of the alley, with hers.

"What's his name?" Toby asked.

"David."

"Do you call him another name?"

"No, just David. He would be ten, if he were alive."

"I'm ten," said Toby.

"Yeah, I kinda guessed that." Her son had reminded him of his own, Mimi supposed. Already she felt her son's illness as if it were afflicting her, as if it were the color of the room, the flu she would wake with tomorrow, the same day she saw the newspaper and Gary's picture in it. Terrence said, "I keep his photo on the mantel, up there with the girls'. We all loved that baby so much. They know they have a brother, he's still part of our life." He began packing up once more; from the foyer, they could hear his companion closing his noisy conversation. "My wife and I separated after David died," Terrence said to Mimi.

"I'm sorry," she murmured, thinking that she could understand that, separating rather than divorcing, unable to bring their marriage to a legal end, unable to document their failure to endure.

"I'll send you these pictures. You feel better, Toby."

Mimi drove to Pittsburg six weeks later thinking not so much of Gary and his picture in the paper as of Terrence, who had taken the picture. She could not stop thinking of him, that there was something she needed to do about him.

Gary met her at the Holiday Inn Express, where they sat in the bar once more. Though they e-mailed frequently, they hadn't seen each other in a few months and were shy. The liquor was for breaking through this shyness. At his house, an hour later, Mimi was taken aback to see the For Sale sign. "You're selling?"

"Sure. I'm sick of this place." He said it as if it should have been obvious: who would want to live in a drafty hovel that smelled like old lady?

"I love this house," Mimi answered. "I can't believe you're selling." Inside, he'd already cleared the rooms of his grandmother's furniture, the shelves of her collections. It was empty, holding only crude basics, the box springs and mattress on the bare floor. They made love, but Mimi was disturbed. Minus curtains, weren't the windows dangerous? She felt for the first time as if she were doing something criminal. Without decoration, the setting seemed merely tawdry, as if located hastily, by desperate strangers on the lam. Gary's gurgling snore grew more annoying, until she could bear it no longer and leaped up to claim her clothing, retrieve her shoes. "I have to get back to my room," she told him, arms crossed, when he roused. "Take me back."

Was it Terrence Rider who had ruined her affair? The imminent sale of Gary's nostalgic house? Driving home the next day, Mimi realized that what she wished was that she could talk to Terrence Rider. She exited the highway and sat on the access road for thirty minutes, listening to cicadas, sweating, deciding what to do. Then she turned the car east, toward Kansas City, and headed for the offices of the *Star*.

* * *

Lillian moved out of Garrett's house before Christmas. They would still be friends, she told Mimi. He was a good man. But she had taken a job in Kansas City, applied for it on purpose and then accepted a cut in pay. It was time to leave Wichita.

"I know somebody in Kansas City you might like," Mimi typed to Lillian. "He works for the newspaper."

Terrence had given her the pictures of her and Toby, taken on that sick murky morning. They were black and white, old-fashioned, and Mimi put them in antique frames. In his cluttered cubicle, Terrence had been unsurprised to see her the day she showed up out of nowhere; perhaps nothing would surprise someone whose baby son had died.

When Mimi looked at the pictures of herself and Toby, she would always imagine the son Terrence hadn't seen grow up. This would lead her to the husband Lillian had lost. And this to the woman Garrett might never find.

As for Gary Silver, brief holder of her heart, Mimi would hardly think of him at all. She blocked his address so that his e-mails wouldn't reach her; it seemed she did the same with her love, simply turned it off. This mystified her: it was as if her need for him had produced him, full-blown familiar stranger, and now the need was gone—without a trace, no harm, no good, as if it had never existed.

"I have a friend I'd like you to meet," she wrote to Terrence Rider now, the connection between him and Lillian taking root in her, an instinct about its rightness that she could practically see materializing before her.

It wasn't until three years had passed—Toby had become a teenager, angular and distant; Mimi's oldest girl was preparing for college—when the Goiter Lady had another visit from the ambulance. This time, they took her away with the lights extinguished, the pace unhurried through the quiet autumn afternoon. It happened during one of Mimi's husband's classes. The Goiter Lady's son had appeared on the scene, and then wandered off. Apparently, he lived in the neighborhood; where had he been all these years, when he should have been advising her to have her cantaloupe-sized goiter removed?

Garrett and Mimi were the last neighbors left on the small house's front walk. Leaves fell around them, as if in slow motion, the air just that thick and still. "I don't think he locked the door," Mimi said.

They entered cautiously, as if under surveillance. The house held nothing that anyone would want to steal. A reclining chair in which you could make out the shape of the woman who had long occupied it, a henna stain from her dyed hair. Dusty porcelain figurines on the windowsills, an odor of burned toast in the air, as well as a cool fermented breeze from the basement, its reminder of old soil, the grave. Mimi and Garrett wandered the place tentatively, ending up together again in the living room, before that indented incliner. Garrett had tears in his eyes.

"What?" Mimi asked, taking his forearms. He held on to her gruffly, with his head lowered, a hug that began with mere sentiment—the woman's death had suddenly hit him, Mimi thought, while passing through her home, breathing the air she had just recently breathed herself—but then the embrace subtly changed. Mimi held him tighter, put a hand upon his warm head as she might one of her children, registering with genuine surprise the strength of her concern, her affection for this man. He did not step away. If anything, he seemed to somewhat collapse, as if he'd been waiting for somebody to stand before him as support. And then he took a step for-ward, so that their bodies matched from toe to forehead.

"Hello," said Mimi. Through several layers of clothing and skin and bones, their hearts were still quite proximate.

"Hello," Garrett agreed. They reminded one another of others. This was the beginning. It was also the end.

DWI

A T AGE EIGHT SHE was entrusted with the Toast-R-Oven, and made her brother his last meal. He was five; it was a hot dog.

Watching him choke Sadie could still recall—his wild eyes, buggy and desperate, the thick knot in his neck like the body of a mouse being digested by a snake. His free hand swam in the patio air, while the other, as if belonging to someone else, clutched at his fine-ribbed chest. Summer, they wore almost nothing, singing the song about short shorts, a TV commercial for depilatory cream. And on an intake of breath—"*We* wear short shorts"—the meat sucked fatally down. Sadie looked on, her own hands full of salty chips. As in most disasters, the atmosphere was saturated with the stuff of nocturnal nightmare, viscous, slow-moving. Even then, she'd been aware of her expression, of the greasy grit of fried potatoes in her fists, as if she were watching herself in a mirror, or as if someone had captured her in a photograph.

It is this same face she pulls when, many years later, she is given the news that her lover has died. Time has stopped, again, animation suspended. She sees herself stunned, yet without undue emotion. Compelled. Riveted. A face caught between acts, in limbo. Her husband sets down the phone, tears in his eyes, and gives her the morbid instruction to sit. He has an unrealistic vision of her. He thinks she needs kid gloves, euphemism.

"Sebastian was killed last night," he says gently, staring deep into her eyes, intimate as a French kiss. He knows she has a special fondness for Sebastian, the youthful friend of the family, the hangdog delinquent twenty-eight-year-old, too young yet to be pitied for his inability to grow up, too young to be a sad-sack bachelor with all the props: filthy apartment, aged bedsheets, nothing but salt and pepper and dusty MSG in his spice rack. She puts on the correct face and utters the proper words for the occasion: horrified but not heart-stricken. Sad but not dying herself.

"Oh, my God." In her hand, unseen, unfelt, she breaks a yellow toy cocktail monkey and pierces her palm. You cannot bandage a palm. The skin won't permit it, something left over from the apes, star-shaped callus, that smooth waxy surface.

Sunday morning, single-car accident, Easter, her fickle secret lover dead on a highway, his vehicle twisted around a bridge piling. She asks if he was drunk, drugged, and her husband says he doesn't know. But she knows.

Long ago, this was the method Sebastian confessed would be his preferred suicide. "Anesthetized," he said, "bam, gone." Sadie told him *she* would plunge from a high, high cliff, given a choice, and he declared that she would suffer. It was the flying that appealed, she said. *She* was the one who would suffer just to see what it was like to fly, first. That was her nature.

"I'm lucky," she insisted, in another of those intimate chats. "Hang around me, you'll get lucky, too."

"Suicide," she tells her husband, under the scrutiny of his gaze, when she has the wherewithal to make a sound.

"You can't know that."

"I can."

In the other room, her son is still seeking Easter eggs, shrieking as he pulls out his pet habitat; there behind the eerie blinking eyes of his two toads the discovery of another foil-wrapped chunk of chocolate.

To her therapist she had confessed her desire that her lover die. "I wish he would die," she said. He had broken her heart; she wanted him dead. Wasn't that passion, too, as in *crime of*?

"Why couldn't he just disappear? Move away? Just because you're embarrassed about the affair doesn't mean he has to die."

Sadie studied him. "Right," she said, which was what she always said to stall. Embarrassed? Who'd said anything about embarrassment? What did it mean that Dr. Rock thought she ought to be embarrassed? Or at least assumed she was, *ought* perhaps not playing a role. *Ought* was something you had to leave in the waiting room, at the shrink's, like a wet umbrella. Maybe he meant that, had *he* had this affair, *he'd* be embarrassed. This was called projection. As was the case with most new experiences, therapy ended up resembling school: vocabulary, irksome effort, anxiety, tests, and failure. Would anything ever *not* seem like some new set of lessons Sadie would neglect to learn?

She'd come here for simple exorcism; her therapist wouldn't supply it.

She wanted Sebastian to die, and now he has. His death makes her think of her first brother, whose vague mortal agent she also feels she had been. Her powers terrify her. No one would blame her; she knows this; yet there it would sit in her body, clot of guilt, organ of bad desire. To prove they trusted her, her parents had brought her a kitten after her brother's funeral. Then they'd had another boy, turned him loose into her care just a few short years later. She knew even then that her sometimes hating him had not killed her first brother. But would loving him have saved him? On Tuesday, after Easter Sunday, when Dr. Rock will ask what is on her mind, she will look down at her nail-bitten hands, resting in her lap, and tell him why she is wearing a black dress. Just a couple of hours after her appointment is this funeral she has to attend . . .

Sebastian's death may mean that she will never give up therapy.

Her other brother, her giant little brother ten years her junior, the spoiled and neglected darling of her parents' bereft affection, had been Sebastian's friend. They played golf. Now he would pallbear. Bear pall. Alongside him would be other fraternity brothers. When Sebastian was an active at the SAE house, Mikey had been a pledge, forced to endure the humiliations of raw eggs and body paint, Sisyphean cleaning chores, and toxic alcoholic carnivals. In the requisite prank of kidnapping an active, Mikey had gone after Sebastian, who submitted gamely to the break-in, the tie-down, the drive to Mexico, the removal of his clothing. Then the two of them had wandered Juarez whorehouses, drinking tequila, bonding in the peculiar male method. In this way Mikey became Sebastian's project, pet, personal pledge. And this was how Sadie knew Sebastian first, as the SAE brother waiting tables at La Isla, her son's favorite restaurant.

Their eyes had caught, and something had transpired, like the flare of a lighter, like the linking snare of two barbed hooks.

They met in old motels, in overgrown fields, at river's edge, on his spongy Murphy bed mattress; he was as bad a habit as a girl could ask for. He was young and carefree, obsessed and sophomoric, manic and depressive, Catholic and criminal, both thrilled and tormented by deception. For a time, the novelty held sway, and then guilt had undone him.

Brotherhood eluded Sadie, its rules and codes. Sebastian's love for her had been eclipsed by some curious commitment to the men in her family whom he also loved: her brother, her husband, even her small son. That he loved her, she did not doubt; that this love could be superseded by loyalty to those masculine others utterly confounded her. She thought of it constantly, when he began to slip away. She had nothing to compare it to, no loyalty, it seemed, larger than passion. February: the slim month of misery, the end of the affair. Still he came to her house to watch television with her husband, still he roamed the golf course and nightclubs with her brother, still he upended her son and dangled him by the feet. He would do none of this with her. He'd stood naked on the blistering Chihuahuan Desert, hair painted blue, hands bound, mouth duct-taped, for her brother and their fraternal order, but he would not even phone her.

And to whom could she complain? To whom could she take this tale of gluttony, her capacious need for excess, and the guilt thereof? No one but Dr. Rock, who refused to do the friendly thing, refused to follow her about, a step or two behind, and badmouth her bad lover.

It had been tempting to tell on Sebastian, spill his unprincipled secret, crack the pristine notion of brotherly solidarity.

He could have been banished; she would have prevailed. These men were *her* men, and she could take them away from him in one gesture. They would rally round her, fierce as rottweilers.

Then there was plan B: she could merely *threaten* to tell, force him to stay away.

But her love was full of hope, pathetic hope like a face at the window, waiting. In life she had been lucky and hopeful. She hoped he would come back. She hoped she would win.

And if she couldn't win, she hoped he would die.

"What's on your mind?" her therapist queried every Tuesday. How could you approach such a question? She thought he'd balk if he glimpsed what was there, inside her, the pure greed, a hunger that would never be satisfied, no matter what was sacrificed to it.

Spring is going to pass without Sadie's permission. She will water the lawn, she will observe the tulips, she'll purchase harbingers of the new, next, season: flip-flops, plastic pool, sunscreen, tonic water. In her mind, however, will grow the tree of thoughts, where squirrelly obsession leaps limb to limb, a closed and busy system, pinwheels in the wind. She will never conclude anything. There was a bed in a boy's apartment, and herself upon it, happy. There was that boy, dead behind the wheel of his car. There were the twin wishes, sitting opposite each other like monkeys: one that he return to her, one that he die. Illicit desires, both. "I feel like it might kill me if you stopped loving me," he'd said last fall. Those words will hang also in the tree of thoughts, alongside his winter escape. She was difficult, and loving her was difficult, and besides, there were these other people, husband, brother, son . . . He was fearful, and jealous, and young beyond his youth. He was scornful and snide and charming and shy; impotent and drunk and furious and weeping. There was her last glimpse of him, entering through the door of her home with a nervous smile, as if he would die were he not welcome, as if her forgiveness would save him.

He would have found the strange shrine at the site of his accident amusing, Sadie will think. The cross that his SAE brothers are going to erect made of balls, solid black 8-ball front and center. Mikey will drive Sadie and her son there two months after the wreck. She'll run her fingers along the pitted surface of a row of TopFlights while Mikey pulls weeds.

"I miss him," her brother will say, simply, bouquet of bitterroots in his fist. Sadie is going to frown. She will be—is, was, has been—missing something, too.

"Driving while intoxicated," his gravestone should read. Like Sadie, Sebastian had had the overwhelming, bottomless-pit-variety appetite for more: higher speed, extra stimulation, supplemental love. There were people who could live a sober life, and then there were those who couldn't, who needed the additional thrilling torque. It was a bad appetite, and without relief. What she will miss—misses, missed—was company in its churning ubiquity.

And, concurrently, ran the urge to be punished. She had asked to be spurned, she sometimes believed. It was her due.

He'd taken strange prophylactic care, Sebastian, in matters large and small, paranoid precaution. For example, on the bumper of his car he had plastered DARE stickers to flatter and mislead the authorities, drove around reciting the alphabet backward, in anticipation of a DWI arrest. Assuming all worst-case scenarios as the ultimate truth, he practiced religiously the preemptive strike. He slept with a gun beneath his pillow. And so sure was he that Sadie would turn off her love for him, he did it first. Like a faucet.

Now it seems she will never be able to shut that valve, end that leak that will not cease.

The summer will hold all the anniversaries: first kiss, first phone call, first fuck. Sadie's gloom will join her in the kitchen, at the table, bottle of gin, deck of cards. Her obsession is going to bore her, but she won't be able to escape it. All the landmarks will be dangerous, the summer moon, the pay telephone, the annual parties of friends. She'll turn down invitations and stop washing her hair. She'll sleep, sweating and unmoving, studying the tortured circle of the ceiling fan, rising only to drive her son to and from holding pens. Thank God for healthful occupation, for swimming lessons and soccer camp, for art class and theater troupe, for computer games and public television and the pet store.

And when her husband finds her crying on the bathroom floor, he will kneel right down beside her, take her in his arms.

"What is it?" he'll ask softly, still believing the best of her, which will be further proof of her good luck.

"I don't know," she'll say. Because time will have taught her a thing or two. It has taught her that she wouldn't have left her lucky life, even had the chance arrived. Yet she won't be able to release her longing, her losing, her truncated love. She'll wish no longer for Sebastian but for her former self, for the life she'd had before he wedged himself between it and her. In that space resides all the trouble. Fantasy and memory, dread and desire, all the invisible intoxicants. That errant glance, in a split second in a restaurant, opened a box of lethal charms, let loose a cabal of harmful follies.

In all the mystic diagnostic maps of the universe, from

zodiac to MMPI, her personality was Romantic. The cards always revealed the Lover.

"We'll go away," her husband is going to whisper in the echoing tiled bathroom. Or is it "This will go away"? It won't matter; he'll swiftly arrange an escape. They'll close the house as if for fumigation, and go—a month where nothing will be able to remind her of her sadness, where everything is white and clean, the clutter of the temporary rather than lasting variety, towels left on the floor, beds unmade, food delivered to the door or table, then hastily cleared afterward.

She will recover, eventually. Long ago, from her brother's death, she'd learned something about her own resilience, a lesson unwanted and undeserved: she kept living. This was not unrelated to luck and hope and love, a possible side benefit, toughness. She'll leave for the month at the beach with a conviction that she will be better on arrival home. She'll turn off lights and lock doors knowing she will switch them on and unlock them a new woman, a woman who has come from there to here, cured. At her son's bedroom door she'll hesitate. The family waits in the car, engine running, enthusiastic chattering, road maps rustling, and here will be her son's two sullen toads, quiet in their tank in the quiet house, about to be abandoned, accusatory. She'll pause only briefly, desperate to leave her misery behind her, desperate to undo a whole string of regrettable knots, from first kiss to last glance. She cannot be bothered by toads. She can replace toads. She will do what the others have done, forgotten their existence, then later come home blameless as everyone else in their death. All year she has had to feed these creatures the live crickets that are their diet. It has been a chore she performed weekly, before therapy, the stop at the pet shop for thirty little crickets. In their baggie they hopped, every week, growing steamy on the front seat, while she nattered on about her obsession to Dr. Rock. This *boy* she could not get over, this *love* her therapist refused to believe was love . . .

"Fuck it," she will tell the toads.

And when she comes home from the beach, from her curative vacation, tanned, calm, wearing linen white enough to be christened in, fully expecting a pair of mummified husks, crusty eyeless shadows, well, there, instead, she will find a single living toad.

"Toady!" her son is going to shriek, gleeful.

Just the one, his fire belly a brilliant red, lungs working in his dry cereal-bowl pond, glossy black gaze, malevolent frightening amphibian. It will seem impossible, and yet, he will live.

In bed the first time, they'd taken a pair of heavy crystal tumblers and filled them with scotch, sat cross-legged on the sheets in underpants. Sebastian's heart beat visibly beneath his pale chest. They both stared, entranced by the literal frailty the pulsing proved. Sadie had no thought of her husband, that trusting and ordinary man, that alibi. When they hoisted those tumblers, knee to knee in the Paradise Motel room, when they knocked them together in a recklessly unavoidable and solemnly desperate toast, it was only fitting that both glasses shattered into a thousand glittering bits there on the white sheets, the pungent spilled liquor, distillate and damp beneath them when they first had sex.

Her son, five years old, the boy who bears an uncanny resemblance to Sadie's long-dead little brother, stands utterly still on Easter morn when he is told about Sebastian's death. Funny honorary uncle Sebastian, beloved and elusive, bad influence and attractive nuisance. He never came when you

182

called, but always when you least expected, never unwelcome, always a delight. Sadie has the strange luxury of seeing her own emotions on her son's face, the naked childish shock that overtakes him like a spanking, the flush of horror, the drained white of realization, the brute physical knowledge that drops him to the floor, egg basket forgotten, foil footballs rolling away, and then the plaintive wail. These are *her* feelings. This is *her* grief, manifest and raw in her little boy—to whom she rushes, this repository of all mysterious unknowable boyhood she cannot own herself, this cage of frail ribs set on wobbling knobby knees, spatulate fingers and adenoidal tonsils, little lost brother, killed lover, hopeless weeping masculine love, her boy, her only boy, the one she clings to as if to save and be saved, her son.

SHAUNTRELLE

I T WASN'T JUST A husband one divorced, but a life. A credit
rating. Certain friends—sadly, some of them small children. The mother-in-law, that innocent bystander. The house,
in this case, with its many indelible vistas that Constance
Vorhees had taken pains to arrange, and would acutely miss.
And sometimes, it seemed to her, she had divorced her own
pronoun, *I*, in favor of the other, *she*. *She*, she sometimes
thought, of herself, and always in the present tense. *Has she
disconnected from her past so completely?*

She hadn't, however, turned loose her city. Houston was hers,
although not this side of it. She'd long been aware that the city
was big and eclectic enough to support as much anonymity as
one could desire. Or fear. Along with the novelty of the south
loop, she'd acquired a roommate, this after many years of the
known quantity: husband, daughter. Dogs. She guessed she had
divorced them, too.

At the front desk of the Laventura a disdainful blond
woman provided her with a handful of devices for entry into
her new life: apartment and mailbox keys, garage gate remote,

car tag, a code for accessing inner sanctums bearing keypads. Up the dizzying garage ramp Constance drove, round and round, seeking out her new stall. On one side of it a racing bike was locked to a fire hose; on the other sat a vintage Mercedes on soft tires, mint green. One of these was her new roommate's vehicle. The voice on the phone, the affect over e-mail, suggested the Mercedes; she had used "y'all"; her cell phone area code was from Louisiana. *Her new roommate is named Fanny Mann,* Constance thought. *To her new home she brings only a suitcase, which rolls along after her like a pet.*

The apartment had a lighted doorbell, a peephole, and was located in a long hallway of such doors. The only distinguishing characteristic was the welcome mat. Some doorways had them, some did not. Fanny Mann's—hers, thought Constance—was bright red, not a speck of dirt upon it.

"Hi there!" the voice sang out before the face appeared. And this was perhaps to offset the startling bandages that covered some of it. "Don't be frightened! Come on in! I'm your roomie, you're at the right place! You didn't know you were moving in with the invisible woman, did you?"

Shaking hands with Fanny Mann is the first physical contact she's had with anybody in a very long time.

"Rhinoplasty," the roommate explained. She wore lipstick, under the antiseptic white strips; her eyes, above, were outlined in kohl, hazel colored, vaguely bloodshot. "In case you were thinking battered wife." Certain other details caught Constance's attention: the manicure, the studded belt, the short denim skirt.

"How smart is it," Fanny Mann was saying as they jockeyed into the too-cool apartment, "to move in with someone you wouldn't recognize on the street?" Was she drunk? No; this, Constance would learn, was her way, to work hard to

make people laugh. Or at least smile, even if only at her effort. It was Fanny Mann's most generous, appealing characteristic; it required a vigilance and preparedness Constance
had rarely encountered, a project like someone seducing a future mate. She was a flirt, down to the makeup and heels.

The apartment smelled overwhelmingly of perfume, a familiar melancholy scent that happened to be the favorite of
Constance's mother, who was dead. Shalimar; the art deco
bottle flashed in Constance's mind. Under the perfume, the
odor of hospital, fresh paint, and air conditioning, the faint
cigarette smoke of someone who took her habit out on the
balcony. The furniture was brand-new, tags hanging from a
few objects, and the art inoffensive, abstract landscapes, vases.
The dining room table was set for two, place mats, plates,
polyester napkins blooming from industrial-strength wineglasses. "I should probably put those away," Fanny Mann said.
"But they amuse me. When I moved in last week, all the lights
were on and the stereo was blaring classical. I kept expecting
somebody in a cummerbund to show up with dinner! I put
the plastic plants out on the balcony, to spruce it up a bit, and
let me tell you, they're *flour*ishing!"

She was older than Constance had guessed, younger than
Constance's mother would have been, yet older than her stepmother. Sixty-two? The body would spill secrets, given a
chance. It was in the leathery arch of her foot in its spike heel,
the automatic lift of the chin to photograph well, the second-
nature way she had with her cigarette, as if she had been born
with a lighted object in her hand. Her accent was lazier than
Constance's, swampier, homier. She was only a temporary
tenant in Houston, here during a forced vacation while her
flooded house was under repair. In a roomy rambling monologue, she highlighted the advantage of her exodus. She was

having her nose sculpted, her face lifted, her skin both lasered and peeled, her fat vacuumed, her tummy tucked, her breasts bolstered, her neck tightened, her teeth veneered, and the spare skin around her eyes snipped away. Her goal, she told Constance, was to more closely resemble the personal ad she'd posted on the Internet. She was limping, she explained, because of liposuction, moving tenderly and somewhat unsteadily on stilettos. In New Orleans, she was a chiropractor.

"I sure wish I could show you a Before picture," she said regretfully. "So you could fully appreciate what's going to come After."

She never knows what to say to sudden intimacies from strangers. Fanny Mann's revelations, and the expectant pause that followed, could seem coercive, as if Constance now owed the woman her own confession. But it was not Constance's habit to make herself available to other people; they mistook her for cold; complete strangers would stop her on the street and implore her to smile. Perhaps she *was* cold; maybe this is what it felt like to be a cold person—even as she felt herself grow warm in the expectant pause now dangling between her and Fanny Mann, that space her own gush of confiding was meant to fill. But to get to know Constance, to grow fond of her, you had to spend a long time hanging around. Her marriage to William had lasted twenty-one years; they had one child, a daughter now eighteen, who'd been so sad to leave for college. The two dogs were also relatively old, brothers, a decade in Constance's care. The boyfriend was her most recent kinship, a love affair of five years. Those beings had been her intimates, and now every one of them had found sudden, utter, devastating fault. *Wouldn't that send anybody to the third person?*

But Fanny Mann didn't seem to mind Constance's reticence; she might not even have noticed it. "I gab enough for two or three fools," she said cheerfully. "I get along great with the quiet type. My husbands were all still-waters sort of guys." She had sufficient warmth, confidence, and imperviousness to float a party. They had located each other online, one in need of a room, one in need of a roommate. Fanny Mann's best friend from grade school—she was of the age, and region, and disposition, to have had the same best friend for over fifty years—who originally promised to undergo similar improving procedures, had backed out at the last minute.

"Cancer," Fanny Mann said, with no less vibrancy. "Stage four, in her lungs."

"That's *awful*." These, besides initial mumbled pleasantries, were Constance's first words to Fanny Mann.

"It truly is." Her eyes, bruised yellow above the bandages, briefly filled with tears. The mascara was waterproof, perfect. "Bless her *heart*," she added, covering her own chest with her hand, her little cigarette wand. "Your room," she went on, continuing on their stuttering tour. The carpet was plush, and caught at Fanny's heels. "Your bath, your walk-in closet, your towels and sheets and butt-ugly bedspread." Corporate housing meant one need only show up—the rest awaited: appliances and their services, lamps and throw rugs and trash cans and kitchen gadgets. Sample-size containers of face and bath and dish and laundry soap.

"Don't answer the land line, is my advice. Some gal named Felicia had this number before, all the calls ask for Felicia, and they leave messages on our machine, too, all POed because Felicia is up to her eyeballs in debt, no wonder she got rid of that number. The thing is, the *ans*wering machine is *not* Felicia's, nor mine neither. The answering machine is *Ray*." She poked the little unit to make it recite its former owner's deep suave voice. "You've reached Ray," he said, enticingly. "And you *know* what I need . . ." Then a chuckle, then the beep.

"That can't hurt, can it? A man answering our phone? I like his sexy voice, too. I wonder where he went, anyway?" As if on cue, Fanny Mann's cell phone buzzed on her hip. She squinted at the screen before declining to engage the line. "And we can get the Internet sometimes, not all the time, and always in a different room. Yesterday the kitchen, but only by the sink; today, who knows?" This accounted for the laptop blinking on the chopping block. The last stop on the tour was the balcony, from which you could see the Astrodome to the west, the hospitals to the north. Directly below: people waiting for a bus. They were six floors away, and Constance could hear them talking, the exclamation and murmur and occasional clear profanity. "I accidentally kicked an ashtray over," said Fanny Mann. "Good lord, what an explosion, glass and butts every which way. Luckily, nobody got hurt, a lawsuit's the *last* thing I need." She held to the railing, balancing on her tiptoes, her head disproportionately large in its swaddling, plus beehive hairdo. She seemed likely to swing over herself, if she wasn't careful.

"Laventura, Laventura!" she sang, lighting another cigarette, mindful of the flame so near her bandages. "I think it means 'Little Wine Bottles,' in Italian."

"I did notice some broken glass around the front door," Constance said.

"Yeah, the neighborhood's gentrifying, but somebody forgot to tell the winos. See there? That fizzling blue light on the corner? That's our local grocery, I call it the No Judgment Store. Everybody buying beer and condoms and lottery tickets and tubs of lard. Whack rags." Fanny smiled, wincing a bit, either from smoke or sutures. "I'm usually the only white woman in the place. The bag boy thinks I'm fine. '*You fine*,' don't you *love* that? Nobody bats an eye, you pick up a carton of smokes and a pack of pork rinds at nine in the a.m. On a Sunday, no less."

Constance returned her smile, relieved, relaxing suddenly as if having finished a challenging physical chore, as if having swilled a stiff drink. Here was a woman with scruples less developed than her own, someone who chose not to be frightened but entertained by her new neighborhood, someone who soldiered on with her elective surgery even when her best friend was diagnosed with cancer. *Lung* cancer—and Fanny Mann sucking on a cigarette. Constance felt light, as if Fanny had spirited away a sack of stones she'd been lugging around. "Maybe I'll bum a smoke," she said shyly.

"*There* you go!" Fanny Mann crowed, expertly tapping the pack so that one jumped out. "There's a carton in the freezer, you just help yourself."

Constance unpacked her clothing that first night in her strange chilly room (Fanny Mann's metabolism, she had apologized, made her hotter than a fritter; did Constance mind the AC on high?), brushed her teeth, plumped her pillows on her new bed, set the alarm. Then what? Her ex-husband would be sleeping on what had been for twenty-one years her side of the bed; he'd always coveted it. Her boyfriend would be fiddling at his computer, the only source of light in his shabby duplex, stoned, busy in the virtual world he most comfortably inhabited. Constance held those images in her mind, staring through them at the wall, still able to smell the vanilla sweetness of Shalimar, which made her picture her mother, preparing for an evening out, back when her parents were the adults and the idea of death, and a stepmother, existed only in a book by the Brothers Grimm. *She hardly recognizes herself in the mirror.* On the other side of the door she heard her roommate rattling in the kitchen, chatting on the cell phone to the best friend, over at M. D. Anderson, "within spitting distance of ol' Little Wine Bottles," her spike heels going clack clack clack, then muffled through the carpet, then the suction of the balcony door, as she took herself out into the sulky humidity for a smoke. It was a life Constance did not have to care about. Her own would reassemble in here, a refrigerated room with ivory walls, starched sheets, dustless and serene as vacancy, and her reflection in the mirror like a portrait hung over the bureau, a woman caught gazing soulfully out, two-dimensionally, from a frame.

She was reading a novel assigned, in a fashion, by her daughter. "There's this book I really liked," Lily had reluctantly offered, when Constance asked how the semester was going. Lily was a secretive, serious girl; she hardly let her mother know anything about her, especially now, since Constance had been discovered to have her own serious secret. Children didn't want their parents to lead private lives; they could not help but be wounded by those.

Constance wasn't making good progress on reading Lily's recommended book, however. The fact that her daughter had enjoyed it, its street-people characters and their drugged, violent existence, alarmed her, interfered with her ability to simply read. Instead, she was taking it in as if in the presence of Lily, self-conscious and with a heightened attention. It was the way she'd felt when Lily was younger, when they watched racy, perhaps inappropriate movies together, averting their eyes as the clothes were peeled or ripped off, as the ravishing sex ensued. Every night Constance reentered the novel's streets of Los Angeles, a city she had never visited in actuality. On those streets, two gay girls, runaways, were making their living as prostitutes. One—Jo—was a heroin addict. The other—Deezy—merely drank. They loved one another, but had sex with men—very graphic, angry sex—and sometimes weren't even paid for the service. They discussed the disadvantage of not working with a pimp, but then reassured one another that they had each other's back. When they reconnoitered, after their separate desperate nights, they wanted only to abuse their respective substances and fall into a chaste embrace.

The book gave Constance nightmares. Although her dreamscape wasn't based on the novel's landscape, it was a consistent place that she found herself frequenting nearly every night. The book operated as a kind of portal. Through it she entered this other world, which was neither fictional Los Angeles nor factual Houston. It seemed to be a city on a hill, with unsteady buildings teetering up its sides, a body of water lapping at its base. There, a boy she'd loved as a teenager often appeared. Corey Forster, who was no longer alive. Like the girls in Lily's novel, he'd had bad habits, and also bad luck, the combination killing him in a car crash when he was only nineteen. In Constance's dreams, Corey Forster was always on the verge of taking her hand, of leading her into a room down a hall. There, she could have him back.

Why, then, did she think of them as nightmares? Because they were difficult to want to leave—No! she would clutch at unconsciousness, behind her waking eyes—and that was somehow worse: being happy in a made-up place in the company of a ghost. The experience seemed insane. Constance was tormented by it.

In the morning, she found her new roommate at the table, its elaborate setting enhanced by a plate of plump muffins.

These were delivered daily, downstairs, Fanny Mann informed Constance. She wore a vivid silk wrap, hair turbaned over her bandages, which were fresh. "Those corporate Barbies in the office hate it when I show up in the lobby wearing my muumuu, but excuse me, I *live* here, they *work* here. These are blueberry and chocolate. Some days we get croissants, some days zucchini loaf. Oh, not *now*," she added, frowning down at her cell phone vibrating on the table. "Poor Lucille. A better friend might have canceled her face lift, espirit de corps and all. But, really, what could I do for her? To quote my daddy, I have no medical expertise, and furthermore I'm not getting any younger." Fanny Mann let the phone burr and buzz its way nearer the plate of muffins. "They got crappy reception over there at the cancer ward, anyway. Everyone else in my life left me but her, Lucille, first my son, then my daughter, next that maroon I married, and after that the next maroons, but never Lucille. Still, I've been waiting a long time to pimp this ride. She said go ahead, the sight'll cheer her up. Over there losing weight without even trying, bless her heart." Finally the phone ceased.

In the night, Constance had woken panicked, unable to recall where she was, and with little to go on. A few small lights in the room, on the ceiling smoke detector and bedside clock, an amber glow from the window. When she opened the vertical blinds, the view was of city night sky, empty yet fuzzy. Before returning to bed, she turned the handle lock on the bedroom door, worried suddenly about sleeping with a stranger on the other side. She read for a while in her daughter's disturbing book, then finally made her usual sleeping journey to Corey Forster's hand, that frustrating hallway located in a tipping house, perched on a cliff above the lapping sea. Corey had driven off an unfinished highway overpass one night long ago, apparently heedless of the orange cones and flashing lights. He had been drunk and high, and probably thrilled at the sudden lack of traffic, the secret shortcut home from a party where Constance had remained. She'd declined his offer of a ride. She would never unsee that vaulting image, one invented by her afterwards, Corey sailing into the air, launched briefly upward before the inevitable plummet. Its actual counterpart, the finished piece of highway that took you to boring Bellaire, seemed significantly less real to Constance than the other.

This morning, Fanny Mann was kind of a welcome sight, jolly and bathed, done up like a tropical bird, offering food and coffee.

"But no newspapers, can we make a deal about that? I cannot abide the news. The most bad news I can take is a peek in the mirror—my grandma would say I look like something the cat drug in and the dog wouldn't eat—and then I'm done. *No mas, gracias.* I got puzzle books and catalogs and *Cosmo*, that oughta do us, huh? Sudoku?"

"Okay," Constance agreed. Was it that easy to forsake the wider world, to give up guilt about her fortunate position in it? Her husband William had been adamant about the paper. Their daughter had developed his habits, every morning the two of them sighing over the war, scoffing at malapropisms in headlines or quotes. His intention had been to educate her, but Constance thought it only made the girl feel depressed and superior, which was perhaps the same thing as being educated.

"You are not wearing those shoes!" Fanny Mann said in horror, when Constance was ready to leave for work. "What size are you?"

"Eight and a half?"

Fanny Mann tottered off to her room, returning with a set of open-toed red heels for Constance. "It's the least I could do for that poor black suit. Now you couldn't possibly be mistaken for going to a funeral. You aren't going to a funeral, are you?"

"No. Work."

"Some day, when I can bend over again, I'll give you a pedicure. We'll have a day of beauty. Where do you work, I forget?"

Constance mentioned the energy office acronym; everyone in Houston was in awe, but Fanny Mann looked nonplussed. She'd never heard of them, which made Constance smile. Her job was sometimes a trial to her; she'd gotten her position there because her father was a senior VP. In the early days, her co-workers had called her the Princess, and so her reputation had been set, a pampered dilettante who didn't deserve her status. If they'd known the truth, they would have understood the miracle of her having been hired: her stepmother, also a senior VP, did not like Constance.

Rather than take the belt loop to the office, she detoured on surface streets through her old neighborhood, just to catch a glimpse of her house. William had removed the leaded stained-glass windows she'd hung in their bathroom, she noticed, finally getting his way; she had shopped for months for those pretty panes, but he claimed they were not opaque enough, that strangers could see him step from the shower. At her daughter's bedroom window was the sponge head of Yao Ming, larger than life-size, faded and stiff from the sunlight. Lily and William had gone to games together, coming home hoarse from cheering; now Lily was a freshman at Barnard. She had left home last fall, which had resulted in Constance's realization of her freedom: her daughter would most likely never live at home again, and therefore Constance did not have to remain there, waiting.

The two dogs lay on the front porch, lifting their muzzles at the sight of her familiar car, some brief motion from each tail, but neither bothering to leave his spot. William would be at his law office, downtown.

The boyfriend was Kevin Kirkendoll; she avoided driving past his duplex, as he might be there. He had moved nearby last year so that she could see him more often, walk those slathering dogs right to his alley door and into his home. When Constance had left William, it was in order to claim Kevin. For five years she'd believed that their secret life was building toward something, that they were preparing a future, one presentable and public, substantial, perhaps painfully garnered, but somehow worth the damage. However, it turned out Kevin hadn't been inhabiting that scenario with her. The day she told her husband about her affair, the day she released the tethers that held the safety net of her marriage, the day she showed up at Kevin's door planning to stay not a feverish hour but the rest of her committed life—well, Kevin panicked. Before her eyes he transformed. Or, rather, he failed to transform. He had wanted nothing to change. He liked the fact of his autonomy, his bachelor life, his only occasional trysts with Constance, the relief of her going away after an hour or, at most, an afternoon. Faced with his alarm, she felt herself shrivel, suddenly aware of how little she had traded her marriage for. This rented dirty space, its frightened occupant. *She feels as if she's let loose of her spaceship, floating in space.*

Losing William to divorce felt to Constance exactly like losing her mother to death: she'd grown to resent the cloying, unconditional love, her own role of spoiled child in its nonjudgmental vapor, and then, as soon as it was gone, straight-away wished to have it restored, surround her like a force field.

Kevin Kirkendoll was younger than Constance; it had been a necessary fact of her attraction to him, her conquest, her bratty activity under her husband's nose. Only occasionally had Kevin's youth worried her. Once he'd made a comment about grown Lily, about her prettiness; he was of an age, his mid-thirties, that had sexual rights on either side of it, to both mother and daughter's generation. Had his comment about Lily been the beginning of the end? The daughter no longer a child, Constance no longer the object of the male glance? It had happened in public, at the mall or on the street, men now eyeing Lily first, then, maybe, the older woman at her side; why wouldn't that same demotion have happened in private?

Banished by William, she insisted on staying with Kevin, lying in the bed she'd made. With her she took one of the dogs, Bruno, who came along gamely enough. But once he re-alized that this wasn't merely a walk, that he wasn't simply being given special preferential treatment this evening (his brother Bob left at home, brooding in a corner), Bruno sidled up to the back door and sat there whisking his tail on the floor, whimpering, occasionally nosing the handle as if to re-mind Constance that it was she with the prehensile ability to get them out of there. He did not like it here; he missed his brother. Constance would scream at him, furious beyond rea-son at his unflagging unhappiness, finally dragging him the three blocks back to her old home, yanking open the front gate and kicking him through it into the yard. Over which he ran with glee, so glad to be rid of her, to be back where he belonged.

She'd stayed at Kevin's only slightly longer than Bruno had, finally exhausted by his reluctance at having her as his guest.

She'd stayed a night at her office, another few with her father and stepmother, a week with friends she had hoped would withhold opinion, then a month at a downtown hotel. *She feels like a fickle princess from a fairy tale, trying out all the options, this door, that bed, detecting flaws in each.* And now she had landed here at the Laventura, with Fanny Mann.

Fanny Mann's face was unwrapped for exactly one day before she returned to the clinic for her next procedure. "I *love* Dr. Fondel's office," she said. "It's perfect, like a cross between a spa and a hospital, everyone real professional, all sanitary in their lab coats, but nobody dying." Constance, accustomed to the bandages, was fascinated by Fanny's exposed features. Her nose, petite and perfect, was very white, as if it had come from some other person's face. When Fanny sneezed, it bled. "Don't look, don't look! I'm a work in progress!" Her cheeks and forehead were blurred beneath a thick application of Vaseline, only her eyes and mouth familiar. She warned Constance not to grow too attached to them, as she was having improvements made in both areas. She packed a set of soft chintz bags and waved with her fingertips at the door.

That night, by herself for the first time, Constance hid in her room, locking the handle once again. She could have tuned into one of the nighttime dramas Fanny Mann had taught her to enjoy, but without Fanny there to provide backstory, the shows seemed nearly indistinguishable from the commercials that interrupted them. This was why Constance had sought out a roommate, having discovered during her time at the hotel that she did not like to be alone. The corporate knives were not very sharp, but she brought the biggest one to her bed. When she couldn't fall asleep—despite three chapters of Lily's novel—she ransacked Fanny

Mann's medicine cabinet (*She's refused plenty of invitations to sample the painkillers there*) and took an OxyContin, letting its loopy undertow suck her down at last.

A few hours later she could hardly rouse herself, but a persistent sound wouldn't let her dismiss it. The doorbell, she eventually determined, having never heard it before. For a few moments she simply sat on the side of the bed, gathering together the strange place, the unfamiliar ringing, and the drugged fog she was trying to operate under. Finally, she remembered the peephole, and this allowed her to unlock her own bedroom door and creep to the front of the apartment.

On the other side of the peephole leaned an exasperated-looking young black woman. She'd been poking at the doorbell, but now she slapped the flat of her palm on the door, just below Constance's blurred eye. "I know you in there, Shauntrelle!"

Constance would not unlock or open up, but put her face to the slit between frame and door and said, croakily, since she hadn't spoken in hours, "I'm not who you think I am."

The woman abruptly ceased. "Shauntrelle?"

"No."

The woman stepped back. Then suddenly disappeared from the fish-eyed confines of the peephole. But Constance could hear the faint ring of another doorbell, down the hall, through the walls, which set off a barking dog.

Now completely awake—the nearness of that stranger, her hand just under Constance's face at the peephole—she lay agitated in bed, wondering whether she should risk another pill. The woman's determination to find Shauntrelle made Constance aware of her own desire to be found, to be sought after. Kevin Kirkendoll had always complained that it was he who had the most to risk, in loving her; never mind her husband

and daughter—he, he had said, had nobody to fall back on, no plan B. He would not hear her when she reminded him that he also had no one to injure, nobody to irrevocably fail. Yet for all his declarations, it seemed simple to let her go. It wasn't Kevin Kirkendoll breaking down her door, calling her name. And neither was it her husband, who'd taken the news of her betrayal quietly, the infliction she made on him one of shock. Complete shock.

When Fanny Mann returned, her chest was bound, her lips swollen, and her eyes hidden behind sunglasses. The Vaseline had given her a terrible case of acne, and she had not tended to her hair, which was so thin and tortured that, unwhipped, unteased, her scalp showed. "Don't look at me!" she insisted, dropping her bags on the living room floor and scurrying into her room. Later, after hours of restorative efforts, she joined Constance on the balcony. Constance had stopped by the No Judgment Store for cigarettes and cocktail-hour food, processed cheese and fancy crackers, gherkins, olives, meat that did not require refrigeration. She made Fanny Mann a vodka gimlet—weak, in consideration of the painkillers— and told her about the nighttime visit from the woman seeking Shauntrelle.

Fanny laughed delightedly, adding it to the names she had already begun calling Constance: Felicia, as in "Felicia, Columbia House is gonna garnishee your wages!" or Ray ("I got bad news about that rubber, Ray") and now Shauntrelle. These were the identities occupying their apartment with them, those who were summoned by the outside world, summoned by some but abandoned by their owners. Who knew why?

"Lord knows nobody's sniffing around here for me," Fanny Mann pointed out.

"Me, neither," Constance said, sighing.

"Was it a messy divorce?"

"No," Constance said. "Maybe it would have been better if it was."

Had Fanny probed, Constance might have explained her wish for a mess, for William to have flown into a rage, threatened a duel; perhaps his fiery passion would have ignited Constance's, in return. But Fanny launched into her own divorce story. Everybody had one, just like everybody had a story about giving birth or crashing a car. The betrayal, the epidural, the whiplash.

"One thing about the Laventura is: Who'd *think* to look for us here, even if they *were* looking?" Fanny said. When she rented the place, from afar, she had been misinformed about the apartment's location; it wasn't, strictly speaking, within walking distance of the medical community, especially if the walker were in any way ill or infirm. It was closer to the Astrodome, which sat across the way like a spaceship. Fanny Mann and Constance weren't members of the Laventura's typical demographic group. Next door to the east lived a night watchman who arrived at dawn to fall asleep; his newspaper lay on his threshold all day, then disappeared in the evening. Across the hall was an Indian medical student, married to another Indian medical student, parents of a small baby who was handed off between shifts. They wore scrubs, entering and exiting, passing the baby, trading bags of groceries or diapers or textbooks. Directly below Fanny and Constance lived somebody who took flash photographs from his or her balcony, the bright quiet blast of light under them every now and then like a spill of phosphorescence, fairy dust, at their feet. At the apartment door next to the parking garage exit leaned a pair of worn cowboy boots, with muddy spurs, their owner—or his wife—apparently unwilling to have the things inside.

"It's true," Constance agreed, "this is not a likely place for me to be." How, then, to explain her lingering hope that she would be rescued from it, regardless? Kevin Kirkendoll, if he put his mind to it, could locate her; surely William, with all his connections, could pull it off. Despite being up high, on the sixth floor, and safe from ordinary intruders, the dedicated suitor could find a way. No matter the locked doors and security cameras and smooth unscalable surface of the building itself—a determined man could storm the castle. The place stood out, not only for its size and grandeur but because it was inhabited, operating, lit up at night. Scattered around it sat empty businesses, their doors padlocked, vines crawling over as if to reclaim them for nature, while on the street loitered the fleet of people pushing grocery carts. This detritus, man-made, earth-grown, was a kind of moat surrounding the building proper, modern fortress, painted a yellow that surely was labeled Tuscan. Once a day, a janitor with a powerful hose circulated, blasting the trash and dog droppings away from the structure's perimeter. You took a risk, exiting the building, walking the neighborhood; Constance had braved it that very afternoon, picking up nonessentials at the No Judgment Store. Men had catcalled, leered; everyone asked her for spare change.

But once she stepped back through the doors of the Laventura—mildly sweaty from apprehension, humidity—she was surrounded by refrigerated air, by soft rock music playing in the elevators and in the gym, piped into the cyber café and corporate meeting suite, even out by the pool and hot tub, the sound track of safety. The contrast to the outside world was so extreme as to equal disbelief, disorientation, dizziness.

Still, Constance believed gestures might be made; imagined, for instance, the biplane that could fly over, a message trailing it proclaiming Kevin's or William's love. They knew where she worked, of course, and could have come there. In expectation of this, she kept an eye out for them: William in one of his gray suits, with his polished bald head, sitting in his Audi. Or Kevin's shaggy blond hair and vintage button-up shirts. Constance loved the wornness of Kevin's clothing, the old-fashioned graphics on his shirts, checks or paisleys or chevrons. He didn't drive a car, so he would have had to ride his bike; her glance eagerly chased any bicycle that flew by. He worked at the public radio station, and she listened to his jazz program, even though he never spoke during it except to mention call letters and megahertz. He'd been the DJ at William's law firm's Christmas party five years ago. His gig ended at midnight, and Constance had offered him a ride, him and his equipment, when his friend with the van had not shown up. It felt good to separate herself from the group of lawyers and their spouses. She'd observed Kevin's amused scorn toward them all evening, could read it in his eyes as he sat behind his elaborate table of machinery, spinning disks, poking buttons, insulated in headphones.

But why should she expect him to put effort into finding her now, when there hadn't been much, on his part, ever? He'd liked having no duties except waiting for Constance to show up. As for William, he was proud. She had forsaken him foolishly; her father had been appalled and impatient, her daughter hurt and embarrassed. Her stepmother had seemed unsurprised, and to take a barely concealed pleasure. At any rate, none of them had inquired about Constance's corporeal location; having her cell number and e-mail address apparently would suffice. In her dreams, ghostly Corey Forster visited and lured, but it didn't matter to him where she lived. *To them all, she is ethereal.*

For Fanny Mann the anonymity was temporary. She would occupy it only long enough to emerge like the phoenix, a brand-new version of her old beautiful self. She consulted frequently with her hand mirror, another fixture on the dining room table, alongside the pristine place settings. In it she gazed at her face, touching here and there, her expression critical. She applied this same critical glance to Constance's face, prescribing Botox and wax, nothing more.

"Maybe we should try Sunday brunch," she said now, feet crossed on the railing, one shoe rocking like a pendulum held by the fulcrum of her big toe. "That's how you meet people. And we could go to Yappy Hour, out there in the courtyard running round in circles, sniffing behinds with the rest of the mutts."

Under their balcony a bus stopped, brakes wheezing, its doors slapped open, then shut, engine roaring and sending up a plume of noxious smoke when it eventually rumbled away. The people left behind, as always, stepped somewhat dazedly into the street, looking around as if unsure what was supposed to happen to them next.

"Wouldn't they have a cow if I dropped a shoe on their head?" said Fanny Mann.

The next time Fanny Mann left for the night, she went to her friend Lucille's bedside at M. D. Anderson. "How do I look?" she asked. She had dressed for the visit, generously spritzed Shalimar, and done her best to cover the fresh bruises around her newly widened eyes. She carried a red silk hankie because her nose still bled now and then.

"You look great," Constance said, wondering if Fanny had always seemed like a person built of incongruous parts, her calves too fine for her feet, her neck too brief, her chest too wide. Had surgery created the freakish appearance, or softened the more extreme original? She called her surgeons miracle workers, wizards, but Constance had no idea how to gauge that assessment.

"Maybe I'll meet a doctor," Fanny said. "Well, of *course* you'll meet a doctor, Fanny fool," she scolded herself. "Maybe I'll meet a *man*. If I do, I'll see if he has a friend, for you."

"Okay," Constance agreed, but without particular enthusiasm. She knew how rare it was for her to fall in love. It had happened only three times in her life, less than once a decade. Corey Forster. Her husband William. And Kevin Kirkendoll. Dead, disappointed, and disappointing, respectively.

Once again, in her roommate's absence Constance felt irrationally vulnerable, aware of every sound in the building, inside the apartment, or outside in the hall. On the street below, screeching brakes, then horns and curses, slamming car doors; in the apartment next door, the dog barked, the night watchman yelled at the animal to shut the fuck up. The elevator bell kept binging, children from another floor playing pranks. And then, hours later, when Constance had finally fallen asleep (another of Fanny's pills, another chapter of Lily's tragic lesbian saga), the phone woke her. She listened as Ray's chuckling, sexy voice took the call, which was not for Felicia but, surprisingly, for someone named Gerald. "Buzz me in, Gerald!" shouted the caller. He was on a street; Constance could hear traffic, wind, the man's breathing and clicking as he pressed an intercom button. "*Dude*," he pleaded, "it's starting to *rain!*"

Constance went to the balcony, opened the door, and stepped out, stuck her hand into the air over the edge. No moisture. Liar. Or maybe he was standing outside a building in some other part of town, some other town, even. Who knew how he'd managed to find Constance, mute audience to his manic anguish? "Mother *fuck*er, let me in! Let me in, or call me a mother-fucking *cab*!"

Constance picked up the phone then. "You have the wrong number," she told the man who was looking for Gerald.

On his end there was a long pause; she could nearly imagine his consternation. "Say what?"

"This isn't Gerald's house. I don't even think this is Gerald's neighborhood."

"Am I speaking with Gabrielle?"

Now Constance paused; another person she wasn't. "No," she said, on the verge of saying her own name. She hadn't said it for a while, to anyone. "This is Felicia," she said.

"Well, hell, Felicia, can't you open this door? It's raining like a motherfucker. Hear that thunder?" From his end came a rumble, hissing and squeaks. But they sounded more like cheap acoustical imitations than a real storm. "Man, my remote's gonna get *ru*ined out here."

"You aren't anywhere near where I am," Constance said. She was sitting now on the balcony, out in the balmy night. Not a drop of rain; in fact, she could make out a few stars, an odd occurrence in the Houston firmament.

"Bitch," he muttered, before hanging up. Constance tried not to feel stung.

The night watchman had named his dog that, "Bitch." Every morning when he returned from his shift, he threw open his front door and called her name with a joyful inflection— "Bitch! Bitch!"—and then ran with her down the hall to the parking garage stairs, the two of them clattering down together, black lab and black man, her barking happily, him encouraging,

"Come on, Bitch! Come on!" cheerful and chaotic. In the night, when he left for work, she would give a forlorn wail, then sometimes a resigned and fading woof, woof, woof.

Once more alert in the lonesome night, Constance took herself around the apartment, seeking an Internet connection, resorting to e-mail. This was where she met up with Lily, who sent notes only in reply to her mother's, not even bothering to adjust the subject line. Constance tried not to burden her daughter with too many messages; it would take time to repair the damage she'd done to that girl, vicarious, what you might, in the current climate, call collateral.

More than anything, what Constance wished was that she would open her computer and it would sparkle like a treasure chest, perched here on the windowsill of the living room. The screen would be radiant, flooding the dark apartment, and a hundred messages would await her. She longed for every single space to be filled with Kevin Kirkendoll, his repeating name scrolling down four glowing pages of her inbox, his name resounding in that lengthy list, the collection of K's like the racket of trumpets, heralding her as she knelt before his declarations, balancing her computer on the thin window ledge, **kevinkirkendoll** vibrating in nearly three-dimensional intensity, *as if she might prick her finger if she touched the screen.*

But there was nothing new, not even spam.

"Where can we go, to show off my new rack?" asked Fanny Mann. Her contractor had been putting the final touches on her home in New Orleans; her aestheticians had done the same to her body, here in Houston. Their time together, hers and Constance's, was nearing its close. "My daughter thinks I'm vain," Fanny Mann had confided. "She thinks all this money on cosmetic surgery should have gone to Oxfam. Her brother, on the other hand, joined the army when he was eighteen. You can't believe the scene I made, weeping and wailing, when he came home in camo and a buzz cut. How'd I produce kids like that, you might ask, a *career* soldier *and* a bleeding-heart hippie? They aren't even on speaking terms. And," she added, shuddering with an afterthought, "my daughter hasn't shaved her legs in twenty years."

Constance was tempted to reply that the truly remarkable thing was Fanny Mann's own capacity to keep caring—about *any*thing, whether it was the size of her breasts or the state of the union. Having some degree of interest in playing the game—putting on the costume, reading the script, saddling up—seemed miles ahead of Constance's own situation. Wouldn't it be simpler to quit?

Instead, she named an expensive restaurant, and what luck? they managed to score a reservation that very evening. In the middle of the main course—braised lamb, new potatoes—Fanny missed the burring of her cell phone, the call that notified her of her dear friend Lucille's death. It had happened that afternoon; only now, in the early evening, had the hospital located this number, the person playing the role of next of kin. And only later still, in the quiet car retrieved from valet parking and then en route back to the Laventura, Constance carefully blinking away her own drunkenness at the wheel, did the equally tipsy Fanny Mann squint at her flashing little screen, recovering the message and then phoning the hospital to receive the news.

"Now she'll never see how it all turned out!" Fanny cried, meaning her surgeries, all these enhancements and rejuvenating procedures. She'd enjoyed dolling herself up for her debut at Carlo's Fine Dining, appearing there with décolletage and beckoning eyes, narrow nose, slim hips in a new red skirt, bruises kindly undetectable by candle light—once more the object of that coveted male gaze, heads turning to follow the alluring Shalimar trail—but the real audience for this metamorphosis had been Lucille, best friend and record keeper. Who else would so profoundly know how to care?

"I'm so sorry," Constance said. *She can never offer a comforting hug automatically. She is a stilted, stunted person.*

"Oh, sugar, it's *ter*rible!" answered Fanny, slumped in the passenger seat. They'd reached Constance's parking spot after the nauseating circling of the garage floors, and now neither opened their doors. "I don't know what I'll do next. I should have *been* there!" she cried.

Constance waited, weighing the two deaths that mattered to her, her mother's and Corey Forster's. She was glad her mother hadn't lived to see what had become of Constance's marriage, or, for that matter, what had become of Constance's father, when he chose his next mate. Neither of those were destinies her mother would have approved; her living would have prevented them. In a more distant past, Corey Forster had offered Constance a ride home the night he died, but she wasn't yet done with the party, it hadn't yet ceased being a good time, an evening of enchantment and possibility. Had he driven her, his route would have been a different one, and he'd never have flown off that unfinished bridge to nowhere. Going with him would have made for an altered future, true, but there was no guarantee of a better one. Was there? "You were a good friend," she chose to say to Fanny Mann. "You *are* a good friend."

"I am a selfish person," Fanny said, wiping her cheeks, smearing her lipstick. "Selfish and ugly. Ugly ugly ugly, that's what my daughter would say. And she'd be right."

"No," Constance said. "No she wouldn't, you're not. I'm sure your daughter loves you. You're very kind." *Is she lying?*

Fanny Mann yanked open the door handle then, igniting the dome light. "You don't know shit about me, Shauntrelle, but I do appreciate you trying to cheer me up." Then she slammed the door and clacked across the garage, amazingly able, given the grief and alcohol and stilettos and still-healing surgery.

Constance sat behind the wheel for another few minutes, allowing Fanny time to enter their apartment, sequester herself in the privacy of her own room, occupy her own solitary remorse. Constance closed her eyes to test her inebriation, now that she was safely out of traffic, home with the engine off. She always thought of Corey Forster when she drove drunk. Now she recalled a more recent fatal evening, another party. Had she not driven away from it with a man not her husband, and if they hadn't both, simultaneously, felt the hour proper to flee that party, which had become, as parties did, suddenly done—the magic demystified, the gig over, the clock chiming midnight—she would never have fallen in love with Kevin Kirkendoll. She couldn't have known that falling for him would mean never being able to reclaim an unfallen state.

This isn't a fresh insight, but death has brought it visiting her once again.

Her time in the care of Corporate Housing would hang like a discrete interlude in Constance's life. It wasn't best measured by days or months; even the rent was prorated, down to the hour. It wasn't a season attached to any known calendar or almanac, nor was it punctuated by a famous holiday. It was situated in the Laventura itself, this spell, and precisely on the sixth floor of that establishment, in a two-bedroom apartment, roommates at strange crossroads. Here, in their garret, they were protected from the riffraff, the neighborhood, even Mother Nature, in the form of floods or biting insects. The lower floors, sometimes, had an odor of rot, the buzz of bugs. That was where the garbage accumulated when it fell from the upper units through the chutes. That was where water seeped to soak into the carpet, from heavy rain, or simply up from the spongy foundation. The city of Houston floated, bobbed, sinkholes opening now and then to claim a piece of terra firma. Over their blighted part of the city presided Fanny Mann and Constance Vorhees, on extended mild evenings. If it had a name, this brief era, it might be Shauntrelle: the season of uncertain and drifting identity, of upheaval and limbo, of anxiety and laughter, of transience and transients, flying ashtrays and painkilling drugs, of tawdry television and baby tomatoes, of furnishings that not only did not belong to them but belonged to nobody, not even to the rooms they temporarily filled. The weather here was ambiguous; dropped into it, unknowing, you would guess late fall or early spring, gentle southern winter; it could be any of the twelve months of the year, unmarked by cycles of the moon or by climate, not a period of time a schoolchild or farmer or politician would recognize. It wasn't even, strictly speaking, biological, Constance and Fanny of different generations and stations, separate crises and wishes. But it was theirs, nonetheless, and it finally had an end.

Constance finished Lily's novel a few nights before the chosen departure day, before the corporate Barbies used the master key to let in the movers, who would haul away the furniture, including the answering machine—so long Felicia, good-bye Ray, and Gerald, and Gabrielle, too. Constance packed the book,

since it was hers, and the instructions from corporate head-
quarters were firm about personal belongings—God forbid
Constance risk sacrificing her and Fanny's deposit—but she
would have preferred to leave it behind. She wanted to forget
that book. Deezy, the novel's drunk, had to mourn Jo, the
heroin addict, who wasn't dead but who might as well have
been. All along there'd been a growing rift between the girls,
one of them more interested in her high than in her beloved,
the other grieving over lost love, over her powerlessness
when faced with someone else's stubborn, subsuming self-
destruction. The reader wanted to reach in and turn Jo the
heroin addict around, convince her of the obvious correct
course, crash her body against Deezy's the way one manipu-
lated dolls, making them hug, settling them in bed together
in the dollhouse so that they could live happily ever after.

Had this exquisite frustration moved Lily? Did those girls'
brutal fates bespeak a truth that, once felt, could not be unfelt?
That was Constance's own experience, not just with favorite
books but in life itself, the disquieting yet unshakable insight,
the step taken that could not be retracted. Constance was desperate to know if her daughter felt like one of those fictional
creatures—Deezy, lover of the living ghost, or Jo, the afflicted
ghost herself—but it wasn't a question she was brave or bold
enough to ask. She was tempted to contact William, seek his
opinion. But she already knew what he would say. He would
default to the obvious: Lily's liking the book merely meant she
was a lesbian. And he would have been satisfied with that,
both the obvious conclusion and the fact of her sexuality.

So, like most other bits of private knotted knowledge, it
would circulate inside Constance, make an appearance now
and then to trouble her, and that's the moment some stranger
might encounter her, wonder aloud why she wasn't smiling.

"You promise to visit?" demanded Fanny Mann on moving day. "I won't leave till you swear." She was set to drive away in her classic mint-colored and -condition Mercedes, having rallied from Lucille's demise. She looked good in her new body, her gay outfit, her coiffed honey-blond hair, ready for a road trip to her refreshed home in New Orleans. "You visit, and I'll introduce you to my future sugar daddy's unmarried son. I have the whole fantasy all worked out!"

"Okay," Constance agreed. They embraced—gently, since Fanny Mann was still on the mend. Her roommate smelled of her—and Constance's mother's—too-strong perfume, an antique odor of romance, bravado, faith. Constance would still be able to smell it later on, driving down the winding ramp for the last time, pulling away from the closing electric gate and the saluting security guard, onto the gritty ground floor and out into traffic, en route to . . . *Where is she, anyway, and where does she think she's going?*

OR ELSE

M Y FAMILY OWNS A house in Telluride" was his favorite, most useful line. And it was a particular kind of girl or woman he used it on, somebody with whom he could not foresee a future. She would one day perceive him truly, with X-ray eyes, and move on. In the meantime, he could take her for a long weekend to Telluride.

She would be impressed by the modesty of the place. "It really is a shack," he would insist during the drive from Arizona, the desert falling away mile by mile, shrubbery and rocks transforming subtly as he ascended, from prickly saguaro and desiccated scrub oak to piñon, then aspen and spruce, those more gracious, greener trees, an escalation of markers by which David had measured his own evolution, from nagging anticipation to delighted arrival, for over twenty-five years. Not much had changed, on that journey: neither for David, nor in the world around him. Yes, traffic in Tucson was worse; sure, Show Low had made a comeback; sadly, a piece of the Petrified Forest was on fire; and some gaudy casino had suddenly landed on the vast moonscape of the Navajo Nation. In Cortez, you detoured through the endless engineering endeavor to straighten out that highway, which used to be sexy 666, but now was newly, inoffensively numbered. Trout farming had become a going enterprise along the Dolores River, square plastic-lined pools in which writhing motion could be detected, as if someone were boiling rather than breeding a great roiling stew of fish. But: the most important things remained faithfully themselves, and David watched them pass as if they were winking at him, confirming their talisman-like confidence in his fortune.

"You're giddy," his current companion noted, in her peculiarly deep voice. When would this voice cease surprising David? "Very cute," it said. On the phone, you might mistake it for a man's voice. Its owner had not seen him this way before, unguardedly enthusiastic, and he knew joy made him appealing, as joy always did, like a child's smile, and also somehow vulnerable, for the same reason. She could hold his joy, that child's smile, in contempt. "You're like a little boy," she said, opening the two windows on her side of the car so that she could smoke. Meanwhile he held tight to the wheel and adhered to speed limits because he wanted nothing to interfere with his momentum, no rules to be broken, no winking signposts dissolved. Then they were at the penultimate turn, the box canyon just ahead, and the little town corralled within, its waterfall tumbling reliably at the precise backdrop center, a landscape painting by a sentimental artist.

"Telluride," he announced in a tone that said *ta da!* "The most beautiful place I've ever been."

"But"—she exhaled, teasing—"where have you been?" And he was too drunk with pleasure to do anything but laugh.

He narrated the noteworthy city sites as they rolled past, those milestones of adolescence and young adulthood: the former train station, where he'd watched, one night in the late seventies, as the firemen set flame to an outbuilding and then extinguished it, which was their tradition. Only later had they discovered that a member of their volunteers had suffered heart failure in the drunken hubbub. And this man was the father of one of the children watching, one of the boys rolling his eyes at the antics of his elders, which were not so different from the antics of the youngsters, who crowded a furtive camp-fire, smoking cigarettes on what had been, then, the rugged other side of the river.

"That's where we used to hang out on Friday and Saturday nights," he told his passenger, pointing at the marble steps of a former bank, its stately window now cluttered with sun-glasses. "Waiting to see where the party was. And that's the bar that never carded, and up there is the historical museum, which we knew how to break into."

"Why?"

He left his wistful repertoire to study her. "Why?"

"Yeah. Why break into a museum? I mean, did you steal stuff?"

"No." Well, yes. But not important stuff. Danielle, he con-sidered, was maybe different from the others he'd brought here. She was older, forty-two to his thirty-nine. Had she outgrown not only brattiness but the memory of its allure? Maybe. Once, in the middle of making love, he asked why she had closed her eyes. "I'm pretending you're someone else," she said. David had ceased motion, no idea what to say; that was what was wrong with him, he was often left in a lull, un-sure of his rights to indignation or hurt feelings, of how a person was entitled to react. "Who?" he finally asked.

"My last boyfriend," she told him, slipping away, pulling a pillow into an embrace between them. "He was a married man, and a lot older than me. He died a couple of years ago, of a heart condition. I don't think of him the whole time, hardly ever, actually, I just was then, when you asked." She'd stared at David frankly, pillow still clutched in her arms. "I sometimes miss him," she added.

"And there's the house," David said now, making the turn that led up to the little home he loved more than any place in the world.

"The house that caulk built," the family fondly claimed. It was dwarfed, these days, by mansions on either side. Forty years earlier, Jack Hart had purchased this property upon the birth of his first child, Priscilla. They'd been campers, the Harts, until Pris was born. Mrs. Hart then put down her foot; she said so whenever the story was retold. "No infants in tents! No diapers in the wilderness!" And so a small house was found, there in a glorious dying mining town, in the heart of that place, on a hill, with views shockingly symphonic from the crooked front porch. The Harts abided by the academic calendar; they fled the heat of Tucson and discovered Telluride, a summer respite, and in it a tiny miners' den with walls made of something called beaverboard, sagging into the ground, there atop a fading community of similar structures, occupied or abandoned by drunken miners and eccentric bar owners, Masons, shopkeepers, future ghosts. "The salt of the earth," Professor Hart would extol. He taught American Studies; his interests were wider and perhaps more catholic than those of many of his ivory tower cohorts. He thought his summer town unpretentious, gritty, endearing. He became an Elk; he agreed to be deputized for the annual invasion of Hells Angels on the Fourth of July. He invited his friends to visit; his offspring did the same. Their home was small and shabby but filled with impromptu dinner parties, bridge games, storytelling sessions over the sticky kitchen table on which always sat a large bottle of red wine.

At the house—like a house in a cartoon, wedged between big bullying structures on either side—David parked, smiling in greeting to his hemmed-in old friend. Whatever the loss of open space—the dog pen, the falling-down shed, the horseshoe pit, the clothesline—nothing for him had changed about the sacred spot that remained, porch slats raggedly grinning. The air was bracing; the lack of oxygen might mean that your breath was literally taken away. Around him the peaks rose in their familiar battleship formations, proximate and daunting. They seemed poised to move, shift on their haunches and shrug the tiny toy town aside. No man-made object could detract from them. It was May, and they were still snow-covered; the aspen wore their nascent green, and on the streets below a resonant silence. Off-season. The collective reverent rest between tourist onslaughts.

Up the crumbling concrete steps David led Danielle; the doors would be locked, their keys long ago lost, but the west living room window would be unlatched. It would squeal when he yanked it up, and then, to prop it open, he would require the use of a tubular cast-iron counterweight that sat, year after year, in a cluster of other rusty or glass objects found on hikes and scavenging adventures, as porch decor. Then, nudging aside the desk that sat before the window, he would crawl through. Inside, David took a moment to breathe in the peculiar scent of this house: coal dust, which still filled the inner walls and pooled at the base of the spongy paneling; stale sunlight as it had been captured through the wavering glass of the western windows; a very faint odor of natural gas from a leak that could never be located; and the simply unique smell of the

Hart family itself. In the living room around him the four easy chairs situated near lamps ("The history of the recliner," Mrs. Hart would say, "before your very eyes." The wooden original, a less ancient brocade-patterned model, a fifties version, and the comfortable but ugly pleather La-Z-Boy. Each with its own nearby lamp; the Harts were readers.) Home.

Then David went to the front door, on the other side of which waited Danielle, who was shivering, staring cross-eyed at the door handle rather than at the monstrous mountains all around her. The elevation was nearly 9,000 feet; from bake-blasted Tucson you had to bring sweaters and wool socks as an act of faith. It was cold up here. At night, the stars devastated the clear, clear sky.

David Chalmers was a liar by nature, and now by long habit. He lied when it wasn't necessary, when it wasn't even advantageous. He lied to amuse himself, to excuse himself, to camouflage himself. The Harts were not his family. He'd been an honorary member, once upon a time, and then he'd been banished, albeit gently.

He had found the family through Priscilla, the eldest daughter, who at age nine, when she was asked, insisted that he was the friend she wished to bring with her for the summer visit. Priscilla was a tomboy, and David was her partner in crime; in Tucson they were prohibited from being in the same classroom at Sam Hughes Elementary. It was they who'd broken into the Telluride museum, along with some local miscreants. At night, they'd occupied the front upstairs bedroom, with its cracked window view of town, the bats that dipped all night long at the green streetlight outside. Late enough, they'd tiptoe through the back bedroom, where Priscilla's little sisters slept, and exit the window there, onto the hillside and into the night. For five summers she'd invited him. And then they were fourteen, and the invitation did not come.

"What happened to your girlfriend?" his father asked that fateful June first, smirking behind his beer and sunglasses. "Have yourself a lovers' spat?" David had no desire or even ability to explain; it was the exact opposite of what his father suggested, not a lovers' spat but the taint of loverly possibility. Pris had never been his *girlfriend*. Until this summer, she hadn't been a *girl*. And now suddenly she was, and she'd invited another girl to accompany her.

He spent the summer imagining himself there, daydreaming his way into adventure as well as ordinary boredom, lounging on the porch with a pile of comic books, waiting for Dr. Hart to announce a project.

Dr. Hart enjoyed having David around. David listened with unskeptical, uncritical attention to what Dr. Hart taught him. He'd memorized the names of the vegetation, the difference between flower and weed; he'd read whatever novel Dr. Hart handed him, reporting back on his confused progress, scandalized, mystified, ashamed; he learned to drive on those dirt roads, his own parents busy eviscerating each other, impatient with him, unable to fathom what it was the Harts liked about him, resenting his ability to escape Tucson for weeks at a time while they were forced to remain, their jobs not ones that permitted long holidays, their friends not likely to have summer homes in the mountains, and the existence of their son a complicating factor in their shared wish to part ways. David only reluctantly introduced them to the Harts, hustling the conversation along as he retrieved his duffel bag on the morning of the first departure. He'd been highly aware of Dr. Hart's taking in his family living room, the giant television, the absence of books or art, and, mostly, his mother's china doll collection, its pantheon standing rigid on their perches, staring back with their ice-cold eyes. Meanwhile, his mother had studied Mrs. Hart, glaring at her tall thinness, her long hair falling in a braid down her back, the easy smile on her tanned face. Mrs. Hart was a potter; her hands were tools, unbeautiful, clay beneath her nails, calluses on her palms. She set her own schedule and followed arts fairs around the Southwest. Her three daughters blinked unafraid beside her, Priscilla, Violet, Lydia. Their white hair was tangled, their knees dirty; the older two already read above grade level and sassed the teachers, and so would the youngest, when it was her turn. They were occasionally kept home "to play in the dirt," Mrs. Hart said. "Just in case they start getting infected by the catty crowd. You know how girls can be," she appealed to David's mother.

"No," she said. "I just have David." *Just.* And as if she'd never been a girl herself. As if she'd been born the hag she was now, lumpen and unhappy, suspicious concerning the lifestyle of her neighbors, those hippie Harts. She and her husband let David go because they had no better options for his summer freedom, and expected the worst of him: delinquency, slovenliness, eventual arrest. They didn't provide spending money: if the Harts wanted him, they could have him, but his parents would never regard it as a favor to them.

Mrs. Hart from then on treated David with a small degree of pity—the moist glance, the gentle pat—which he accepted like any rescued creature. He was not proud, he knew that. She kissed him good night as she did her girls, the four of them tucked in upstairs where the cabin's air was stuffy and warm, the pitched ceiling directly overhead, decorated with their own childish artwork, the very walls their canvas, naughtiness and eloquence, crisscrossed by webs and spiders, which the Harts never killed, the old records of folk songs spinning on the player set before the open doors of the two bedrooms, the girls singing along to all the shocking lyrics. David learned those songs, too. His favorite starred a rube who returned nightly to his home, only to be told by his scheming wife that the evidence he found of infidelity was nothing more than his drunken imagination. Not a horse in the yard, but a cow; not a coat on the rack but a quilt; and not a head on the pillow, where his ought to be, but a cabbage. "But a cow with a saddle?" the befuddled fool would lament. "A quilt with pockets?" "A cabbage head with a mustache I never did see before," the four of them would gleefully conclude the tune at top volume. In the morning, Mrs. Hart would ask how they had slept and serve them pancakes. Every day, pancakes, studded with berries; like the dope in the song, David hadn't known pancakes came from anything but a box, or that there was such a thing as butter instead of margarine, or that syrup from its maple source ran thin and tart, nothing like the gluey stuff he got at home.

Then they were set free, out the front door to rush wild in the empty town. Down to the river, out to the mine, up the hills, into the few businesses that lined Main and where all the shopkeepers knew their names. David pretended to be the brother. He wished it with all his heart. At night they played kick-the-can with the local children, hiding behind sheds and burn barrels. When the curfew siren sounded, they'd head home, spend the next hour or two all four riding the propane tank in the side yard, that warm echoing horse, or rocket, or motorcycle, while the air cooled around them.

For five years the weeks he would spend in Telluride stood for David as an annual pinnacle, time that he anticipated and then consumed, a blend of ritual as he absorbed it from the

Harts, and anomaly: the year the visiting dog bit off a chunk of the Hart dog's ear; the summer the city dug a hole in the front yard to fix a water line and failed to fill it in, an oozing pond into which Dr. Hart and his visiting graduate students planted a pair of sticks, clothed in pants and shoes, as if someone had dived in and stuck. These summer weeks were when David felt most fully himself, trotting alongside Priscilla down the rocky streets, plunging their skinny arms into the mail slot at the museum in order to turn the lock, climbing at midnight up the slender path beside the stream to a large flat stone they considered their own, reclining there shoulder to shoulder, talking without thinking while stars fell overhead. Priscilla encouraged in him a frankness; perhaps she encouraged it in everyone. He hadn't spoken without forethought since his long-ago beginnings as a liar. And he hadn't done it since.

David pulled the cord for the kitchen light, a foreign familiar coin cool in his palm, beneath which sat the house's modest hub, the table. Here was where he'd learned the rules of bridge, Mrs. Hart always recognizing his anxiety just before he made a fatal error in play. Here was where, after a morning of painting or plumbing or weeding or roofing, he joined Dr. Hart for lunch. Sandwiches on bread made by Mrs. Hart, soggy combinations David's mother would never have dreamed up, and his father wouldn't have tolerated. Hummus. Shredded carrot. Basil leaves. What the Hart family called stinky-feet cheese. Beer. And afterward the afternoon, a warm haze, a certain kind of clicking bug hopping drunkenly through the air . . . So strong was the sense of the past, so deep was his desire to have it restored, David for a moment forgot with whom he'd come today. Danielle. She was asking in her hoarse voice about the bathroom, about making a fire, about what they might do for dinner, which she called, like a man, "chow." David immediately set to work with the necessary homecoming moves: plugging in the refrigerator, pulling bedsheets from the upper cupboards, running the water long enough to clear rust from the lines.

"This is a cozy room," Danielle said, after she'd emerged from the bathroom, toilet gurgling behind her. She stood at the door to Dr. and Mrs. Hart's bedroom.

"My room's upstairs," David said. He had never yet spent a night on the adult Harts' bed. He was willing to break into their home, but he was superstitious about sleeping where they had slept, having sex where they had had sex. "The view is better up there," he said, which certainly must be true, now that the mansion next door had blocked any kind of view or light from the elder Harts' bedroom window.

He and Danielle went up together, single file on the steep, noisy treads. In the front bedroom, where he'd spent five summers with Priscilla, and then one, in secret, with teenage Lydia, when he'd been her brief lover, he sat on the edge of the bed and creaked open the window, which, like the one downstairs, had its own distinct complaint. Cool air poured in like water. The moon was rising over the mountains, a glow there opposite the lingering glow of the setting sun.

"Once I found a bat hanging in here," David said, "before we put up screens." This story wasn't his but Priscilla's. She'd screamed, the black thing attached to her wall like a leather glove.

"It's incredible," Danielle said, blinking cross-eyed as her face encountered a web. "Smart investment, buying this back when."

"It wasn't an investment," David said, bristling as he always did when this dull observation was made. "They didn't buy it to make a profit."

"Yeah, okay, but most people wouldn't have hung on to it. Most people would have cashed in." And then, backing up, she asked, "They?"

"Before I was around," he said.

Dr. Hart had allowed David the use of the house one winter when David had tried to move to Telluride. He'd failed at college, been refused at both his mother's and his father's now-separate homes with their newly constituted second families, the fleet of stepsiblings he scorned. He found a job with the Telluride transit company, driving away three days a week in a truck he could barely control, returning the next day with the goods he had accumulated down in the larger towns. Film reels, liquor, coal, hardware, groceries. Without him, Telluride might fail to function. He had felt like a legitimate local for the three months that this idyllic situation stuttered along, like Santa when he arrived and threw open the truck's back doors to reveal its bounty. Then in November he crashed, rolled off the hillside on black ice, a delivery of beer cans and lumber spilled four hundred feet, and that was the end of his time as town hero. The men who worked at the gravel quarry at the bottom of the hill made off with the spoils; David could only crawl from the cab and shout ineffectually, clutching his broken arm, gasping around bruised lungs: Stop thief! Although his rent was free, he had no money for utilities or food or fun. He'd had to return abjectly to Tucson, gas for his own vehicle siphoned with a section of garden hose from somebody parked in the street. He'd not known how to leave a house in the winter; the pipes froze and burst, and a brood

of skunks moved in under the floor. When the Harts returned, as they always did, on June first, they'd had to stay in a
hotel for a few days while the plumbing was replaced and ver-
min evicted. David also came to understand that he hadn't
been particularly tidy as a tenant, either. "I don't blame you,"
Dr. Hart assured him. "But I wouldn't bring any of this up
when you see Judy or the girls." With horror, David remembered the pornography he must surely have left under the upstairs bed. Who had discovered that?

Beside him Danielle sneezed, five loud times in a row. "I
may be allergic to your house," she said. "And don't you ever
bless anybody when they sneeze?" As she stepped cautiously,
duck-footed, down the steps ahead of him, David had an ugly
temptation to plant his foot squarely between her shoulders,
deliver a powerful kick.

"Why's your room painted purple?" she was asking. "You
some kinda gaylord?"

He'd known the Harts' schedule so well as to have engineered
a pity pickup, one season. They always arrived on the first of
June; he'd positioned himself, as hitchhiker, on the highway
just east of Rico. This would permit neither too much nor too
little time with the family.

He envisioned their drive as he made his own journey. He
hitched from Tucson days earlier, accepting a long, lucky ride
on a band bus with a bluegrass group booked at a bar in Telluride. Although that was his ultimate destination, he begged
off at Rico, spending two nights camping on Scotch Creek. It
snowed both nights; his small holey bivouac sack was frozen
every morning as he hatched himself from it. By the time the
Harts' white van appeared, David had been offered a half

dozen rides; had the Harts driven by without stopping, he might have later sought them out for revenge, torched their little piece of paradise.

But they pulled over, as he had trusted they would, and he managed to hide his exhausted lingering and near hypothermia long enough to pretend utter astonishment at this incredible coincidence. This was two years after his stint as Telluride transit driver; he claimed he had a job waiting him, a place to crash, friends looking forward to his arrival.

Lydia and her best friend were along with the parents, that year. The other Hart girls were coming later; they had jobs, boyfriends, summer school. Only Lydia was still fixed in the family routine. She would be a high school senior in the fall; her best friend was a dark beauty who greeted David with an automatic seductive move of her knees as she made room for him and his damp belongings. Swinging himself into the vehicle, he witnessed an exchanged glance between the Hart parents; he wished he could convince them he was someone worth admitting back into the warm circle of their family. Prodigal? Wasn't that a role he might claim?

"Pris is getting married," Lydia informed him over her friend's presence. "At the house. Me and Violet are maids of honor."

"Violet and I," said Mrs. Hart.

"Wow," David said, trying to hide his hurt feelings. Nobody had notified him. And now nobody was inviting him. A pregnant pause filled more than a few miles. The teenage beauty allowed her bare thigh to rest against David's, although all he could think of was Priscilla, his old best friend. When they left him at the bakery—No, he wouldn't take money, although he might stop by for a drink, later on—he began immediately devising some way to become integral to the wedding. Lawn boy? Caterer? He had until the summer solstice to figure it out.

And the friend, because girls were cutthroat, would be the key, leading Lydia to sneak him into the house, through that same back window and into her bedroom, that purple place, and into her bed, which had once been Pris's, in order to claim victory in having seduced him. Twenty-four to her seventeen years, he closed his eyes during sex, an apology running in his mind like a prayer. For a couple of weeks, he lived upstairs without the Hart parents' knowledge, like a stray cat, padding softly across the floors, climbing in and out of the back window, eating the food Lydia and her friend brought for him, crawling into bed beside her and lying when he said he'd always liked her best.

In the morning, David's eyes flew open. He'd heard the west window screech downstairs. He looked to the pillow next to him, where he expected to find Danielle, snoring mannishly away, but she was gone. Maybe she was climbing out of the house, finished with him.

Before he could pull on pants he heard the women meet, the vague scream of surprise on either side, the confrontation. This was backdrop to his swift calculations—through the upstairs window he would go, down to the car, out of town. But wait: no key! Then another flashing plan, the one story that would convince two people of his innocence. Palms flattening his hair, he wondered which sister it was, hoping for Lydia, who was the naughtiest Hart, the spoiled baby with whom he'd had shaming sex. He arrived at the bottom of the stairs just as its door was thrown open. Violet.

"David! What the *hell*? I wondered whose car that was, with the Arizona plates."

He moved to embrace her, which would have been acceptable

to placid Violet, except that she seemed somehow armored, wearing a backpack and carrying a shoe box.

"You're early," David chose to say, hoping that bluster might cover his trespass long enough to hustle Danielle out of earshot. "It's usually not until June first. This is Danielle, but I guess you met, I heard the yelling." Meanwhile, he made a whirl of himself, filling the kettle, lighting the gas. "I told your dad I was coming, but maybe he forgot to mention it?"

Violet didn't respond for a moment. She wasn't as fast on her feet as her sisters. Finally she said, "When did you tell Dad?"

"Maybe a month ago?"

Violet turned to Danielle. "What's your name, again?"

"Danielle," said Danielle. "Danielle Graham."

"I'm Violet, and this is my family's house. Welcome," she added, looking down Danielle's long bare legs under her nightshirt.

"Coffee?" David asked, having the absurd thought that this might not end badly, that Violet might allow him to escape utter humiliation. She had asthma, and sometimes disappeared from social exchanges in order to attend to her own respiration.

"Sure," Violet said, collecting breath, returning to them. "I don't know why I decided to drive all night."

"Lotta wildlife on the road?" David asked, fussing with filters, cups, potholders, avoiding Danielle's curious expression. Unlike other women, she had a patient observing personality, the same one that had been bemused by his childishness yesterday, the one that today studied him for clues as to what was going on. She was a nurse, and she didn't panic, not at the fact of bodily fluids, not at the arrival of an emergency, not at the sight of any human facial expression. She had seen them all. Would that get him off this hook today? Or more fully snag him?

"I almost hit a dozen deer," said Violet. "I was starting to think it was the same one, following me, throwing itself out in the road like a joke. And its sidekick, the same dumb skunk." She set her box on the table, shrugged out of the pack, then pulled her knitted duster around her and fell, sighing, into a chair. As a middle child, she'd been accustomed to being left out. She was neither oldest nor youngest, and neither was she a boy, which would have been a Hart novelty. Perhaps she felt redundant. And as for David, he'd first been Pris's friend, leaving Violet with little tagalong Lydia, and then it was Lydia with whom David was close. Violet read books; she sometimes grew bored and tattled. David had always thought her the dud Hart, the least necessary of the bunch. Along with the asthma, she had a wandering eye, her left, that nudged toward her skull. Because of imperfections, she had always seemed approachable, to be a *nice* person even if she wasn't, actually, a nice person. You might be misled by the wandering eye, as if her attention or intelligence or humanity also wandered, as if she had only to be half attended to.

Violet let him serve her coffee. Via chitchat, she and Danielle had discovered they were members of the same twenty-four-hour gym in Tucson, although Violet, lazy, rarely used the place, and Danielle's routine there was odd, given her shifts at the hospital.

"I'm here to plan Lydia's wedding," Violet addressed David. He forced himself to focus on the eye that reliably strayed. "Mom and Pris and Lyd are coming tomorrow, and then Pris's husband and kids the day after, with the fiancée."

David had seated himself at the head of the table, aware suddenly that his feet were bare and frozen, that he ought to have started a fire, that Violet hadn't mentioned her father's arrival time, that he was looking away from her face to the box she had set on the table, and that the label on it was that of a mortuary. There would be the wedding in a week, Violet was saying, but before then, before the men and children arrived, the women were going to spread Dr. Hart's ashes.

"What?"

"Dad died," Violet said, adding, apologetically, "last December. Pancreatic cancer. It was very unexpected." She was studying her coffee cup, which was one her mother had thrown, years ago; all of the cups and plates and bowls and trivets were of her making, mismatched seconds that she'd not been able to sell. There was a mug in the cupboard that had been David's, once upon a time.

He blinked at the white box. The box could have held shoes, or a pastry, perhaps letterhead. He felt specifically as if his body was repulsing the news of its true contents, like the wrong end of a magnet. The box on the table, the table in the house, the house in the town, the town in the canyon. And the man, in the box. David was dizzy. "Christmas was awful," Violet was saying, "but I think we're all getting used to it. We thought we'd take him up to Blue Lake. He always said that was his favorite spot. Although I'm not sure Mom can make it up there, anymore. Arthritis. She's a potter," she explained to Danielle, "so it's really especially cruel to have arthritis."

"I didn't know," David finally uttered. *Cruel*, he noted; maybe Violet had found religion, believed now in some figure who'd *cruelly* afflicted her mother with arthritis, Violet's own peculiar brand of rebellion against passionate atheist parents. "Why didn't you tell me?" he finally said, interrupting an exchange the women were having. Danielle, he'd overheard, learning it for the first time, was an orphan.

This time Violet performed her unique blink, one eye closing just before the other. "His obituary ran in the paper," she said at last.

They should have notified him, he thought, he should have been personally told. How was it they could not understand his affection for them all, his need especially of Dr. Hart?

Violet said, gently, "I think you probably ought to get out of here today. I don't really care that you're here, but it's not going to be cool with Mom or Pris."

He never got away with anything, David thought. If it wasn't an officer of the law actually pulling him over, it was a ticket in the mail, the indisputable evidence of his vehicle, flying by a camera, traveling many miles over the limit. What a person might eventually ask himself was, Why did he feel a need to break rules, tell lies, have things to get away with? Why couldn't he, in some definitive way, exhaust or outgrow childish defiance?

Upstairs, bundling their belongings back into their bags, David preempted what he believed would be Danielle's outrage by saying, "Don't say anything, okay? Just don't say a fucking word." She was his responsibility, witness to his humiliation, a woman with a horsey face—big square teeth, oversize jaw, hair she tossed like a mane—five hundred miles from Tucson, where she belonged. When he first saw her, he'd wondered if she was a former man. And now she was stripping the bed, methodically removing what they'd just last night spread out together.

"We have to wash these," she said. "It's the least." Downstairs, she assured Violet she would return the sheets by noon, leave them on the front porch. David glanced at the broken-handled mug atop the refrigerator, where the quarters were kept for the washeteria, and then his gaze crashed into Violet's, whose eyes had also gone automatically to the money.

While the sheets churned, David took Danielle to his favorite bar. The bartender was the same as previous years; she said hello without true recognition of him, the generic hospitality of a tourist town. He began to tell Danielle about the local character who rode his horse through these very doors, reliably, every year, when she stopped him.

"You already told me about that."

"I did?" He wondered if he'd also told her about being beat up behind this bar, if he'd trotted out that particular tall tale, the explanation for the divot in his forehead, from the time he'd taken a header in the alley and then blamed his scabs on two mythical men, his false beating. He touched his scar and raised his eyebrows.

"Yeah, I heard all about that, too. You know, I'm beginning to feel like I could diagnose you."

"I don't want a diagnosis." But then he discovered he'd rather know it than not. "All right, what?" He was ready to deny being a compulsive liar.

"You perseverate."

"I don't even know what that means."

"Not knowing doesn't exempt you. You live in the past, you revisit the same things over and over. This place is nothing but a big nostalgia trip for you. I don't know what the story is with you and that family, but—"

He inserted himself here, "Messy breakup with Violet," he lied. "The others—"

"I. Don't. Care," Danielle said. He could tell from her expression that she didn't. The details bored her. Neon beer lights turned her face green, then yellow. She was as mechanically unmoved as one of the machines she manned at the hospital, merely charting a human condition. "Just for a change, how about you ask me something," she proposed. "How about that?"

"Okay." David thought a moment. "How old was that other boyfriend?"

"Seventy," she said.

"Wow."

"My parents were spinning in their graves, a man as old as them. But I loved him with all my heart."

"Why?"

"Why?" Danielle leaned back, focusing on David's face. "Two questions in a row. It's a record. But whatever. I'd rather visit my weird situation than hear about yours. So I loved Franklin because, when I talked with him, I always imagined that we were wandering around in a big house, a big house with endless rooms, and every time I thought we might encounter some closed door, in one of those rooms, instead we would find an open one. Open doors, open doors, one after another. That's why I loved him."

David imagined the house, the wind circulating through those rooms, doors swinging on hinges.

"You can't smoke in here," the bartender came over to tell her, as soon as Danielle had lit up. "New law."

She suddenly laughed. "I love drinking before noon," she declared.

"It's a great high," David agreed. "The altitude really helps." He was tempted to tell her about the BIOTA club—*blame it on the altitude*—but was afraid he'd already done so.

Back at the washeteria, they couldn't locate their load of sheets and underwear. Every machine was empty, the row of washers with their open mouths, the row of dryers hollow bellies. "What the fuck?" David said. The floor was damp, a smell of chlorine, a cool breeze through a broken window. There was nobody to appeal to, the business a self-service one; upstairs were apartments, blameless tenants. "*You* tell her," he said to Danielle. She shrugged, willing. Her record was still relatively clean. He watched from the street as Danielle banged on the front door. When Violet answered it, she sneezed into the sunlight.

"*Bless* you," David heard. Then the two women went inside, the door banging behind them. David waited. He studied the garbage can, latched the clip so that bears wouldn't overturn it, swept with his foot the accumulation of concrete rubble at the bottom of the steps, swiped his hand on the creosote treated light pole just to have the odor on his fingers. Finally Danielle emerged.

"What took so long?"

"None of your beeswax. I wrote her a check, she can buy six hundred thread count. And then we exchanged numbers. We might share a trainer this fall."

"I don't actually know what you're talking about."

"You're in shock," Danielle said. "I've seen it before."

"Shock?"

"The dead dad?" *Duh,* her tone said.

Dr. Hart. David saw him suddenly at the kitchen table, a few of his university cronies alongside, bearded and complaining around the glowing wine bottle—bastard politicians, pretentious films, popular potboilers, historical rogues, critical tirades turned into a competitive sport—while Mrs. Hart floated around humming, serving food, salving childish wounds, changing records, locating pajamas and lighters and answers to all manner of esoteric inquiry, Who the hell was that poet? Where oh where was the blankie? Even then, when David was a young boy allowed to sit beside Dr. Hart, to sip at the wine if he wanted, to occasionally receive a fond pat on the back, he had recognized the difference between Dr. Hart and those others. Concerning a certain slim confounding novel that Dr. Hart had just the day before handed to David, one particular colleague had sneered, "Is that any good?" A gauntlet, made of contempt.

"Well," Dr. Hart had said, tipping his head thoughtfully—humble, shy, sagacious—"*I* liked it."

"I liked it, too!" David had declared, heart swollen with pride, confoundedness forgotten, pledging loyalty to his king. The table laughed, and he felt himself shrink back to proportion: skinny boy on a quaking stool, parrot or ventriloquist's doll, squawking sidekick to the great man.

Still, he *was* a great man.

"Keys?" Danielle said, out of nowhere. Apparently she had been waiting, palm out, fingers wiggling. "I should drive."

It snowed that night. They stayed at a lodge on the edge of town, down by the river, by the former train station where an outhouse had once burned. David opened his mouth to tell the tale, then couldn't remember whether he'd already told it, and didn't want to be scolded for perseverating. Diagnosis indeed. He did appreciate Danielle's accepting the change in plans. She did not seem shocked by his deceit, and she had a functioning credit card to offer at the front desk. David himself was consigned to cash, which he readily provided—what he had of it—promising to make up later what he owed.

"No reason to ruin the weekend," Danielle had said. ER nurse: David had to admire her unflinching willingness to roll with the punches. This, too, reminded him of a man. When she undressed, he watched from the back, mentally sheering off her long hair so as to see only the wide swimmer's shoulders and narrow hips, calves overmuscled, feet perhaps flat, certainly large. Then she dropped her hair and swung around, her breasts dispelling any lingering sense of manliness.

"I think it's only fair to tell you that I'm not using protection," she said, in the middle of sex.

David laughed, relieved to be in the throes of someone else's story, whatever weave of fabrication that allowed her to think her admission, at this late date, honorable. "Duly noted," he said.

"I was pregnant before, with the married man, and I aborted. I really wish I hadn't. It's my big regret. Franklin," she added.

The image of that man had been taking shape in David's mind, a dead man like Dr. Hart, and that's who he was thinking about as they finished having unprotected sex.

Danielle wore one of David's jackets when they went out walking on their third and last evening in Telluride. He was glad to do something for her, clutching at any small favor. They stopped by the trash cans outside the Hart house, snow falling once again around the warm glow of the window. The tentative green of spring would not be killed by this storm. It was a harmless piece of winter, an errant cold cloud making a pit stop here, committing no permanent damage. Inside were the women, the mother and three daughters; Judy Hart still wore her braid down her back, silver now against her bronze face. She smiled, sitting at the head of the table, facing the window, where she would see only her own reflection. Others crossed the small space, moving from stove to sink to refrigerator, a tight choreography with which David was intimately familiar. But now strangers filled the space, two men, and two little boys, Pris's children, who would no doubt be put to sleep in the back bedroom upstairs, under the drawings made by their mother and aunts. And by David. His scrawlings were up there, too.

"Looking in like this reminds me of a snow globe," Danielle

said, quiet and low. "Except we're in the snow, and they're in the globe." There'd been drinks with dinner; David held her hand happily, quietly. He wished Priscilla would step onto the porch and discover his happiness; he needed to display it, to prove it. At least the sons-in-law hadn't taken Dr. Hart's place at the head of the table. At least that hadn't happened.

He saw Lydia embrace one of the men, from the back, lean over him and put her face beside his. Her hair was the same bleached straggle from childhood. It was her mother who had discovered David and Lydia in bed, one morning long ago, only days before Pris was to be married, when David was officially an adult and Lydia officially not. Judy Hart opened the door after rapping briefly. "Lyd?" Then closed her eyes at the sight of David's bare chest. She hadn't been angry; she was a kind, kind woman, whose disappointment was far harder to bear than her anger. "Let's not tell your father," she suggested to her daughter, still standing there at the door, eyes averted. "I'm afraid he won't understand."

Danielle asked him, "Do you wish you were in there, instead of out here?"

"No," David said. And then he was reviewing his response. It was a lie—or else it wasn't.

WE AND THEY

I.

We were the neighborhood atheists, famous all around the block for being bad. Our large family was not the result of Catholic faith and we didn't attend Blessed Sacrament church or school, despite the fact that it was a stone's throw away from our house. We threw stones, so we knew. Every weekday morning the children would pass by our home, girls in plaid pleats, boys in blazers; by day's end they'd be askew as scarecrows, suit jackets tied around the neck by their arms, knee socks sagging at the ankles. BS, the school was called. "BS, BS, BS!" we could shriek, cursing yet never in trouble. BS! It seemed these children had to put up with it all the livelong day. We liked to envision them, formally clothed, at the mercy of the nuns, those archetypal old maids, brandishing their legendary yardsticks, taking out their sex-starved torture on their well-appointed students. No wonder everyone left BS so bedraggled.

Our parents—one a lapsed Baptist, the other a disenchanted Episcopalian, both with doctorate degrees—complained about the Catholics in two modes: the generally philosophical (over-population! sexism! idolatry!); and the locally inconvenient (Blessed Sacrament's endless tolling bells, and the traffic, cars parked perennially up and down the street). These conjoined when the church expanded—they didn't practice birth con-trol, of course they needed more and more and more of everything!—and tore out two historic homes to build a larger parking lot. My mother cried when those houses fell. She stood in the street weeping at the sight of the wrecking ball. At our dinner table there was no winning for the Catholics. We de-spised them, and our most proximate target was the Pierces, perfect embodiment of all that was wrong.

Naturally, the Pierces disapproved of us, too. For one thing, our father had been divorced, and the two oldest children in our family were the products of that first marriage. Moreover, his first wife had been Jewish, so those two sons could claim their Judaic heritage (although they—lazy, irreverent—never did). Also, we were obviously politically liberal; the bumper stickers on our (old, foreign) cars all proclaimed affiliation with causes the Pierces could not abide. We didn't think war was healthy for children or other living things; we wished that the military had to hold bake sales to finance their bombs. Every four years a new Democratic candidate's name would replace the faded name of the last loser we'd promoted on our vehi-cles and in our yard. We attended Wichita's public schools—College Hill Elementary, Roosevelt Junior High, and East High—instead of BS. My parents taught at the city's com-muter college and threw loud parties. If our guests parked in front of the Pierces' house, we would hear about it the next day—early. Bottles busted on their sidewalks must surely have been our fault; the beloved family cat they could not now find had certainly been stolen or run over or sacrificed in a satanic ritual by the likes of us.

Our feud with the Pierces reached a fever pitch upon the arrival of the two youngest members of our household, the adopted mixed-race brother and sister. They showed up near Christmas in 1975, like gifts, our projects to see us through adolescence and my parents' midlife crises. "Nigras," the Pierces called them, as in "Where'd you get the little nigras?" It was Helena and Celeste Pierce, holding two of their nephews, who stood behind the bars of the wrought-iron fence that chilly winter morning. My sister and I stood scowling in our front yard; what the hell were we to do with such ignorant unkindness? Weren't these Pierces violating some rule in the big Catholic handbook? We each held a small black child in our arms, our new relations done up in holiday velvet; otherwise we might have hefted stones and waited for the traffic to clear so that we could hurl them at our neighbors' foolish skulls. We were, all of us Landerses, awfully good aims.

"Prejudiced!" we screamed back. "Racist!" Early in life our mother had sat us down for a talk about race relations. Then, we'd been guilty of repeating what we claimed we'd learned from one Pierce or another when chanting Eenie-Meenie-Miney-Moe, the part about catching "a nigger by the toe." We were instructed to substitute "tiger" for the forbidden word. And to try to correct anyone who was savage enough to say otherwise. Our mother's earnest instruction hung between me and Portia that Christmas of 1975; we'd never been comfortable trying to educate our peers. True, we'd been as uninformed, once upon a time; we, too, had used the N-word in ignorance. "Some people," our Pollyanna mother told us, "simply don't know what they're saying is offensive. They might whistle 'Dixie' without thinking about what it stands for, just because they heard it somewhere and thought it was a catchy tune. Or they might hang the Confederate flag, just because it was a tradition, something they didn't think about. So these same people might use the N-word not knowing. Do you see?" We could see, when she described it; our mother was famous for over-explaining her points, patient to the point of patroniza-tion with us, her children, as well as with the remedial readers she taught at night school.

Yet how likely was it we could effectively communicate the intricacies of civil rights to the young Pierces making faces at us this Christmas day from the safety of their front yard? Never mind the reinforcements back in the house proper, the two-to-one ratio of Pierces to Landerses that was always a factor. In an out-and-out brawl, they'd take us easily. Traffic cut through this current standoff, and what those drivers would have seen if they were looking was that on either side of First Street two preteen girls holding toddlers in their arms were shouting insults at the pair across the street. "Racists!" we yelled at the girls. "Nigras!" they taunted, shaking their hind ends within the shelter of their wrought-iron fence. "Lookit the purple nigras!"

We called our adopted siblings "the little fellas," and they joined us when they were one and three years old, both in di-apers, wide-eyed, terrified, their white father incarcerated for having murdered their black mother. The fatal argument was not to be discussed; these toddlers had apparently witnessed it. They were called Otis and Angel, not names my parents would have chosen but certainly not changeable since they were among the only words Otis knew, his and his sister's name.

We didn't like our neighbors, but we envied their number. It was possible that my parents' adoption of Otis and Angel was influenced by the Pierces. The perfect presentation they never failed to flaunt, stair-step children, a sea of yellow hair and creamy skin, straightened teeth and uniforms. Over there, they favored saints when they christened their children: Mary, Michael, Paul, Teresa, John, Christopher, Jude, James, Helena, Celeste, Luke, Jason, and Matthew. As houses went up for sale across the street, the family pounced. They took over the block, tore down dog pens and garden boundaries, little privet hedges and fences, so that a common yawning yard emerged, on which they laid sod, installed a swimming pool, and rolled a tennis court. Were they a different kind of family, you might have labeled the place a commune, but with them it was more like a country club, the entire block across from ours, exclusive Club Pierce, enclosed by its tall black iron fence, a full perimeter cage with posts like upturned swords, spiked like the boundary of a foreign country or a prison yard. The children used keys to enter.

Only Jude presented a hitch. He had been born with Down syndrome, eyes off kilter, tongue too large for his mouth, face lit always with a surprised smile. He was the middle child; the Pierces had not been daunted. Instead, they soldiered on and had six more. Thirteen children: unthinkable. Nearly twice our strength. Plus, they perpetuated their own teams. By the time Luke was born, Mary was pregnant; her own children, and Michael's and Teresa's that followed, simply supplemented the family coffers, a sequence of grandbabies joining the uninterrupted assembly line of Pierces, one blond mop after another. They believed in evening constitutionals, which often coincided with my own family's cocktail hour. In the summer dusk, we watched from our porch swing and ratty rattan chairs, holding up highballs or Hawaiian Punch as they passed, a parade of strollers and full-bred dogs, every Pierce a freckled white-blond specimen, each perfect except Jude, who, alone, always raised his hand and sunny indiscriminating face to us.

If we ever wanted to feel appalled by our antagonism, we had only to see that boy's starfish hand and optimistic smile.

The condition of adopting Otis and Angel was that brother and sister not be separated; their family members on both sides had long ago written off the doomed relationship between murdered mother and felon father. On paper—in fact, *newspaper*, where we first saw the children's picture—you'd never dream of separating the one-year-old girl and her three-year-old brother. In the picture, the boy held his baby sister wrapped in a blanket so that her face didn't show. He looked up through ringlets of hair with a pair of enormous pleading eyes. Clearly, he would hold onto this baby until someone trustworthy arrived to relieve him of the duty. He loved his sister, and his obvious love for her was what made you want to save them both.

"I've never seen an uglier infant," my half brother Cecil said. We were driving home from the agency, he and Stuart and I in the car following the sedan where the rest of our family rode. My half brothers, ages nineteen and seventeen, had been invited along to formally celebrate and seal the adoption. I was eight, insanely glad to be riding with the big boys, hysterical in the presence of their mordant wit.

"Now the murder is starting to make more sense," said Stuart.

"In the paper, she looked normal," I said. "But then in person . . ."

"That's how they get you," Cecil agreed. Someone was always out to "get" Cecil and Stuart and our father. "That's how they get you," they would say knowingly to one another. In the beginning, the three of them had lived without the rest of us. We heard about those years now and then, references as if to a secret society, a brotherhood that had been eclipsed by the arrival of our mother and then us, eclipsed but not forgotten by its three exclusive members.

Later at home when I said publicly that the baby was undeniably the ugliest we'd ever seen, looking to Stuart and Cecil for confirmation, I was not only sent to my room, but given the most dismissive of sniffy looks from the two of them. "I am a*shamed* of you," my mother hissed before closing my bedroom door.

When you closed doors in anger, in shame, at our house, the plaster trickled inside the walls. It was the sound of despair.

Otis was a beautiful child. His skin was smooth and caramel colored, his eyes like big butterscotch disks, his hair soft and coiled in ringlets into which you couldn't help wanting to twirl your fingers. Here was gorgeous genetic alchemy, a breathtaking specimen, sweet, even-tempered, sensitive, charming, protective of his sister, quick-witted and kind and impish—could there have been a more perfect child? And naturally, and unfortunately, his parents had not stopped while they were ahead. Wasn't that the perpetual human condition, not stopping while you were ahead?

The second time around, they concocted Angel, her name surely an appeal to heaven, a futile prayer. The parents were neither ugly nor pretty, but whatever small morsels of comeliness either possessed had been totally spent in Otis, leaving Angel bankrupt.

Her skin was eggplant hued like her mother's, yet pimpled

like her father's. From him she'd also received the small skull, close-set eyes, and negligible chin and lips. Square in the center of her face was her mother's large flat nose. She'd been born early and underweight, an aggrieved colicky baby who had never really done what the doctors called *thriving*. Later she developed eczema and was prone to desperate scratching fits that made her look possessed, plagued by invisible demons crawling on her flesh, or perhaps merely mad at herself. Moreover, she seemed gloomy, was easily wounded, walked around suspicious of others, clinging to her belongings and scowling when touched, profoundly impolite and averse to being corrected, no matter how gently—as if her unattractiveness, contrary to conventional wisdom, were more than skin-deep.

Her first sentence: "Leave me *'lone!*"

It was hard to like her. Our family, from the beginning, made a pact to love her, which was easier. Loving someone was a gesture like jumping into a black hole, and its terms precluded all sorts of requirements that were essential in other relationships, such as pleasure or reciprocity.

Most important of all was Otis's devotion to Angel. It was through him that we'd first come upon her, and it was through him that we continued to endure her. His was a character capable of sustaining two. His trembling smile alone would have earned him our fierce indivisible support.

Loving someone as unlikable as Angel also bought our family a lot of moral high-handedness. It was a special card and we each had our own rendition. We sometimes used it like a credit card, and other times played it like a trump. How we liked to spurn the bigots and racists. How we liked to not answer the unasked questions about our unusual family constitution. Unlike our hypocritical neighbors, those Pierces who thought nothing of overpopulating the world and depleting its natural resources, we would take in the already-existing children, house the needy, blend the races. "Nigra," they taunted through the black fence bars of their compound across the street. "Little niglettes!" and we clung ever more proudly to our new charges.

II.

Angel's best friend in our house was Jackie, the black maid. Our parents didn't believe in hiring a housekeeper; they were of the opinion that cleaning up after yourself was one of the cornerstones of conscientiousness. But Jackie had been a maid in our mother's family until Nana had been put in the nursing home. Jackie needed a job; we were obligated. Two tenets competed—the one dictating that a person, a family, clean up after itself, and the one that said you didn't bail on a commitment. Jackie had long ago stopped being a very good maid. She was our grandmother's age, roughly, and could no longer see much of the grime she was supposed to be getting rid of. She couldn't lift the furniture or wash the dishes; glasses and plates regularly shattered, escaping her quaking hands. Once she had also cooked the occasional loaf of bread or pot of stew, but the dials on the stove began confusing her—on, off, high, low—and so she mostly tottered around the place stacking paper. That she could do. If you brought the laundry downstairs, she could sort it, generally, and run the machine, more or less, and then take the warm clothing out of the dryer, separating it into piles. Stacking, folding, separating. These were her chores. Never mind that the back door was left wide open on the coldest days, or that the books in the library were shelved according to color and height. The wool sweaters had to be hidden or they would be laundered and shrunk. The stemware had to be washed and put away before she arrived. Important papers—bills, contracts, grades—had to be tucked into drawers or they would disappear in the heaps of newspaper or magazines or catalogs. She was seventy when we adopted Angel and Otis, far too old to look after toddlers. Yet she was the only one in the house who knew what to do with Angel's hair.

Angel would stand trapped between Jackie's knees, her hair being tamed into cornrows across her head. Jackie's burled fingers worked easily through the hair, pacifying a wildness there that was reflected in Angel's face. She frowned, that girl; she was born with worry wrinkles etched upon her brow. Behind Jackie's thick smudgy glasses, her eyelids lifted and lowered slowly. She couldn't see what she was doing but she was doing it very well, making order out of chaos, stroking balm on something inflamed. Angel let Jackie touch her as a mother ought to have been permitted. Our mother was not allowed this. Like us, she could only witness it from a distance.

When Jackie died—one day en route to our house, some crucial vessel in her heart or head went tragically *pop!*, sending her vehicle crashing into a light pole—Angel was ten. Her response was anger, predictably enough, but an anger so specific that each of us reached the same conclusion: She believed we'd killed the woman. And done it with the sole intention of punishing Angel.

Her life was about being punished. When I was older I surmised that her white father perhaps doubted his paternity of this dark, dark child; he might have used Angel as evidence in the crazed case that led to killing her mother. Could you expect a person to fully recover from such a situation? Could you complain that she seemed to have an absence of joy? Of light?

Angel did not possess a sense of humor that any of us recognized. We teased, and she didn't understand teasing. You could think it was on purpose, her refusal to be jolly, her declining to perceive that we played pranks as a way of showing our affection, her rejection of our overtures. We tricked one another, we were sarcastic. We loved irony and gallows humor. We whistled through the graveyard. It was the way we got along. But she insisted on having her feelings hurt, on consistently being injured by the slightest sideways remark. Only Otis could make her smile at her own foibles, and this reluctantly. I don't think she meant to act as our collective conscience, but it was the role she ended up playing, the wet blanket, the drag, the bad sport, the tattletale. Until she was old enough to acquire some bad habits of her own, she spent her time notifying my mother of ours. When we were late coming home, when we smelled of cigarettes, when there'd been a secret overnight guest in one of our bedrooms. We hadn't liked her name when she arrived—ridiculous, something you'd name a poodle as a joke—and then later it came to embody all forms of judgment: The Angel, we called her. The Angel on High.

Years later I would see her walking home from East High, always alone. She hunched herself into her navy pea jacket, one she'd found in the attic, and that she wore proudly. Should we tell her it had been an *authentic* navy coat, that it had gone to the Atlantic during World War II on our father's back? Probably not. She did not wish to claim our kin, not in the house, not anywhere. She maybe had no peers, I thought, not anybody who was very much like her. But wasn't that the situation with every high-school-age person? The solitude? The utter conviction of a nihilistic universe? Yet all of the rest of us had had friends. Our parents prided themselves on operating the fun house, the place where teenagers felt welcome, accepted, the choice location for holing up, for hanging out, for feeling like they could be themselves. "Have a party!" our mother would plead. "Invite anyone you like!" They went out of their way to understand our friends, to be sympathetic, kind adults in a world of the unkind, the selfish. Our mother had all sorts of creative plans for gatherings we could throw, transforming one of the basement rooms into a dance hall, or making a haunted house with the ancient coal chute opened as the scary entrance. Our parents were by nature social beings, gregarious and empathic, rabble-rousers, peace marchers, block partiers. By and large, our friends envied us. We all lived at our home well beyond the time that most people fled theirs.

But Angel never wanted to have friends visit. We embarrassed her, we deduced; we were to be avoided. She skulked in and out after school, leaving notes, coming home on time but from where, we couldn't really be sure. If you pushed, she might mention a name. "Candy," she finally came up with. That was the name of her best friend.

"Invite Candy over!" my mother crowed. "Let's have her to dinner."

"She won't come," Angel said.

"Well, ask her first and then let her decide," my mother persisted. "Does she eat meat?"

"She eats meat," Angel said, suddenly smiling to herself. We should have known this meant something.

We couldn't ask if Candy was white or black; we couldn't ask anything of Angel, really. On the designated day—twice postponed by her work schedule (she flipped burgers at the Arby's across from East High)—Candy was due at six thirty. My mother and father had cooked together, recipes they had pulled from a collection of cooking magazines and that were, always, the fare when guests came to dinner. Not really teenager food, the meal was probably meant to indicate their honest efforts at making Angel's friend—and, by extension, Angel—feel special.

The doorbell rang at six fifty. I answered, finding a middle-aged black woman in a hairnet standing on the porch. I assumed she was Candy's mother, and looked behind her, to the street where a dark blue sedan was parked, for Angel's friend. "Hi," I said, "I'm Angel's sister." When the woman scowled, I added, "Adopted sister."

"You're adopted or she's adopted?"

"She is."

The woman nodded, the two of us looking around each other in search of someone else, waiting for the next thing. "I'm sorry to be late," she said.

"That's okay," I said.

Still, for a few beats it did not occur to me to assign this strange woman her identity. This was Angel's friend Candy. Candy was not a teenager but a woman. A woman who worked at Arby's near East High. A woman who'd just gotten off her shift and, now that I was looking *at* her rather than *around* her, I saw was still wearing the telltale brown and orange uniform. She was here to eat dinner with my family. "Come in," I said. "Let me find Angel," I told her, leaving her in the living room holding her handbag as I raced through the dining room, where Portia was setting the table, to the kitchen, where my father was wrapping bananas in sliced ham and my mother was shredding Swiss cheese into biscuit dough. The greenery in this strange meal was asparagus in pineapple lemon sauce. The dinner was never served without all of its parts. Even the most finicky of the family enjoyed it, and guests always made positive surprised noises as they chewed at the stuff.

"Is it her?" my mother asked. I said it was, then added that she was a lot older than we had thought.

"How old is that?" my father asked.

"Old," I said, just before Portia brought our guest into the kitchen.

"This is Candy," my sister said. "Where's Angel?"

Since Candy was my parents' age, I thought it only reasonable that Portia and I go scout out our sister. Had the situation been reversed—a teenage guest—our parents would have left her with us.

Around the table that evening sat most of the family, minus Stuart (graduate school, Rhode Island) and Cecil (shacking up across town with a stripper). I was in college, my third year pursuing a major that would land me in my parents' shoes, if I was lucky: teaching English composition. Portia was floundering, still living at home despite having graduated high school. It was she who had discovered Cecil's girlfriend's job as a pole dancer, showing up at the Kitty Cat Club to audition for the position herself. Her failure and lostness were making her fat; she performed the jobs that our old housekeeper Jackie once had, and about as effectively. Otherwise, she watched TV and snacked. Raymond, the youngest white Landers, was a senior at East, where Otis was a junior and Angel a freshman.

Through the years, there had been various configurations of alliances at our house. First it had been the big boys— Cecil and Stuart—against us, the younger three. Or sometimes it was boys versus girls, Portia and Angel and I laying claim to the larger bathroom with the tub, forcing the boys into the basement shower. Now and then it was brainiacs

against athletes, or Mom's defenders against Dad's. Angel and
Otis had been their own little subset, separate from us the
way Cecil and Stuart sort of were. That couldn't be helped.

At the table that night, however, a new division popped up:
Angel and Candy against all the rest of us. If it had been an
athletic match, Otis might have been the referee, committed
to neither side, but knowledgeable about both, sitting judi-
ciously, perhaps a little anxiously, in between a few opposi-
tional forces.

Candy lifted a peel of ham from around its banana, leaving
the fruit naked as a penis on her plate. She made quite a face.
Angel burst into laughter. The rest of us also made faces—big
surprised question marks on our foreheads. Angel never
laughed. As a group, we decided not to be hurt about Candy's
rudeness (this was a certified gourmet meal; it came out of the
magazine named that same thing), but to be inspired by Angel's joy. After all, we'd tried for years to get her to laugh at us,
to mock with us. We were utterly game for being the butt of
a good joke.

"This what the white people eat?" asked Candy. She was
way too comfortable, as a guest, and I gave myself permission
to dislike her. I had only recently acknowledged that I did not
like Angel. I loved her, but I didn't like her. My lack of affection for Candy was not nearly as prickly as it was concerning
Angel; in fact, I more or less luxuriated into it, as one might
any forbidden naughtiness—a huge dessert, a dirty movie.
Candy said, "I always knew it'd be different on this side of the
tracks."

"Which side?" I said, eager for the challenge. My mother
gave me what we all called the hairy eyeball.

"The rich side," she said.

"We aren't rich."

Candy gave me a droll look, meant to make me reconsider what I'd said. But we weren't rich, despite the big house in the neighborhood that had, by then, 1990, taken a surprising upswing. The Pierces had continued to purchase and rehabilitate homes across First Street, and Blessed Sacrament maintained its steady (growing) population and popularity. *They* were affluent; *we* weren't. Hadn't she noticed the cracks in the walls? The sticky, chipped surface of the dining table? The vague odor of dog? I could personally tour her around the house and yard, show her the dripping faucets, the water stains, the rotting wood of the carport, the pigeon guano all over the drive, the pieces of tile roof that had fallen and smashed, the patch of poison ivy and the tangle of broken bikes and swings. We were schoolteacher shabby, hippie holdovers. Crumbling Acres, our dad called the place. "Freaks," the neighbors had named us.

"Where do you live, Candy?" asked my mother. Despite being a noisy group, we weren't question-askers, in general, in my family. We told stories, instead, and they were successes or failures depending on the degree to which the rest of us found them amusing. We were conversation snobs, in fact, all of us except Angel (she sat sullen through most meals, poking at her food and watching the clock) and our mother, who'd grown up as the baby of a group of nice but dull people who coddled her. She had manners, our mother; she smiled and asked questions the rest of us would have denounced as deadening small talk.

Candy said, "Why? You gonna visit me?"

Again, Angel laughed.

"Ha ha," Candy said, "I'm just fooling with you. I live down by the root canal." Now it was my brothers' turn to laugh, both Otis and Raymond: the root canal! In the eighties the city had constructed a freeway and a giant drainage ditch beneath. It was named the canal route, and there'd been a flurry of civic indignation flying on the pages of the newspaper. "Down there with the other poor folk."

Hers might have been one of the houses suffering under the onus of eminent domain; this would have given my parents an opportunity to extend righteous indignation on her behalf. But she went on to say that the root canal had most likely increased the value of her home since her drug-dealing neighbor had been forced to move away. Now she had only vagrants to contend with, those who lived under the overpasses, taking advantage of the thin trickle of green water sliding over the canal's concrete floor. "When I'm gonna meet the boyfriend?" Candy suddenly said to Angel.

We all turned toward Angel. She wasn't laughing now. Now, she looked just like she always did: smoldering, held hostage in a house of fools. She snarled something Candy apparently understood, giving her a knowing "Uh-huh" as a response.

Boyfriend?

"You met him, haven't you?" Candy said to Otis. And it was clear from Otis's reaction that he had indeed met the boyfriend. Even blushing, caught and guilty, he was still beautiful, our Otis, still the favorite child. I think one of the reasons neither Portia nor I had moved away yet was because we would have missed Otis. He liked to sit on our beds and hear about our days. He complimented our clothing and found us fascinating. He enjoyed riding along on errands, making entertaining comments, giving us heartfelt, unexpected affection in the form of hugs or homemade gifts. He was everybody's favorite and nobody begrudged him the place of honor. It was as if we'd elected him, as if we'd formed a fan club around him. So no one would hold it against him, keeping a secret. Only he seemed to find it awful. He gave Angel a frightened glance. And the look she fired back merely increased his misery.

"May we be excused," Angel said, shoving back her chair and rocking the table. She took her own and Candy's plates to the kitchen, where she made a racket running water over their surfaces, then tossing them into the dishwasher. "We're going out," she shouted from in there.

Candy had risen from the table casually, maybe a little tiredly. She was thick in the waist, her cleavage pushed up beneath her hideous uniform. When she passed my chair the smell of Arby's followed, old grease and the food that went into it. "Bye everybody," she said at the door. And they were gone.

Poor Otis. We all looked at him. There he was with those mournful eyes, still after all these years waiting for somebody to relieve him of the burden of his baby sister.

III.

"I saw him shoot her," Otis told me, one evening near Christmas of his senior year in high school. He was referring to his real father, and what he'd done to his real mother. Otis and I had been paging through college catalogs; he was being heavily recruited, which made him sad; he didn't want to leave home. His biological mother had been an honors student at North before she'd quit to get married, have children, lose her life. His biological father had died on death row of hepatitis before he could take his turn on the table. Neither child had ever wanted to visit him, although our parents, being who they were, had made the offer. "I sort of remember that night she died," Otis told me. "I sort of do, and I sort of think I invented it from what everybody told me." He'd climbed into his sister's crib. There'd been chasing, and there'd been deaf-ening sparks. That's where the neighbors found him, when the noise of the fight and the gunshots finally drew them out. There was Otis, hugging Angel, staring out between the bars of her bed.

They'd lived in the same neighborhood Candy had, a house now bulldozed, nothing there now but an immaculate slab of concrete.

"I just remember that I was in Angel's crib," Otis said. "I was so embarrassed to be in a baby bed."

"Honey," I said. No one could bear his tears.

Angel's boyfriend turned out to be a Pierce. He looked like all the rest, cloned from some perfect original model, another in the assembly line—but he was, apparently, their prodigal son, a self-declared black sheep. Jason: he'd been kicked out of Blessed Sacrament, then out of Capon Mount Carmel, next out of Southeast, and had landed, finally, at the bottom of the heap: East High. Which is where he befriended Angel, out behind the vo-tech building, smoking pot.

Poor Otis, who had to tell us this on the bizarre evening that Candy had come to dinner. The secret had given him a rash on his neck, which he worried with his fingers. Portia and Raymond and I sat out in the driveway, his audience late at night that fateful spring, witnessing our beloved brother painfully betray his millstone sister. The problem was that Angel was pregnant. So predictable. Now what?

Raymond, eighteen years old—still a virgin, we were sure—scowled, perhaps evaluating his own relative lateness of bloom. "Is she sure he's the father?" he blurted. We gave him the notorious family withering glance.

"We'll take her for an abortion," Portia and I declared. Our parents need never know; we were adults, we could raise the money, drive the car, ferry the girl from trouble to safety easily, so easily. I'd had an abortion, Portia had had one, no doubt our mother had had one, back when, during some summer of love. It simply wasn't the end of the world, we assured Otis. It was so easy.

"She doesn't believe in abortion," Otis said. As a group, our mouths hinged open, the stunned confusion hanging there like a common word we might all utter. She was fifteen; did she have a right to *believe* in anything? Wasn't that kind of a big-person claim, *belief*? Had none of our bleeding-heart liberalism or feminist-empowerment rhetoric rubbed off? Couldn't we talk her out of it?

No, as a matter of fact, we could not. We tried. And she enjoyed our efforts. It might have been the first time in our life together that she relished conversation with us. First Portia and I approached her.

"You'll get fat," we said. "You'll have to drop out of school." She would be ostracized, embarrassed, shunned, ridiculed. To each of these she listened dully, letting us know she either already suffered such things or looked forward to the eventuality. We weren't prognosticating anything new or loathsome.

"*I* like babies," she said, as if we didn't.

When we failed to make progress, we were forced to notify our mother.

Our mother had faith in literature the way others had faith in God or America; she put herself in its hands the way patients did their physicians; she prescribed it, she preached it. She was ever-ready with a book title, when the occasion arose. As youngsters, we'd been required to read *The Bluest Eye*, in order to understand Angel's future issues with her race. During my suicidal junior year, I was given *The Bell Jar*, just so I'd know that my mother knew what I was going through. When

Portia had no boyfriends, my mother handed over *Rubyfruit Jungle*. "She thinks I'm a lesbo!" my sister shrieked. For weeks, we called her the crack snacker.

What would our mother recommend to Angel now? Not that Angel would read it, but what book would lend itself to this dilemma? We were surprised to find our mother stumped. No book, merely tears. She cried and cried, our naive, stunned mother; she understood this event as a signature failure on her part. She had not parented this child well, she had proven to herself that all the best intentions in the world could not prevent disaster. She wept not only for this personal letdown but for all that it stood for: If she, doing everything within her power, working with all her heart and soul, couldn't improve the life of one black female child in late-twentieth-century America, what hope was there for the world?

This dismal sight elicited from Angel only boredom. She looked upon our mother's heaving shoulders and rolled her eyes. She jumped up when a horn blasted outside: Candy had come in her nasty sedan to take her away.

Nobody at the Pierce house had a clue, not even the boyfriend, the black sheep, the bad seed, the father. Jason.

He'd been a naughty youngster, that one, notorious for not exactly breaking into neighborhood homes but sneaking into them, and not for *removing* things *from* them so much as merely *moving* things *within* them. Doors in our neighborhood were often left unlocked, and, except for ours, the houses were full of valuables. Jason couldn't exactly get caught because he wasn't exactly guilty. Brazenly, casually, he'd walk in, lift a vase or wallet or record, place it elsewhere, rearrange the medicine cabinet contents or turn on a faucet, place all the mantel photos on their faces, then walk out. Did he feel entitled? Was he merely curious? Could it be criticism? Hard to say. He seemed to want to play the role of poltergeist. And surely that was part of what attracted Angel to him.

He humiliated his family, he enraged his father. He'd gone through cars the way he'd gone through schools, crashing and burning, earning himself tickets and hearings and fines and failures to pass various tests. Neighborhood rumor held that next year he'd be consigned to military school in Roswell, New Mexico. Ship him out, shape him up.

Angel asked only Otis to go with her to the Pierces' when her pregnant mind remained unchanged and her secret could no longer be kept. They crossed First Street on a Sunday afternoon, cars still clearing from the morning's service at Blessed Sacrament. It was April, blustery, pink buds on the pink-bud trees, sticky blue eggshells on the sidewalks beneath the wind-shook nests of robins. Angel hadn't asked a favor from any of us for a long while. Her brother couldn't have said no.

At the bars of the Pierce gate they rang the bell, spoke over the intercom, then were met halfway up the path by Jason, who grinned to see them there. Stoned, already headed toward the worst-case scenario—his future as a buzz-cut boy in a faraway school without girls—he thought he had nothing to lose.

Jude Pierce was the oldest child still living in the main house. He would always need caring for. When his parents died, he would move in with one of his brothers or sisters; there would always be a spot for him nearby. He was setting the dining room table, helping with preparations for the family meal that would come later, two dozen attendees, all of them his kindly kin. During the clumsy conversation that took place in the parlor, Jude moved around the table murmuring to himself, "Two forks left, little then big, one knife, one spoon, and *you* spoon, for ice cream, on top." It was a tune. It was his chore. He smiled sincerely to see Angel and Otis; they waved reflexively in his direction. Mrs. Pierce looked back sadly to our siblings. She'd suffered a stroke a few years earlier; her left eye slanted down, a permanently poignant expression even when she smiled. Her husband still had enough energy to fuel an empire, spawn an army, but Mrs. Pierce seemed depleted, spacey, surrounded by something intangible, like lovely music, or toxic gas. Otis didn't want to bring her bad news.

"Your house is pretty," Angel said, glancing around. This place would awe her as our place never had. All of our effort—and what she really wanted was opulence, tradition. Antiques, wallpaper, decorative floral arrangements, framed landscapes of bucolic nature instead of our art, the crude nudes and splattery abstracts. She stood before the ticking grandfather clock, admiring its polite quarter-hour chime.

"Thank you," said Mrs. Pierce in response to the compliment. On the doorway between parlor and dining room was a series of crayoned lines, dozens of them, names and dates alongside. The growth chart of the monstrous family. Mrs. Pierce had followed Angel's glance. "Now, I can't just paint over that, can I? But look at how dirty the wall . . ." Her stroke had left her conversation filled with ellipses. From the kitchen, on the other side of the dining room, came the clatter of cooking, pans, voices, water running, laughter. The Pierce women were fixing Sunday dinner. The rich odor of long-cooked beef filled the place, that, and furniture polish, history, the calm sound of a ticking clock.

"Let me tell you right off that I do not support school fundraisers," Mr. Pierce said as he entered from another room, hands in his pockets. "Simply a policy, nothing personal. I pay taxes—"

"No sir," Otis said. "We're not collecting money. Our mother doesn't let us do that, either."

The Pierces might have been surprised to hear that our two families agreed on anything. But our parents never permitted any of us to canvass the neighborhood begging for funds. We knew better than to bring home candy or wrapping paper or scented candles. Jason Pierce leaned back on a fragile settee, legs spread, smirk on his face, hair a length that surely made his father want to grab and yank him upright by it. He may have believed he was clued in on the circumstances of this visit, revelation of his illicit fraternizing. He'd maybe enjoyed the thought that he could still astonish his mom and dad, still injure them anew. A black girlfriend would send them around yet another bend, and he would relish the spectacle.

"I'm gonna have a baby," Angel said. That's how Otis reported it later, neither an angry nor timid announcement from Angel, yet one that precluded any other option. She met their eyes. They met hers. The five of them in the room—Angel and Otis, the Pierces, Jason, Mrs., Mr.—sat waiting for the words to collectively make sense to them as a linked and relevant message. Jude was still singing his service-setting song, moving methodically, duck-footed, around the vast beautiful table—legs like the paws of lions, vines scrolled along the wide lip—and farther away, the grown daughters in the kitchen spooned vegetables into bowls, whisked gravy at the stove, unwrapped wax paper from cool, pale sticks of butter. And then the pieces fell into place in the parlor, as first Jason, then Mr., and finally Mrs. Pierce understood the equation Angel had drawn in thin air with her words.

It was Jude, listening as he worked, who broadcast the announcement to the house at large: "She's gonna have a baby!"

he shouted cheerfully, as he threw open the sideboard for cloth napkins. "That chocolate girl's gonna have a baby!"

IV.

She dropped out of school and she moved across the street. She demanded our parents give her written permission to marry Jason Pierce and then invited none of us to the ceremony, not even Otis. It was he and Jason who moved her belongings, the two of them trudging up and down our stairs, Jason pausing to gaze around himself, as impressed by our house as Angel had been by his, then waiting at First for the traffic to clear, the gate at the Pierce manse held open with a small lawn ornament, an angel, ironically enough.

Angel refused to pack her possessions in suitcases or baskets, insisting on trash bags or grocery sacks instead, as if we'd always thought of her as a future homeless person.

Angel Pierce gave birth in August, during a tornado warning. Jason, newly wed, newly a parent, did not have to go to military school in Roswell, after all. He got his act together and reentered East in the fall. When he came home from school, he found his mother and wife doting on his daughter, named Teresa, after her Catholic grandmother. She was a pretty baby. She looked like her uncle Otis, flawless.

"She's a good mother," Otis told us. He was the only one invited to visit; he brought back surprised accounts of Angel's placid happiness, her having found peace and joy and other greeting-card feelings, her reading, of all things, the Bible. This was one book our mother would never have thought to prescribe. We could go over to the Pierces', if we wanted, stand at the gate and ring the bell, but we weren't particularly welcome. Our mother and Mrs. had embraced at the hospital, at the child's birth, tears in their eyes. They shared a grand-child in common; they were now related. I suppose we were all related, though only Otis by blood.

That fall, Raymond left for college in California. Portia rented an apartment three blocks away with a new boyfriend. Only Otis and I remained at home, in the ramshackle hippie house with our parents. I'd never come up with a good enough reason to move out. It was a capacious place, and I liked my family. My father was beginning to forget things, big impor-tant things, like who we were and why we were bothering him; I told myself my mother needed my help and company; she had placed her faith in family, and I didn't want her to be fully disillusioned.

My bedroom faced First Street and, across it, the main Pierce house. On the other side of an upstairs window there, Jason and Angel and baby Teresa slept. At night, Otis came and sat on the radiator beneath my window, looking out. He would leave, too. I would be the last. The church would even-tually offer to buy our house from us, as they had every other one along our street, and after my parents were gone, I would stubbornly, stupidly, decline.

For a short while, back in the late seventies, I'd been part of a city-wide volunteer busing campaign. We were integrating the schools; I was twelve, sent as emissary to Brooks Junior High, which was 90 percent black. Everyone else in my fam-ily either drove or walked to the schools nearer by. I rose early, made myself French toast, then walked two blocks away to wait for the bus. I considered it my duty, riding nauseated on the bus for more than an hour a day; my parents were proud of me. In a few of my classes, I was the only white person in the room. The white dairy lady in the lunch room always gave

me an extra ice cream, sorry for me. I was enjoying my mar-
tyrdom right up to the afternoon I got beat up. Punched in
the face, just for being myself. How could I explain to that furious ring of black girls that I meant them no harm? That I
was on their side? Simply: I couldn't.

When I came home bruised and self-righteous, my mother
was adamant that I not blame the girls but the whole of
American history, our original slave-owning sin.

My brother Cecil provided me with a switchblade, an object I never used, but nevertheless enjoyed knowing sat in my
purse alongside my lunch money.

My bedroom faced north, the coldest direction. We'd
stopped heating the third floor, the extra bedrooms, one by
one as my siblings left home. The icy winter blasts shook
through my windows, waves of chilly air. I didn't mind them.
I'd learned to sleep that way, warm in an insular bundle of old
blankets. When we adopted the little fellas, before Cecil and
Stuart moved away, when Jackie sometimes fell asleep on a
couch and accidentally slept over, when the house was as full
as it would ever be, Portia had slept in here with me, the only
time I'd had to share the place. We'd talked at night, gazing
dreamily over toward the Pierce house, both envying and dis-
paraging their reputed seven bathrooms, their swimming
pool, their fleet of cars from their father's Cadillac dealership.

Now, Otis looked out that same window. Now Angel was
on the other side of the street, on the other side of the bars
enclosing the Pierces' vast yard, inside that giant lighted craft.

He'd been riffling the pages of college catalogs, trying to
imagine the various rooms and futures he might occupy. He'd
also been trying to decide if he truly recalled the night his
father had killed his mother, or whether he'd invented that
memory, that past, he and his sister huddled in a crib watching

through its slats a bath of blood, the most awful act in the world. I would have done anything for him. I hoped that at least this moment, the two of us at the window, would seem solid to him, the present, verifiable.

Angel's baby had been baptized that afternoon. Down at Blessed Sacrament, her large extended family as audience, Otis our lone emissary. They'd walked home afterward, as they always did after church. Had we been looking out then, we'd have seen some fancy blond grandson pushing the wheelchair holding the matriarch, prodigal Jason carrying the newest Pierce, and dark Angel borne along on the sea of white dresses and coats and gloves, a brilliant smile on her face, her hair straightened now, held with ivory combs. *That's how they get you*, I could imagine Cecil and Stuart pronouncing, the grand occasion of it all, the regalia and pomp, the inviolable beauty and bigness, the numerous wealths involved that had *gotten* our Angel.

And then we'd have seen Otis, splintering off at our house, walking up the frost-heaved front walk alone.

"I'm here," Otis said, leaning his forehead against the chilly glass. "And she's there." Another vaguely unimaginable situation.

"*We're* here," I insisted. And because he had always been good, Otis didn't disagree.

PEOPLE PEOPLE

Elaine's sister tricked her into answering the phone. *Private*, the caller ID read, and of course, enticed, Elaine engaged the line.

"Lainey, things are *awful*," her sister began. *Fine, and how are you?* Elaine's husband's voice replied. She'd been married to him for so long that he spoke to her even when he wasn't anywhere to be seen. His voice in her head was sarcastic, the devilish side of a pairing that traditionally also featured an angel, characters on either shoulder, nattering away.

Elaine's sister Martha had never understood the friendly overtures others used on the phone. "I'm in a real pickle," she went on. "I'm being crucified." *Unavailable*, the phone call from Martha usually read; Elaine always saw it as *Unavoidable*, and answered in that mood. Today she had just gotten into the car, on her way to the gym to pay penance on the treadmill, to later lie baking in the sauna. It was four thirty on a gloomy Friday; instead of turning on the engine and pulling out of the driveway, she reentered the carport and then the house, poured herself a glass of wine in the kitchen,

and declined to switch on lights. A dark spongy cloud had
been sitting on Houston for three weeks now; it almost felt
like a real winter. The temperature outside said that the wine
ought to be red.

"Crucified for telling the truth!" Moral indignation, so much
her sister's MO. Martha was setting up the context of her current disaster, which was taking a while. Preamble. Background.
Disclaimer. But the significant information Elaine had learned
growing up with Martha, the narrator. She was snoopy, jealous, a gossip, self-righteous, and had no control over her ap-
petites. She was also a genius, and that trait had overshadowed
and excused the others for many years. A foundation had gone
so far as to assign her the title, capital G, and put her on payroll.
This official designation had then been parlayed into a kind of
bidding war among universities for Martha's talents; at the moment, she was between gigs, trading her way up an academic
ladder, one endowed chair for another. Meanwhile, she'd been
invited to host a session at a think tank. Holed up in a moun-
tain town in Colorado with other geniuses, her own dream
team, gathered at her request, brainstorming, conjuring ecological rescue of what was either a wetlands or a swamp, depending on who you asked, Martha the honorary hostess of an elite
and peculiar gathering. *Par-tay!* crowed Elaine's husband.

Elaine, settling on a kitchen stool, taking a first bracing
swallow of wine, listened to her sister describing her peers
and their specialties, occasionally digressing to qualify an expertise or define a word Martha couldn't imagine Elaine would
understand. Elaine pictured the dramatic personae in lab coats,
nothing but lab coats and horn-rimmed eyeglasses. *Cut to the
fucking chase*, her husband said.

She has the gift of gab, another voice chimed in, this the one
of Elaine's dead father, in reference to her dead mother. It was

a patient sardonic voice; it spoke directly to Elaine, through memory and affection, under the softening influence of wine. And this was how Elaine always ended up forgiving her sister, by remembering the ways in which she resembled their mother, and by the way she, Elaine, admired herself most when she played the other part, that of their tolerant father.

The gist of the crisis was that Martha had ratted out two of her current brainiac colleagues who'd been conducting an adulterous affair. "For *ten years*," she said, outraged, and somehow secure that Elaine would agree. "I mean, *everybody* knows, absolutely everybody except the spouses. The grown *son* of the man knows. These two go to conferences together, meet up in Berlin and England, all over the freaking globe, and mostly people just assume they're a couple, that they're married—they even get invitations addressed to both of them, to weddings and brises and such stuff—but in fact they're not married, not to each other, but to other people, innocent people who, it seems to me, have the right to know what's going on behind their backs. Wouldn't you want to know?"

Elaine had focused on Martha's use of the word "freaking" instead of "fucking." Her husband didn't understand why people did that. *Either say the word, or don't, but substitute?* He found it juvenile; on the weekends, he performed at an open-mic comedy club, droning mock-folk songs accompanied by an out-of-tune guitar. His sister-in-law Martha was a sometime subject of his routine. "I would want to know," Elaine told her sister, just because it was the easiest thing to say. Her husband, in fact, had once had an affair. With Elaine. He'd left that first wife in order to claim Elaine. She couldn't exactly condemn the practice, since they'd had a happy marriage. But what business was it of her sister's, to expect Elaine to air dirty laundry now, twenty years later? Frankly, Elaine didn't even think it was particularly dirty. Just dulled by use, like most laundry. Like most lives. *Fat cow*, her husband's voice said. Fatness frightened him, and Martha, in addition to possessing a high IQ, was what the doctors called morbidly obese.

On and on she went, Elaine's sister, recounting the tale of how she'd been wronged, *she*, the one who should have been praised for bearing the truth, for notifying the wife of the philandering husband, as well as the husband of the whore. But no, that wasn't how her so-called peers at the insular think tank thought of it. Not at all. Instead, they'd rallied round the adulterers, and found Martha, *Martha*, the pariah. Their hostess, whose get-together they had spoiled. Where was this sad story going, Elaine wondered? Where in the world did Martha think she'd end up, in the saddle of her high horse, whinnying there on her high road?

"So now they're after me," her sister said. "I don't feel safe." The Alpine town in which her gathering was taking place comprised fewer than ten thousand people; she could not make herself anonymous. Also, she was the only large person in all of Colorado; her IQ was amazing, but her BMI was abysmal. She stood out. (*Endowed chair*, said Elaine's husband. *Well-endowed chair*.) Her handpicked group was holding secret meetings without her. Hateful e-mails were arriving, hang-up phone calls, a dirty disposable diaper left on her doorstep.

"What?"

"I know! They're targeting me! Something awful is going to happen!"

And so Elaine extended the invitation for her sister to visit, to escape, to hide out in huge and indiscriminate Houston. *Holy fuck*, her husband's voice said. *I hate when she's here*.

* * *

"Think of it as our own little witness protection program," she told her husband, Eddie. *Little?* he mouthed. If she mentioned that he might be secretly gleeful, that Martha was fodder for stand-up material, he would hold it against Elaine. He didn't know that she noticed when he was angry, the way he gave her the finger while pushing up his eyeglasses, that she recognized rebellion and discontent and contrariness simmering in him. The two of them were preparing the house, their modest bungalow, removing or covering mirrors, as Martha wouldn't tolerate them. Unlike many fat people, she did not conceal her gluttony. She was not a furtive eater, nor was she a woman hiding in heavy makeup and flowing robes, sporting pedicures and hairdos and jewelry, those one-size-fits-all fashion statements. Rather, she refused to consider herself as a person with corporeal traits; her two published books featured no author photo. She was a mind, housed in a large ravenous body, outfitted in comfortable clothing, functional as fur on any mammal. If you weren't careful—*"Avert the Gaze!"* one of Eddie's little ditties was titled—you'd catch a scary glimpse of overtaxed flesh.

"You and Martha would make good Before and After pictures," Eddie said.

"Which would I be?" Elaine asked, flapping sheets over the bed.

"Depends. You could be After the Stomach Stapling, or you could be Before the Tragic Thyroid Malfunction."

"We looked almost exactly alike, at birth. Our baby pictures are hard to tell apart unless you have some other object around, like a certain dog or the other one of us, to tell which baby you're looking at." Elaine thought: Babies are Before; Adults are After.

"Well, at least we can share a bed this time," her husband

said. Their son had left for college that fall. Martha was too big to sleep in his single bunk, or on the couch, so she always ended up in Elaine and Eddie's bed. Eddie was tucking a tablecloth around the full-length mirror on the closet door in their room; Elaine had taped wrapping paper over the master bath medicine cabinet mirror. Last time Martha had visited, Eddie had served dinner on the wedding silver, a piece of sabotage Elaine hadn't registered until it was too late—Martha glimpsing herself as she served up the last of the pork loin, her face there in the prune pottage. Eddie was a brat.

"I miss Danny so much," Elaine said as they stood in their boy's doorway. His belongings stirred her, the posters, the instruments, turntables, computer, mementos, faded curled photos. He had a very small endearing habit of touching things gently as he moved through a room, not like an obsessive compulsive, but like a ghost ascertaining his presence in the physical world. Missing him made Elaine dizzy. He used to play, every single morning before school, just to get everybody in the mood for the day, the Beatles' "Here Comes the Sun." On her clavicle, at the place where as a true-blue American grade-school girl she'd daily thrown her hand to pledge allegiance, she had had Danny's tiny toddler handprint tattooed. She covered that spot now with her palm, and her husband put his lips against her opposite shoulder, where, in the same sentimental season, she had had his kiss tattooed. Her boys, on her body, her only life.

But such heart-stopping moments as these could undo Eddie; inside his nervous antic surface ran a substantial stream of sap. He did not like to have it tapped.

"So she felt it was somehow up to her to do the right thing," he was saying, of Martha. "She didn't have enough on her plate—does she ever, ha ha ha?—what with the extinction of gnats and runny glaciers and blighted bushes and whatever the hell else those pointy heads are up to their ears in, she had to go wag her tongue?"

Martha's tongue; it was a powerful muscle. "Sustainability," Elaine said, quoting her sister's mission, uninterested in its full meaning. "Just sustainability."

"Oh, she'll sustain," said Eddie. "She'll do more than *sustain*."

"She's my sister. She has no one else. What was I supposed to do?"

"Really though, if she thinks somebody's going to push her off a cliff for being a pain in the ass, she'd already be dead."

"I know."

"Killed a thousand times over. Will you wear that thing I like to bed tonight?" Eddie asked, perking his eyebrows, nodding toward their son's bunk, where they would sleep. For the last month, he had been unemployed; he was working hard at his own morale.

"Sure."

Martha arrived in a rental car, carrying a throwaway cell phone. She'd told no one where she was going, paid for her flights with cash, routed herself through two unnecessary airports, Indianapolis and Tampa. The think tank would have to finish its meeting without her. "*I* have the hard-drive," she gloated; she had flounced out of the state and taken her toy with her. As soon as Elaine served lunch—spaghetti Bolognese, French bread, Chianti—Martha started over with the saga.

Ava, the female adulterer, was, like Martha, a biologist. She had three small children, all living in Philadelphia with their father, also profoundly pedigreed. The male adulterer, Jonathan, was an eco-architect from Los Angeles. He was significantly older, the father of a son now following in his footsteps, who was privy to the father's dual life. Jonathan's wife was ill, in a wheelchair, thereby making divorce morally unsavory. Also, neither Ava nor Jonathan seemed to find their situation problematic. They loved their families, they notified anyone who cared to hear it. They loved each other. They led two lives. "Do they think just because they're brilliant they get to be above the common courtesies of human relationships?" Martha demanded of Elaine.

"I don't know. Maybe?" *Doesn't Mabel Dick here think so?* asked absent Eddie. Martha's sweatsuit was stained with food; she hadn't washed her hair in days. When she flew, she refused to purchase two seats.

"Are you kidding?" Martha said. In her opinion, their superior minds, their current superheroic mission, ought to bind them more completely to integrity, rules, decency. Not superficial ones, it seemed, but sacred ones.

"That's something I've noticed about literature, too—" Elaine started to say. All those novels and poems of the past, guilt and consequence, ethical object lessons for the reader. Yet their authors: all just as fallible and fucked-up as anybody else.

"I'm such a naïf!" Martha wailed.

"So *that's* how it's pronounced," Elaine said, repeating the word. Growing up, she'd been the Pretty One, since it was obvious that Martha would be the Smart One. They had no other siblings, and their parents had devised a divide-and-conquer strategy, the mother always protecting Martha, the father Elaine. In high school, Elaine had lied and said that they were twins, identical, and now look: her big fat left-behind-two-grades sister Martha. And trim, cheerleading Elaine. "I'm *ashamed* of you," her mother had declared, learning of this lie, Martha blubbering and horrified. Later that evening, her father had tapped on Elaine's bedroom door and invited her back downstairs to watch a Marx Brothers movie with him. They shared a guilty fondness for slapstick. Lazyheads, he named them, their team of two. He would have approved of Eddie, Elaine often thought; it was tragic they'd not met until her father was too addled to fully appreciate him.

"How old are her children?" Elaine asked.

"They were all born during the time of the affair."

"Yet they aren't Jonathan's?"

"Apparently not."

"That's kind of admirable, keeping things separate like that." Elaine was truly impressed: having babies with one man, a love affair with another, preserving the gene pool while also kindling illicit passion. Not to mention the research agenda. "Is she pretty?" Elaine asked, that somehow being of the essence.

Martha scowled. "I don't know. She's tall. She has a lot of hair which is always falling around her face and getting in the way. Yellow," she added, before Elaine could ask.

"By which you mean blonde."

"I guess." There was red sauce around Martha's mouth. She looked like a child, inflated. Despite everything, it was a pleasure to cook for someone who enjoyed eating as much as Martha did. For years, that had been the way Elaine could most easily make contact with her sister: food, and their parents. Once, Elaine had thought that her son would provide some sort of binding force. Love of him. But Martha wasn't interested in children. She hadn't liked them when she was one herself. To her, children were as tedious as other humans, minus manners. She had always been solitary. "People are boring," she would say. "Why be bored?" The think tank session had seemed a godsend, this handpicked tribe of like-minded souls, bankrolled by a billionaire in Colorado who collected ideas instead of art or real estate. Martha had been giddy with the prospect, unboring others!

And now it was spoiled.

"Why did you tell?" Elaine asked.

"If there's one thing I know," Martha said, doing a cursory wipe of her sauced face and hands, "it's that knowledge is power." *But ignorance is bliss,* said Eddie; "Adios," he'd announced that morning, disappearing who-knew-where. Now Elaine could not decide whether to respond to her sister's smugness or to her tomatoey helplessness. In high school, the same problems had doomed Martha's social life, Teacher's Pet, Goody Two-shoes, the Fat Girl who didn't even have the Great Personality, nor friends to tout that selling feature. Elaine sighed, ambivalent as usual, and probably seemed simply dumb. She had never envied her sister's gifts, not given what the cost appeared to be.

Martha traveled light (*not literally* . . .), a briefcase, two laptops, some books, and another sweatsuit, a toothbrush and a rock (natural deodorant) her only toiletries. She had in her possession a letter that allowed her access to every library and special collection in the nation. After lunch, she drove away to put that letter to use. Elaine did the dishes, pressing her hipbones up against the rim of the sink, relieved to feel their sharpness. In addition to the job she held publicly, at the high school, she held a lifelong secret second one: the work of her body. She studied it, she exercised it, she starved it, she removed its imperfections, then decorated and costumed it. She crossed her arms to touch her tattoos. Nobody could see these, the marks of her beloved. Explaining them to Martha would be impossible. Martha hadn't even believed in getting her ears pierced. "Self-mutilation," she'd declared, thirteen years old.

"Barbaric." But she didn't understand much about the holiness of the body, Elaine thought. She only knew how to be bound by it.

Because Eddie was deaf in one ear, Elaine thought maybe he wouldn't hear what she could as they lay in their son's bed at night. Martha had been with them for a week.

"Is she crying?" Eddie whispered.

"Maybe laughing," Elaine hoped aloud. She feared masturbation. It was not something she wished to posit to Eddie; this was her sister's only sex life. (*A virgin!* Eddie would rejoice, and Elaine all over again was relieved for never having shared this fact with him.) Tonight's loyalty made her flush with both pity and pride, as if she were performing for her parents. *Their* parents, hers and Martha's.

Eddie's half-deafness was from having stabbed a chopstick into his left ear during a drug trip in college. He'd been sober since. Semi-impaired, he got things usefully wrong, heard "terrorist" when the passenger beside him on the plane had said "tourist." At least he could find his problems funny, Elaine thought. He went to meetings when he was anxious. Lately, since being "let go" at the ad agency, since the arrival of Martha, he'd been more religious in attendance. Elaine imagined they liked him at AA and NA; he could try out his ballads, strum, strum, get a laugh. His code name for his sister-in-law was The Extenuating Circumstance, so that he could make fun of her in her presence. For Martha's part, she seemed to believe he was referring to some sexual shenanigan he and Elaine shared. What did she have to compare it to, the secret language of people who slept together? It was a term of endearment, as far as she was concerned, a pet name, a physical position involving rubber toys.

"Poor Danny," Eddie said then. "All those years, he probably got an earful of us." And Elaine understood that Eddie wouldn't have missed what was really going on on the other side of the wall. Moreover, he'd put it in his routine, try it out at the church basement, then take it on the road. A ballad was writing itself, a happy hum revving in Eddie's mind. She couldn't stop that engine, either. For one thing, Eddie was just naughty enough to do what she requested he not do; and for another, he was unemployed and therefore on the downside of his personality, tails instead of heads: selfish, defensive, and paranoid rather than gregarious, fun-loving, and gallant. In this mood, making sport of others would be his protection. "Is nothing off limits?" she had once asked him, near tears at having heard him sing about, in many refrains, her father's senility to a room of drinking, guffawing strangers. It had literally pained her, in the heart; who was this cruel man? "Do I really want to be married to someone for whom there are no sacred cows?"

Eddie had burst into laughter, high with success, applause. "You're such a total *teacher*! Even when you're mad you can't dangle a fucking preposition."

To balance this memory, to view the other side of the coin, she had only to recall the day her dad had died. She had found Eddie hiding in the car, sobbing over the steering wheel, a face he was trying to keep from her. He was afraid of his tenderness. He had been punished for showing it, once upon a time. She had no doubt that he had wept similarly when he'd driven away from Danny's dorm in Austin, having delivered him there after a ride of jokes and bonhomie, breakdown in the breakdown lane.

"Maybe she's doing crunches?" Elaine said as the bed continued to squeak.

"You just keep thinking that," Eddie replied, patting her shoulder.

Elaine mistook the voice on the phone for her son's. "Danny?" she said, instantly happy, simultaneously wary of bad news.

"I'm P. J. Cotton," the boy said. "My father is Dr. Jonathan Cotton. From the conference."

"Oh." Elaine recalibrated to begin lying for her sister, who had gone to the neighborhood Fiesta for provisions.

"I'm trying to locate Martha. She won't return my e-mails. I even wonder if she's reading them. I'd like to explain to her about my parents. If I told you, would you tell her?"

"Maybe," Elaine allowed. Had she just given away Martha's location? Was this kid a genius, too? They weren't psychic, she scolded herself; in fact, most of them were closer to the opposite, like Martha, obtuse to the workings of social interactions, annoyed by and numb to the nuance of subtle personal transactions. They were not people people; they often smelled bad and muttered to themselves. P. J. Cotton told about his mother and her condition, which was advanced MS. He was living with her, in Los Angeles, and caring for her while going to school.

"What are you studying?" Elaine asked, thinking of her own son.

"Pre-med," P.J. said. "And ergonomics."

"My son's probably going to major in philosophy," Elaine told him. In his bedroom, she'd come upon his various shrines, one only visible from her side of the bed where she and Eddie had been sleeping. A red candle surrounded by tinfoil, a little Buddha statue, fat as Martha, grinning peaceably.

"Anyway," P.J. was saying, "I just wanted to tell her, I did tell her, in my e-mail, that my parents have always had an understanding. My mother's severely disabled, and she gave my father permission a long time ago to find someone else. I mean, she knew this was a contingency. It's okay. It's an acceptable situation. Well, it would have been better if she hadn't had to hear about it. I think she preferred not thinking about it." He paused. Elaine imagined the woman in the wheelchair, a supple mind at the mercy of a clumsy machine. Jonathan's son said, "But really, she's fine. I just wanted to tell Martha that, because they'd like to have her back." For a second it dawned on Elaine that the hard drive was the true reason for his call. But her thoughts veered toward his family life, his mother in a wheelchair, his father leaving the boy at home, the amazingly adult responsibility he seemed to have assumed without a hitch. Did P.J., like Danny, still enjoy video games? Noodle around all Saturday afternoon on an electric bass? Text message endlessly with his friends? Somehow she didn't think so.

"What about the other children?" she asked suddenly.

"Other children?"

"The children of your father's mistress, the children in Philadelphia, those three little kids? What about them?"

The silence with which this was greeted made Elaine's heart begin to race. She had spilled a secret. Not only that, he might now know she knew where Martha was. Would he come to her house? She could feel him mentally packing what would undoubtedly be very little luggage to come do some unknown amount of harm.

"I'm an idiot," she whispered into Eddie's right ear that night, in bed.

"Honey, I didn't marry you for your mind."

"What made her think there wouldn't be consequences?"

"If you tell her he's coming, then she'll go away," Eddie said. "I can only see this as win-win."

"If she goes away, I may never see her again," Elaine replied; her parents would spin in their graves. "Clearly she can easily disappear." Eddie didn't bother to make the obvious joke, nor endorse that eventuality, also, as win-win. Martha didn't even have to show up at her next campus until the year 2010. "Marquee value," she had explained her status on the department's masthead, despite her absence in its classrooms. "Why does she think they're out to get her?"

"Because she's a paranoid freak," he answered. "Same reason she wears sunglasses and a hat when she goes out the door, as if that equals a disguise."

"How big is a hard drive?"

"I'm imagining it could be hidden in a body cavity. I'm not *enjoying* imagining that, but that's what I've got."

"We're harboring a fugitive."

"A *huge*-itive," he said. "It'd take a harbor, too. You're lucky you don't have to hang around all day with her. She's like a bad cable station that I can't turn off." For three and a half weeks he'd been treated to Station Martha, which was tedious and/or disgusting; Eddie was bored by the saga of Ava and Jonathan; like most men, he preferred car chases to soap opera. "*And* she refuses to shut the bathroom door. *And* she snacks endlessly. I think she's trying to bug me, flaunting herself all over. I think she wants to catch me looking, and then catch me being repulsed. And I'm starting to feel like I'm going to give her what she's asking for. There's this odor. I feel driven to drive. I'm up to a pack a day, by the way, which is a disaster." He coughed, to illustrate.

"I'm sorry." Elaine counseled at a charter high school; she had office hours, an alarm clock, meetings, paperwork, a personal trainer for daily neutralizing: certified excuses to escape. Often these last weeks, when she came home it was to a vivid silence, the kind of quiet as if doors had just that moment been slammed, slammed as coda to other noise, voices raised in irrational insult, the startling barking of dogs.

Yet her sister and husband greeted her benignly enough.

"Plus," Eddie went on, "I'm really sick of hearing how fucked-up Texas is. If she doesn't like our air, hello, go breathe somewhere else." Of course, Martha would find fault with Houston. Elaine was accustomed to her contempt, her amazement at the abandon with which Houstonians, Americans, spent their money, took for granted their luck, exhibited their entitlement. "What would she have us do?" Eddie asked. "Sell our belongings, send our money to Africa?"

"Yes," Elaine said. That was exactly what Martha would want. Martha herself was exempt, owner of a mind full of ideas and good intentions, dedicating her life to improving the conditions of others, possessing no property, handed about from one institution to another, like a national treasure. She could eat veal; she could drink bottled water. But others had not paid their dues. This was clear.

"So now she's going to find out what happens when you act like some sort of god," Eddie said. "Some mere mortals are going to be pissed." Her sister had evicted herself from her clan, those other gods on Mount Olympus, including her adulterous enemies.

"He didn't sound pissed," Elaine said, referring to P.J. He'd sounded exhausted. He'd sounded like a good boy who understood and loved his parents.

"She's a know-it-all who doesn't know shit." He rolled over to bite Elaine's neck. "Well," he conceded, "she knows *some* shit. She's been doing some research for me, showing me her skills. Potions, lotions, notions," he said, and, to preclude interrogation, then added, as further distraction, "You've lost weight." He ran his hand along her thigh. It hadn't been unpleasant, sleeping in this small bed together night after night. Waking to see what their son had seen all those years, faces in the shadows and cracks and curtains, the dramas there he might have imagined. Elaine didn't mind having a caretaking mission, in the form of her sister, to listen to and feed; without Danny, she'd been a little at loose ends, the evidence indisputable that time would render her obsolete. And her sister's presence had shifted the tension in the house away from Eddie's unemployment; he was probably already worrying about how things would shift back, when Martha left. Then he'd resume his defensive face when he greeted Elaine at the end of the day, anticipating the question she actually never asked. "I'm a loser, baby," he would say, scraping at his guitar, "so why don't you kill me." He collected unemployment; he filled out applications at places he thought he'd left behind ages ago, run by bosses whose type he'd given the fuck-you-forever finger. This floundering restlessness could only last so long; there'd been a time or two before, when he'd fallen into a funk, once ending in a love affair with Elaine, another time in a short stay at the hospital, where Elaine and Danny had visited. "Daddy's sad," Elaine had told their son.

"Sad," four-year-old Danny had agreed.

"I tend to not eat when she's around," Elaine said now. "Food sort of stops seeming like fun."

"It's because she chews with her mouth open. Her mouth is always open, the yawning maw."

"Since she was little," Elaine agreed. "Young," she corrected. "What are we going to do if that boy P.J. shows up at our front door?"

"Invite him in. Watch the fireworks." Eddie rolled carefully over and they lay back to back, proximate, compact. Tomorrow night he would go to the comedy club. He had had that glint in his eye all evening, that fever of a new, funny, mean tale to tell. His routines depended on victims. *She has two Ph.D.s. Yes, folks. Two. Room enough for two inside this double-wide.* His last ditty had been Santa in the Off Season. All around Houston you could find him, the large homeless man with the scruffy red jacket, the unkempt beard and crazy white hair. He'd be pedaling a slow bike, butt crack in full view, balancing a basket of aluminum cans, or lazing around in his ratty black boots in front of the video store with the other itinerant workers, waiting for somebody to drive up and hire them. One day in foggy January, Santa had stepped out of the bayou in front of Eddie's car: a near fatal accident, Santa shaking his fist and cursing. Now, just in time, Martha had arrived at his front door.

"Eddie," Elaine whispered to the dark of her side of the bed, "you know, when we started going out, I knew about your wife, but she didn't know about me. Eve," she added, the first Mrs. Eddie. "I never felt bad about that, but maybe I should have. I didn't know her. I thought I was saving you from some sort of witch. I thought she didn't understand you." Elaine kept whispering, her eyes closed, flush with remembering how imperative passion had been back then, how irrelevant the wife, the marriage, those obstacles to her happiness. Obstacles, or enticements? Hadn't she always liked winning, in the realm of female competition for the man? Hadn't she started with her father, making him fonder of her than his other daughter, practicing?

"Was I having an affair, or was it just you? I mean, not being married myself, does that count? And do you have to be an adult to be an adulterer?" she spoke ever more softly. She'd forever been glad there weren't children from that first marriage to consider. Long ago, her hairdresser had told her that if she ever decided to have an affair, she shouldn't tell anyone, not one person. Elaine had thought that the woman knew something, since Elaine had just that very month begun her affair with Eddie. Around her head snipped the angry scissors, Elaine unnerved, agreeing eagerly, meagerly with the hairdresser: mum's the word.

"Did you feel bad for your wife?" She knew Eddie wouldn't respond, that he had fallen asleep with his deaf ear exposed, or that his pretense at having done so was very convincing.

She left him there and went to find Martha, who was busy on her computers, ambidextrous clattering. She'd turned Elaine's and Eddie's bed into a kind of mission control, surrounding herself with books and Post-it notes and reading glasses, on the night table an assortment of small plates and cups and spoons and candy wrappers and Kleenex. She shut one machine's lid, a graphic photo of a surgical procedure—tiny instruments holding open the flayed skin of a human face—snapped flat when Elaine came in, caught doing something. This aided *sustainability* how?

"What's up?" Elaine sat at the bed's end, resting lightly there. The room smelled different, like electric power, like feet, like dust, no longer hers and Eddie's. It seemed smaller, minus the mirror she was accustomed to consulting on the door to the bathroom. She adjusted herself as she always did for a mirror, posture, tipped chin. Her sister was a kind of mirror, an image staring back, an opportunity for self-correction.

"Does he want me to leave?" Martha asked, blinking behind unflattering eyeglasses, the lenses of which were thoroughly smudged.

"No," Elaine said. "Of course not. Not at all. No no no. What makes you ask that?"

"I don't know. Sometimes being in the house with him

seems like two enemies in a cage at the zoo." The elephant and the mouse, Elaine thought. The snake and the rabbit— only, which one of them was the snake?

Martha said, "He thinks I'm listening in to his phone calls. He thinks I care about his marijuana."

"He only smokes tobacco," Elaine said, sighing.

"Pot," Martha insisted.

"Have you ever smoked either? Have you ever smoked anything? Eddie smokes when he's anxious—it's hard to be unemployed."

"Why hide behind the carport?"

"Because he knows it makes me worry. Not because it's illegal." Martha opened her mouth to disagree, but Elaine went on, "Not because it's pot. Not. Pot."

Her sister peered thoughtfully at her. "What do I care what he smokes?" She scratched furiously at both sides of her head. "I don't care what he keeps under that rock, I don't care about getting my money back, I don't flipping care who he talks to on the phone, or who he meets at the end of the block."

"The end of the block?" Elaine frowned, trying to imagine what went on in her home when she wasn't there, trying to sift through Eddie's version and Martha's, taking into account their relative biases as narrators. "He said you've been helping him do research."

"Any idiot could do it. But you can't expect to navigate the Web if you can't spell. He *is* more friendly when he's high."

"He misses Danny. He needs a job." Elaine felt the defeating weight of Eddie's trouble descend upon her, right alongside the irritating heft of her sister. When Elaine had told her aged and failing parents about her plans to wed, her father had hugged her, *marriage* a word he could still recognize as salubrious.

Her mother had made an ominous prediction. "You think you'll fix him, but you won't."

"Why should I care about Eddie's BS?" said Martha now. "I've got my own problems. Everybody back at the session blames me for this big to-do over Ava and Jonathan. I mean, really. How can I go back there, with them all so resentful? But how can I *not* go back? It was my idea in the first place!"

"Has something else happened?" Elaine asked.

"Ava's husband wants a divorce," said Martha. "And custody."

"Oh dear." Elaine had wondered about the big-haired blonde, those little children, that woman who, in Elaine's mind anyway, had it all.

"Yeah, he trashed the house, I guess, tore up the wedding pictures, ruined her clothes. Told the kids Mommy was a monster. He's forced her to go back to Philly, so everything in Colorado is at a standstill. Our benefactor is furious, *furious!* He called me a buttinski! But at least somebody else thought it meant something. The infidelity," she added.

"Besides you, you mean?" Her sister was a virgin, Elaine reminded herself, in addition to being a buttinski. Martha knew a million indisputable useful facts, and could fashion them into solutions to environmental troubles the world was only beginning to recognize it would encounter and therefore need solved. She possessed superior knowledge, there was no denying it, but she also appeared to be hanging on to a really feeble fantasy, a strange romance. This was probably predicated on their parents' long peaceful marriage, and it wasn't sophisticated or developed or tried, even. It was purely hypothetical. Her heart, that literal muscle, worked extremely hard, having to support a busy brain, pump twice as much fluid through its chambers because it was running a very big organization, but for all its labor, for its undoubtedly over-large size, it hadn't been wanted or taken by anyone, not in the crucial, unliteral, valentine-shaped sense.

"Isn't there even one person there who you think of as a friend?" Elaine asked, squinting, hopeful. "One ally?" Martha pondered the question objectively, as if the implications weren't embarrassingly personal.

"No," she said, as simply as she would have had someone asked if she owned a pet, or liked anchovies. "I *thought* I would. I admired their work. I respected their ideas."

Which left Elaine as her sole, albeit flawed, human cohort. She might have been tempted to embrace her, but Martha had cracker crumbs on her chest, her hair was oily and awry, her glasses made her eyes tiny, and there were inch-long whiskers growing from her chin. When they were young, they'd shared a bedroom, and it was Martha's slovenliness Elaine cited when she insisted she'd rather sleep in the basement, never mind the spiders. It could all be washed, she told herself now, the pillowcases, the tabletop, the rug. Washed, or replaced. *Purge*, she thought, a word that often had been her reaction to the spectacle of her sister.

In the morning, before Eddie rose, Elaine visited the overgrown back of the carport where, sure enough, a large rock concealed a Baggie full of weed, pipe, and lighter.

It wasn't the son, P.J., who came to their home, but Dr. Jonathan Cotton himself. The six-week intensive session had ended. Martha had missed her own party; those intellectual gods on Mount Olympus were descending back into their regular lives. Dr. Cotton had sojourned hundreds of miles south and east; for more than an hour, Elaine sat with him in her living room, failing to make conversation, serving decaffeinated tea and tiresome soy crackers. He reminded her of a praying mantis, all folded elbows and knees between coffee table and couch, blinking abstractly at his environs, no interest in or, perhaps, ability at small talk. Eddie had left a note claiming he was "running errands"; Martha was at the Rice library. A spring storm rolled through the city, blowing leaves and flowers and sticks through the streets, causing the lights to flicker, and that became their merciful subject. Dr. Cotton helped Elaine unplug the more sophisticated electronic equipment, pausing to evaluate Eddie's elaborate collection of CDs.

Finally, the back door banged open.

Eddie came in chewing gum, wadding an alcohol wipe in his hands, took one look at Dr. Cotton, and asked, "Has anyone ever mistaken you for a coke dealer?" Only Elaine knew that Eddie wasn't trying to be an asshole; that was often her predicament, with her husband. She was so grateful that they had Danny, somebody else indubitably on Eddie's side.

"I thought you might be Martha," Elaine said. But Martha would have identified Dr. Cotton's California plates on his hybrid car and simply driven on. It was possible she would not come back. She had her carte blanche research letter and a laptop with her; what else in this world did she need?

"I resemble a drug dealer?" Dr. Cotton asked Eddie. "How so?"

"Sorry," Eddie said, waving his hands, erasing the air. "Sorry." Elaine knew it was the doctor's eyes, their maniacal bulbousness. It was probably a medical disorder, and unquestionably rude to inquire about. She herself had been wondering how it was this very unattractive man had managed to capture the love of two women, the tragic gracious wife and the gifted mistress. His charisma so far eluded her. "Kidding,"

Eddie added, nodding now, putting together the pieces. "You're a friend of Martha's, huh?"

"I am. A colleague from the institute. The wetlands project."

"One of the bog people. Another think-tanker. A tink thanker." They shook, and Eddie sat cross-legged on the floor in front of the coffee table where Elaine and Dr. Cotton's empty teacups rested. Despite the chewing gum and the hand wipes, Elaine could smell marijuana. She hated Eddie's need—both of the drug, and of hiding it from her. *You think you'll fix him . . .*

Eddie said to the professor, "I bet you're the guy who designs mud huts, the one she has the crush on."

"What?" Elaine said, while Jonathan Cotton blushed, protruding eyes focused now on his lap. *Three* women! In five seconds, Eddie had cleared up everything that had been messily perplexing Elaine for the last month.

"Earth shelters," the professor corrected, then admitted, "It really did get sticky."

"Sounds like it," Eddie said sympathetically. "Martha's got zip in the way of experience with relationships, nada, zilch. *If* you know what I mean." And how, Elaine wondered, did Eddie himself know what he meant?

Dr. Cotton heaved a sigh. "It is a mess, no question. But that's not why I'm here. She has to return the hard drive. The institute is ready to hire attorneys. I'm here to keep her from being prosecuted."

Elaine's cell phone rang then; on its face, *Private. Unavoidable*, she thought: her sister. "Excuse me," she told the men.

"Jonathan's there, isn't he?" Martha said breathlessly. Elaine stood under the carport, watching water cascade onto the drive, into the street, along the curb, sludge, petals, mud—ecological mayhem, a sight Martha abhorred, yet Elaine thought it kind of pretty. Inside, without her there to prevent it, stoned Eddie would be telling Jonathan about the noises Martha made at night in her bed, relishing his own weak power, that of humiliation, the cornerstone of humor.

"Where are you?"

"Around the block. What should I do?"

Elaine had never been able to mentor Martha. Her sister and their mother had always scorned what Elaine knew—those feminine pastimes of lipstick and gossip and flirting and crying, praising and hugging and lying, of remembering a thousand birthdays, of having an arsenal of costumes, complete with matching undergarments and shoes, handbags, facial expressions, strategies. Martha met such information with utter and stunning disdain. As teenagers, Elaine had been taking notes from magazines—order fish on a date and you won't eat as much, busy as you are with the bones!—while Martha was spending her days at the morgue or the radio station, doing ride-alongs with the dog catcher or the bookmobile librarian, and when asked in company what she wanted to be when she grew up, would say "A phlebotomist," and then patiently explain what that meant. She had gone off to clear-aired Alpine Colorado to puzzle the problems of a microcosm, to extrapolate those findings into a macro vision, to play her part in a miracle.

Yet here was simple unrequited love, thwarted romance, by which she'd been blindsided, brought to this: at night tucked beneath her sister's blankets, consuming saltines by the sleeve like a sick person; during the day a frightened fugitive parked in a rental in a rainstorm.

"He wants the hard drive."

Martha was taken aback; Elaine could hear her frowning

confusion. As if Jonathan would come this distance for anything other than official business. "Don't you want to talk to
him?" she asked gently.

"Heck no!" Better to avoid him. Better to have never felt a
thing. And of course, better to have ratted out those illicit
lovers, gone public rather than private. Not *her* shame, but
Jonathan's and Ava's. Not Martha's pain or heartache or mor-
tification, but theirs. "Make him leave!" she pleaded.

"I will."

"Apologize," Elaine instructed her the next day over eggs and
bacon and bagels. Jonathan had driven away last night with the
hard drive in hand. No bigger than a videotape, it was slipped
out of Martha's briefcase and into his own. He had glanced
around the cave she'd made of Elaine and Eddie's bedroom,
picking up a file card, squinting at it, then replacing it, his lips
moving. By now he was en route to Philadelphia, chasing Ava.
He'd confessed to Eddie that he knew she would choose the
children, the marriage; he'd detoured to Texas at the behest of
the institute to appeal to Martha and her conscience, to avoid
the personal devastation in favor of the greater good. "Learn
from your mistake," Elaine said. Martha paused, a forkful of
food stalled midair. Elaine couldn't put a thing in her own
mouth, watching Martha eat; she could barely drink her coffee.
Her body had become light and angular, its bones and veins
prominent, something fascinatingly dwindling. She studied it
at the gym, at the dermatologist's, at the dentist's and hairdresser's and in department store dressing rooms, in all those
mirrors as she went through the motions. To her sister she said,
"You shouldn't have told, say that you're sorry." Jonathan had
informed them that Ava's children were three girls, blonde and
betrayed, eight, six, four. Elaine didn't need a photograph to

imagine their tearful faces. They only wanted their parents. Simple math, Mom plus Dad, minus anybody else. *"Are* you sorry?"

"I'm sorry everyone's blaming me," Martha said stubbornly.

"Well, to be fair, it did seem like everybody was doing okay with it . . ." Knowing that Martha had loved Jonathan, and been rebuffed, was embarrassing. *How many elephants can we get in this room?* Eddie would have said. Her heart went out to her sister, but her sister wouldn't accept it.

Martha consumed her last bit of bagel gloomily. She drank her juice, then frowned over her absolutely spotless plate. "That tasted good."

"I'm glad." Elaine loaded the plate in the dishwasher, rinsed the glass, refused to offer more. It was time for her sister to leave Houston. "They'll forgive you, you'll forgive them, your reputation will remain intact. You have bigger fish to fry. Hang your head," she advised. "Get on with your life. Mind your own business." There were endless platitudes, and for good reason. Elaine could have gone on all day.

"You're saying I should have kept my mouth shut? That they were better off not knowing?"

"Exactly. Remember what Daddy used to say? 'The closed mouth catches no flies'? Jonathan's wife didn't need to hear about Ava, Ava's kids didn't need to see their daddy tearing up the wedding pictures. You made a mess, it could have been avoided."

"If only I could eat my words, instead of candy?"

"Right."

"To quote your husband."

"That sounds like Eddie."

"That, and a bunch of other stuff he thinks is so freaking funny. The Woman with the Golden Face."

"What's that?"

"His little song. 'There's a hole in Mama's face where all the money goes.' I am getting so sick of hearing him practice it, sometimes it just keeps running in my head." Martha rolled her eyes. "He's got a tin ear. Haven't you heard that stupid song?"

"I don't think so."

"'Inflatable Doll'? About implants and lipo? 'Suckin' it out and pumpin' it in, pastry queen with the vacuum machine'?"

Elaine flushed; she had an impulse to reach for her breasts, those saline pouches installed years ago, after Danny was weaned.

"No." She swung her head back and forth, hoping her sister would, as usual, miss the sudden appearance of tears in her eyes. "No, I haven't heard that."

Martha took a breath, ready to sing the rest, then stopped herself.

"What?" Elaine asked. "What else?" Again Martha inhaled as if to tell, and then resolutely closed her mouth. Sealed her lips. In her eyes, too late, Elaine saw everything she wouldn't say.

A NOTE ON THE AUTHOR

Antonya Nelson is the author of eight books of fiction. Her works include *Female Trouble* and the novels *Talking in Bed, Nobody's Girl*, and *Living to Tell*. Nelson's work has appeared in the *New Yorker, Esquire, Harper's, Redbook*, and many other magazines, as well as in anthologies such as *Prize Stories: The O. Henry Awards* and *Best American Short Stories*. She is also the recent recipient of the Rea Award for Short Fiction and is a recipient of an NEA Grant 2000–2001 and a Guggenheim Fellowship. She teaches at the University of Houston and is married to the writer Robert Boswell.